Vodka Four
a novel

Jennifer Elliott

VODKA FOUR
A Canby Blue Book/November 2008
Published by Canby Blue Writing

Copyright © 2008 Jennifer Elliott
Canby Blue Writing and its associated logos are
trademarks of Canby Blue Writing

VODKA FOUR is a work of fiction. Names, characters,
places, and incidents are the products of the author's
imagination or are used fictitiously.

No part of this publication may be reproduced, stored
in a retrieval system, transmitted in any form or by any
means, electronic, mechanical, photocopying, recording,
or otherwise, without prior written permission of the
publisher and author/illustrator.

For information regarding permissions, write to CANBY
BLUE WRITING at canbyblue@hotmail.com.

ISBN: 978-0-615-26097-6

Library of Congress Number:
Printed in the U.S.A.
First Printed November 2008

Front cover art: Mike Mitchell

*For my parents, Ken and Cindy,
and my sisters, Krissy and Becky.*

29 and counting ...

Heather knew why she was single. She knew why a former high school homecoming queen was still single. She knew why the girl with such striking green eyes that compelled strangers to compliment them was still freakin' single.

Heather never told anyone her secret. She was ashamed she had judged a perfectly nice and lovely person whom she barely knew. Her parents and sisters would be disappointed. Her closest friends might even disown her. Yes, Heather was ashamed, embarrassed, and mortified.

Heather was a freshman in college, studying in her dorm room when her mom had called to check in. After talking about her classes and asking about her three younger sisters, the conversation had turned to news about other people they knew.

"April Robertson got married over the weekend," her mom had said.

"April Robertson," Heather had repeated, thinking about the familiar name.

"Mrs. Robertson the librarian," her mom had explained. "Her oldest daughter, April."

Heather remembered. Mrs. Robertson was the kind head librarian who was friends with her mother and was a member of the same Lutheran church Heather and her family attended. April Robertson was vaguely familiar to Heather. She had seen April in church and around town, but they weren't friends. Not that April wasn't nice or friendly, she was just quite a bit older than Heather. To a college freshman, April was an adult.

"How old is April?" Heather had asked.

"I think she's 35," her mom had replied.

Pathetic was the first word that popped into Heather's mind. At age 35, April Robertson was getting married for the first time.

"That won't happen to me" were the next words that followed in Heather's thoughts. *That will never happen to me.*

Heather was crowned homecoming queen in high school. From the time her father allowed her to date, Heather's weekends were filled with dinner-and-a-movie dates. She was too pretty, fun, and charming to be single. She wasn't even 21, and Heather firmly believed she was going to find her future husband in college.

Heather had her future mapped out. After dating in college, her wonderful future husband would propose to her, with a big sparkly diamond ring, and she would ecstatically say yes. They would be engaged for about a year. Their wedding would be elegant and perfect. Then during the first couple years of marriage, they would travel around the world to go bungee jumping and skydiving, swim with sharks and dolphins, and immerse themselves in different cultures. With their adventures behind them, they would start a family. They would have beautiful and well-behaved children. Heather would love her life as a loving mother and dedicated wife.

How naïve and stupid she was back then, Heather thought as she was preparing to turn 30. She firmly believed God was punishing her for thinking April Robertson was pathetic for getting married at age 35. Because she had judged April, God took away the life Heather had planned. Because she was conceited and vain, she was still single at age 29. She didn't even have a boyfriend. Because she thought April was a loser, Heather had to watch all three of her younger sisters exchange wedding vows before her.

Since that conversation with her mom, Heather fell to her knees numerous times and promised God that she would change and not judge people. She prayed He would lead her to her soul mate. She prayed the guy she was dating would be "the one." She prayed she would get married before she turned 35.

Heather felt she was no longer that silly, vain, and stupid college freshman. She believed she was a mature adult who thought of others' feelings. She changed not because she wanted to get married, but because she wanted to become a better person. She didn't want to present herself as shallow and cruel.

Although she was 29 and single, Heather loved her life. She had a great job. She was surrounded by great friends and family. She had two beautiful cats who unconditionally loved her. She was leading a good life. And she was grateful that society's attitude about dating and marriage had changed a teeny teeny bit. Single women in their late 20s weren't marked as losers or lesbians, and bets were made when anyone younger than 25 (who are now considered "kids") got hitched.

Heather thought about the April Robertson comment from time to time and wondered whether God was still punishing her for being vain and stupid. She even thought about apologizing to April for thinking such a dumb comment, but the revelation would only ease Heather's guilty conscience. April definitely would not benefit from knowing that an acquaintance — a stranger now — thought she was a loser so many years ago. So, Heather nixed that idea.

Every time a relationship ended, numerous questions flooded Heather's mind. Why did she attract such losers? Why did men change for the worse after she had fallen in love with them? Was there something wrong with her? Why can men be such assholes? Did her parents think she was a complete failure for not marrying and having children? Would she walk down the aisle before she was 35?

CHAPTER 1

Monday, January 3

"Oh crap," Heather Kincannon grumbled as she closed the door to her one-bedroom apartment and stepped onto a freshly snow-covered sidewalk.

Due to hitting the snooze button on her alarm clock too many times, she was running a little late. Had she known that it was snowing, she would have left for work a lot sooner. And she would have grabbed a scarf and matching cap.

Heather continued grumbling to herself as she backed her car out of the garage and headed to work. About 15 minutes later, she pulled her car into the business' back parking lot and saw her co-worker, Morna, arriving at the same time.

"Good morning, Heather," Morna cheerfully chirped, walking with her to the back door of the business. "How are you today?"

"I'm doing OK," Heather replied. "I didn't know it was going to snow today."

"I don't think anyone knew," she said, opening the back door and walking in. "But what do you expect when you live in Amery Lake?"

Heather smiled and made her way to the front of the store, where her beautiful and elegant desk waited for her. She hung her dark brown wool coat in a nearby closet and reached for her keys that gave her access to her apartment, her car, and the business. As she unlocked the store's double doors, she looked out of the doors' windows to see snow falling on a peaceful parking lot in Amery Lake, Wisconsin.

Amery Lake was a city that boasted three colleges — a technical college, a state university, and a Lutheran university — and two established medical centers. The city wasn't too big for people who wanted to get away from bigger well-known cities, such as Madison or Milwaukee, however, the city wasn't too small that people needed to drive elsewhere to find fun activities. But what Amery Lake was best known for was its extravagant and expensive balls.

The Carrington House — an elegant and historic hotel — threw two elaborate parties a year. Very generous donors would receive two personal invitations. Being dressed in Sunday's best was hardly appropriate for the Carrington balls. Black tuxedos are required during the winter ball and white or gray tuxes during the summer. Women carefully planned their attire months in advance. The wealthier women shopped for new ball gowns while the less wealthy usually spruced up old bridesmaid dresses or found an acceptable dress during the homecoming and prom seasons.

Heather never attended the grand event but had heard stories from the women who shopped at Lexington. She heard about the never-ending fountain of champagne flowing into a pyramid of expensive glasses. She heard about the poker room, the beautiful dance hall, and the sitting areas where guests can talk and nibble on endless trays of expensive hors d'oeuvres. A large elegant balcony overlooked the gorgeous and immaculate garden and water fountain.

Heather had no desire to go even when she had the opportunity. Her boss, Wesley Lexington, generously donated to the Carrington House and received several personal invitations. Heather had no desire to spend a fortune on a dress (she'd probably wear once) and accessories to surround herself with people she didn't know. She wouldn't know what to say to the mayor of Amery Lake and other local and surrounding area officials nor would they want to talk to a lowly administrative assistant at Lexington.

Vodka Four

"Are you insane?" Gretchen, a part-time administrative assistant who took over Heather's position at night, had asked a couple of years ago. "You turned down an invitation to go to the winter ball?"

"It's not a big deal," Heather had said, organizing her desk. "Who am I going to take? And who would want to talk to me?"

"Will could go with you," Gretchen pointed out, referring to Heather's boyfriend at that time. "And who cares about who will talk to you? You're there to gawk at everyone else and indulge in the extravagant food."

Heather made a noise and rolled her eyes. "If I took Will, he would definitely make an ass out of himself. One, he can't afford to rent a tux with his Walmart paycheck. Two, he wastes his money on those stupid online poker games. He can't even afford to take me out to a nice restaurant. Three, even if we did go, Will would make an ass out of himself by overindulging in the free champagne and believing he's good enough to play poker with the wealthy. He would lose his money in a heartbeat."

Gretchen shook her blonde hair as she sat in Heather's chair. "I can't believe you passed up the opportunity to go to the winter ball."

"I would rather spend my money on something else than go to a ball where I don't know anyone and would have a boring time."

"You would look so pretty in a beautiful ball gown."

"Yeah, I know, but I'm not going unless I have a good reason and if I have a presentable boyfriend."

"Will's not a presentable boyfriend?" Gretchen asked curiously.

"I wouldn't take him to the winter ball," Heather explained carefully, choosing the right words. "Think about who usually goes to the balls ... the wealthy. Will is by no means wealthy and really doesn't work hard. He works for $8 an hour behind the jewelry counter at Wal-Mart. He has no ambition to look for another job, but that doesn't stop him from bitching about the job he has. Instead, he wastes his days drinking and gambling."

During the third week of dating Will, Heather realized he was never going to be a presentable boyfriend. Like what most women would do when they first meet a new guy, they attempted to envision a future together. With Will, Heather couldn't see herself bringing him home to meet her parents and sisters. And if she did, she would have had to coach him on what (or not) to say. Even without meeting her three younger sisters, Heather had figured they would disapprove of him, and to an extent, she wouldn't blame them.

"Why are you still with Will?"

"That's a very good question," Heather said thoughtfully, pulling on her coat and leaving her workday at Lexington behind her.

Lexington is a popular (and the only) formal department store in Amery Lake. Once the Carrington House started throwing elaborate balls, Wesley Lexington's father, Blake, saw a lucrative business opportunity. He opened the store to cater to the wealthy that shopped in Madison, Milwaukee, or the Twin Cities. Over the years, the store expanded to include expensive but comfortable casual wear.

On a normal business day, four full-time salespeople took care of the men's and women's departments while others filled the night and weekend shifts.

"Penny for your thoughts," Morna said sweetly, setting a full coffee cup on Heather's desk.

"Thank you, Morna," Heather said. "You didn't have to bring me coffee. You're too sweet to me."

Wesley's sister-in-law, Morna Lexington, worked as the store's accountant and human resource director. Wesley's father first hired her as a part-time administrative assistant. She eventually became a full-time administrative assistant before

Vodka Four

trying her hand as a full-time sales associate. She worked with Wesley and his brother, David, and David and Morna fell in love and married. David had no desire to work at the store once he entered college. He studied business and construction and now owns and operates a construction business.

"Well, I didn't see you in the break room when I went to get my coffee fix. So, I thought I would bring your morning cup."

"Thank you," Heather repeated and smiled sheepishly for being caught staring outside. "I was just thinking about how beautiful the square looks when it first snows. Sounds lame."

"Not at all, sweetie," Morna said reassuringly. "Enjoy the moment while you can before the salt trucks ruin the scenic view."

"Thank you for the coffee," Heather said as Morna returned to her office in the back room.

Heather was the only full-time administrative assistant and worked Mondays through Fridays and occasional weekends during the busy season. Two part-time assistants covered the paperwork and telephone lines after 5 p.m. and when she called in sick or went on vacation.

College students and aspiring fashion designers longed to work at Lexington because of the flexible hours, good pay, great discounts, easygoing boss, and opportunities to mix with the wealthy. Around the college campuses, Wesley Lexington was rumored to be a very generous man. He offered two employees the chance to attend the Carrington balls, gave generous Christmas and end-of-the-year bonuses, and provided excellent references. Nobody wanted to be on his shit list.

Wesley was not an ignorant man. He knew the majority of applicants were looking for bigger and better opportunities. He didn't hold the goal against them, but he wanted to provide professional customer service. The last thing he wanted was gold-digging employees with hidden agendas. So, Wesley carefully and personally selected his employees.

Heather was surprised when Wesley called to schedule an interview and was nervous as hell when she met him. Although she had dressed confidently in a sharp pin-striped dress and jacket, looked professional, and remained calm throughout the interview, she felt she belonged in a different working environment as she sat in front of Wesley and Morna, who were immaculately and confidently dressed.

The interview went well, with Morna rattling off the description of the position, the benefits package, and how to earn vacation and sick hours. Wesley asked her about her strengths and weaknesses and what she would do in certain scenarios. Heather proceeded with her three questions she always asked during interviews: what is the dress code, what is the hardest part of the position, and what do they expect from her.

Then Wesley had asked Heather a question she was not prepared for, "Where do you see yourself in five years?"

She had no idea. She didn't know whether to lie about wanting to climb the ranks in the business world or tell the truth.

"I have no idea," Heather had answered honestly. "Personally, I love the Amery Lake area and plan to stay here for as long as I can. Professionally, I honestly don't know where I want to be in five years. For now, I like working as an administrative assistant because I excel in this area."

After the interview, Heather had thought she blew her chance. As she replayed the interview in her mind, her answer to the surprise question wouldn't have changed because she honestly didn't know where she wanted to be in five years.

Wesley called a week later to offer her the position. He liked her honest answer about not knowing where she wanted to be. Her answer was refreshing compared to the other applicants who gave him some bullshit answers. Wesley had

Vodka Four

a knack for picking good hard-working employees and rarely had to fire anyone.

Heather truly loved working at Lexington. During the busy seasons, she didn't mind picking up extra hours. Wesley was more than happy to pay overtime to make sure his customers were happy. Satisfied customers made return appearances and recommended Lexington to friends and family.

For the next hour, Heather organized weekend paperwork and read customers' e-mails on her computer. She was so engrossed reading customers' praises that she didn't notice Wesley and the full-time sales associates wandering onto the floor room.

Wesley Lexington liked to see his floor room immaculate. He was an organized man and didn't care for sloppiness. The men's and women's casual wear were hanging perfectly on expensive racks that dotted the burgundy carpeted floor room. Lining the back wall, a huge closet contained the expensive suits and ball gowns that built Lexington's good reputation. At the end of the day, the night-time supervisor closed and locked the closet doors to hide the pricey merchandise.

Wesley watched the sales associates huddle around Heather's desk. She was informing them when the first scheduled customers were coming in and which associate needed to be ready.

Wesley smiled as he watched Heather run down the schedule. Hiring her was one of the best decisions he had ever made. Based solely on her appearance during her interview, he was ready to send her a "thanks for interviewing with us" letter. Her rail-thin frame and youthful look made him guess that she wasn't legally allowed into bars. He was wrong. According to Morna who quickly befriended Heather after she was hired, Heather had just turned 25.

During the interview, Heather had remained poised and confident. She didn't even blink when he asked her where she wanted to be in five years. She answered honestly, and he liked that. Her three references raved about her organizational skills, professionalism, and maturity. Still believing she was an underage drinker, Wesley hired her anyway.

No one could blame him for his first impression either. At first glance, most people believed Heather was in her early 20s and stared in disbelief when told that she'll turn 30 this year. The only average characteristic about Heather was her height. Her long legs gave the impression that she was of supermodel height, but she stood at an average height. An extremely high metabolism and occasional exercise kept her naturally tanned figure slender. What caught most people's attention were her piercing green eyes that complimented her oval-shaped face.

Heather loved experimenting with her naturally straight and dark brown hair. Throughout her five years at Lexington, the length, style, and color of her hair have all changed. Wesley remembered she had curls at one point, sported blonde highlights, and dyed her hair dark red. Now, remnants of dark red could be seen in her straight dark brown hair that barely touched her slender shoulders.

Wesley liked Heather and enjoyed working with her. She was mature, had a great sense of humor, and refused to be bullied by anyone — even him. Her maturity was evident in the way she dressed. Most girls with her frame made sure their thongs peeked out and believed showing some skin was sexy. Not Heather. She was always and completely professionally dressed. Today, she wore black dress pants and a white turtleneck sweater that fell to her hips. Her hair was pulled into a low ponytail, and her sparkling green eyes were hidden behind black-rimmed glasses.

"Morning, Heather," he greeted, walking toward her always clean desk. Arranged to her satisfaction sat a flat screen computer and keyboard, a framed picture of her sitting with her three younger sisters and a second framed picture of her two cats.

"Good morning, Wesley."

Vodka Four

"What's on the agenda today?"

"Mr. Lambert comes in at 9:30 a.m. He is looking for a tuxedo for the ball," Heather read from her computer screen. "Robert is going to meet with him, and Christopher is going to take care of Mr. Silbaugh, who also needs a new tux."

"Will you be attending the ball this year?" Wesley asked, knowing she would turn down the invitation.

"Ah, no," Heather said. "Thank you for the invitation, but I will once again decline."

"Any particular reason?"

Heather shrugged her shoulders. "Not really. I don't want to be in a room full of people I don't know and don't want to talk to. That and I don't have a date."

"I find it hard to believe that you're single."

"Still haven't found the lucky guy, I guess."

"Then the guys you have dated are all fools."

Heather looked at Wesley and smiled. She enjoyed hearing him berate her ex-boyfriends. Made her feel less like a loser for being a single 29-year-old.

"Thank you, Wesley. My sisters have no doubt that I will meet the man of dreams someday."

"You have smart sisters," he said. "What else is on the agenda?"

Heather also believed he operated the store well, treated his employees fairly, and was open to new ideas. Heather admired Wesley's work ethics and family values as a happily married man with four adorable kids. Those characteristics were what she needed to think about whenever she found herself drooling over Wesley's incredibly fine features.

Standing a few inches over six feet tall, Wesley was an image of a successful and wealthy businessman. His naturally wavy dark blond hair was always cropped short. A few lines on his handsome face indicated his older years, but the rest of his body revealed a fine physique kept in shape by running five miles every morning before dropping his children off at school. His blue eyes sparkled when he was in a good mood and darkened when he was pissed.

"Will you tell me when Mr. Whittaker and his son are here?" Wesley asked, as he started walking toward the two full-time men's sales associates, Robert and Christopher, who were straightening the suits in the closet.

"Not a problem, Wesley," Heather said, picking up the ringing black cordless telephone cradled in its base behind her desk. "Good morning. Thank you for calling Lexington."

CHAPTER 2

"How was your holiday vacation?" Heather asked before shoveling fried rice in her mouth.

"It was OK," Christopher Milling replied in the traditional guy manner.

"What did you do?" she pressed.

"Spent Christmas with my brothers and my friends."

Heather looked at Christopher, who was pulling apart a crab rangoon. Christopher was a 25-year-old who has worked as a sales associate at Lexington for six years. He started out as a part-time associate while he studied business administration at the state university. The idea of working at a department store didn't thrill him, but he had heard about the great benefits and discounts and saw Lexington as a launching pad for his career. However, when Christopher accepted the full-time position, his social life decreased significantly between working and going to school full time. So, he left school a few months later.

At least once a week, Heather and Christopher or other friends would meet for lunch at China Garden Buffet or order from other restaurants. This morning, due to running a little bit behind, Heather completely forgot to pack a lunch. She had no problem talking Christopher into going out at noon.

Despite the expensive suit and tie, Christopher was the typical college student who liked to hang out with his friends at the bars, play poker at the casino, watch ESPN as much as possible, and fly to Las Vegas at least once a year. A self-proclaimed bachelor for life, he has been single for about a year after ending a three-year relationship. Since the breakup, Christopher has been on a few dates that never led to anything more. Too much alcohol was one of the biggest reasons why he rarely hooked up with a woman.

When Christopher had too much to drink, his memory became fuzzy. On several occasions, his friends continuously harassed him the next day for not taking a good-looking and very willing woman home with him. Christopher had several opportunities to go home with someone, but too much alcohol always prevented him from getting laid.

"Tell me about Vegas," Heather pushed.

Christopher shrugged his shoulders. "I got drunk, placed bets, and won a little bit of money."

"How much did you win?"

"About five hundred. Not a big deal," he said. "Nick won about two thousand."

"Really?" Heather asked. "How did he do that?"

"He won about a thousand by putting a dollar into some random slot machine, and then he won the rest by betting on sports."

"Nice."

"Yeah, I thought so."

"How much did you bring?" she asked.

"About a thousand."

"Did you see naked women?"

"I don't know what you're talking about," Christopher said, smiling sweetly.

Heather laughed.

"Yeah, I think someone saw some boobs."

"Once again, I don't know what you're talking about."

"Yeah, I think you do, but I will let it go. I can't imagine a group of guys going to Vegas and not see strippers. Please. I may not be a genius, but I'm not stupid."

"Never said you were."

"Was there ever a time when you weren't drunk?"

Christopher paused for a second. "Uh, no."

"Was there ever a time when you were sober?"

Vodka Four

"When I was sleeping."

"Did you ever have to deal with any hangovers?"

"Not really," Christopher answered. "The hotel that we stayed at provided us with free drinks. What were we supposed to do? Turn them away?"

"Well, I'm glad you had a good time."

"I had a great time," he said, smiling. "The first night I was in Vegas, I called everyone I knew. Because my phone was on roam, I used my brother's cell phone to call people. I called my roommate, Tamara, at 4 a.m. and left a message on her phone telling her that I was in Vegas. I think I called about a dozen people and left similar messages at 3 or 4 a.m. I called one of my friends, Shorty, almost every day in the early morning. I think I called Tamara and her friends a couple of times."

Heather laughed with delight.

"When I got back to Amery Lake, I had about a dozen messages on my cell telling me that I'm an asshole. It was great."

Heather laughed again, but felt a little jealous and maybe disappointed that Christopher didn't call her. But then again, her friendship with Christopher really didn't exist outside of the working hours at Lexington. On the rare occasion that they ran into each other outside of the store, they exchanged the friendly "hellos" and "how are you doings."

Despite talking for hours about their high school and college days and their friends, Heather barely knew Christopher. She knew, for some reason, that he didn't liked to be called Chris. Not even his closest friends called him Chris instead they either used Christopher or nicknames, such as Milly. Part of her yearned to be included in Christopher's circle of friends, but his partying lifestyle brought her back to reality. Despite having an easygoing relationship at work, Heather and Christopher were also two different people who led different lifestyles.

"I was so drunk," Christopher continued.

"You're an alcoholic," Heather teased.

"No," he defended. "I'm a binge drinker. There's a difference. And I'm barely a binge drinker."

Heather made a small grunting noise. "Christopher, you go out almost every weekend and get drunk with your friends. You may not be an alcoholic, but you are a binge drinker."

Christopher looked like a typical college student. He kept his reddish brown hair cut close but let the hair around his chin grow for a few days. A clean face is what he preferred, but sheer laziness kept him away from a razor and mirror. Except for when he slept, Christopher always wore contacts on his dark green eyes. He never liked to wear glasses and preferred contacts due to roughhousing with his buddies and playing sports. His love for sports kept his average athletic body in decent shape. Heather suspected that if Christopher cut back on his alcohol, he wouldn't have a small beer belly that was unnoticeable to the untrained eye.

"How was your holiday?" Christopher asked.

"I had a good time," Heather said. "Santa gave me everything I wanted."

"Did you have a good time at your sister's wedding?"

Heather smiled at the thought of herself dancing madly on the dance floor with much younger and eligible men.

"Yes, I did," she admitted. "I got a little drunk in front of my parents. I don't think they were impressed with my ability to suck down drinks."

Christopher chuckled.

Heather's youngest sister, Sarah, rang in the new year by marrying her college boyfriend of three years in a farming town in Minnesota. Heather was truly happy for her younger sister's special occasion, but she felt like the biggest loser. The oldest of three younger and married sisters, Heather had nothing to showcase her success. She wasn't married, and she didn't have

Vodka Four

adorable children. All she had was her happiness with two cats and a job she loved.

Despite feeling like a loser, Heather had a great time at Sarah's wedding. She talked with relatives whom she hadn't seen in years and hung around with her younger and always fun cousins. And she looked absolutely fabulous in a shimmery silver dress Sarah picked out for her bridesmaids.

"Was that the first time your parents have seen you drunk?"

Heather nodded.

"You see, my sisters and I were good girls growing up," she explained, pausing to thank the waitress who refilled the water glasses. "But once we entered college, all of the rules changed as expected. All of us did the usual thing ... party, drink, skip classes."

Heather was about to ask whether Christopher's parents had ever seen him drunk, but then remembered his parents died when he was 15 years old. She didn't know the details and never pressed for more information. The only family history she knew about was that he had two older brothers who lived in Colorado and Las Vegas.

As Christopher was paying the bill and Heather was shrugging into her jacket, two young men walked into the restaurant.

"Milly!" one of them exclaimed as Christopher slipped his wallet into his back pocket.

"Hey, Ryan," Christopher greeted. "What's up?"

"Time for lunch," Ryan said and then looked at Heather. "Hey, Heather."

"Hi," she said easily. "How's it going?"

"I'm hungry," he answered. "Is he still paying off his debt?"

Heather nodded, with a devilish grin.

At the start of the national football season, Christopher bragged about his extensive knowledge of the sport and predicted he would do well in the annual office pool. So, Heather — knowing next to nothing about football — challenged him to a weekly lunch bet. Whoever correctly picked more winning teams chose the restaurant while the loser had to pay for lunch. Heather wanted to prove to Christopher that having an extensive knowledge of football didn't matter.

Because she didn't know statistics, players, or anything else about the sport, she used the mascot theory — which team mascot was tougher or which mascot she liked better. Bengals, jaguars, panthers, and lions were likely picked to win because Heather believed felines were fierce animals. When she couldn't decide who was tougher between a buccaneer and a raider, team colors then became a factor in the decision-making process.

Although Christopher would never admit it, Heather believed her mascot theory worked. She won the first week of competition, and Christopher was the winner the second week. The alternate-winning pattern followed them throughout the football season until the end when Heather triumphed with a just a few more overall points.

"Good girl," Ryan said, with a smile.

Heather smirked at Christopher, who rolled his eyes.

"Did you guys have a good time in Vegas?" she asked.

"Hell yeah," Ryan exclaimed, holding up a hand for a high-five from Christopher.

"Heard you won some money, Nick," she said, eyeing the guy behind Ryan who remained quiet.

He shrugged. "I had a good time."

"Lucky bastard," Ryan said, winking at Heather. "He's walking past a dollar slot machine. Puts some money in, and wins a thousand bucks."

Heather laughed as Ryan pretended to pout and playfully hit Nick in the shoulder.

After exchanging goodbyes, Christopher and Heather returned to work and Ryan and Nick were seated at a table.

Vodka Four

After piling their plates from the buffet, they returned to the table.

"Christopher's a lucky bastard," Ryan said, between bites.

"Why?" Nick asked.

"Because he gets to work with Heather every day."

Nick smiled. He wasn't going to deny that Heather was hot, but he didn't understand why she was still single. Nick knew at least a hundred guys who would be willing to commit to her. Stories of Heather's failed relationships and wild tales with her girlfriends traveled next door to the sports store where he and Ryan worked. They also used to work with one of Heather's ex-boyfriends before he moved to California to be closer to his ailing mother.

"Why hasn't Christopher hit on her?" Ryan wondered.

Nick shrugged. "I don't know. Maybe he doesn't think he has a chance with her. Or maybe he doesn't want to date someone he works with."

"How long has it been since he broke up with Leslie?"

Nick mentally counted the months before answering, "About a year, I think."

"I can't believe he ended it with Leslie, too," Ryan said, shaking his head. "She was pretty and had huge tits."

Nick smirked as a mental image of Leslie and her breasts appeared in his mind. Sex was Ryan Wells' favorite subject. He loved hearing stories about other peoples' torrid affairs and sexual experiences. Not that Ryan needed to live through other people, he simply liked talking about sex and didn't mind sharing his fair share of tawdry tales.

Despite being 27 years old, Ryan didn't act or look his stated age. During the week, he was a full-time sales associate at Amery Lake Sports. During the weekend, he spent his time and money at the bars or strip clubs. While Ryan had no desire to settle down and start a family, he had no issues being in a relationship and committing to one woman. He enjoyed being a boyfriend and being pampered by a girlfriend. But as soon as questions were asked about where their relationship was headed and what he wanted in his future, he ended the relationship. Ryan simply liked having a good time. Marriage and children weren't in his immediate future and weren't his idea of having a good time.

Like Christopher, Ryan looked like a typical college student. He stood about average height with a muscular build. When Ryan wasn't working, he usually wore a baseball cap to hide his thinning brown hair. Contacts usually were worn over his blue eyes, but silver wire-rimmed glasses were used often due to laziness. He also thought he looked intelligent whenever he wore glasses. Beer and hard alcohol kept from him having a hard and lean body, but league sports kept him from becoming too flabby.

At first glance, women normally didn't give Ryan a second look due to his ordinary looks, but his easygoing and charming personality usually won them over. He was a natural flirt who loved talking to women. He had an easier time talking to women than his roommate and one of his best friends, Nick Reed.

Shy and quiet easily described Nick. But once people learned more about him, he was talkative and easygoing. Ryan recalled numerous occasions when women asked him about Nick's eligibility. Women were drawn to Nick's aloof manner, but his serious and studious look usually kept them from approaching him.

Nick was almost six feet tall with a muscular and lean body. Although he usually accompanied Ryan and Christopher to the bars and strip clubs, Nick had his limits. Not that he was opposed to having a good time and getting liquored up, he wanted to spend or save his money on more important stuff, such as cool electronic gadgets or a huge flat screen TV. He kept his body in shape by working out every day and participating in league sports. His light brown hair was kept

Vodka Four

short and perfectly combed. Nick felt lucky that his blue eyes didn't require glasses or contacts.

Nick liked his life. He enjoyed working at the sports department store and the nightlife with Ryan and Christopher. However, he missed being in a relationship, missing the warmth and company the most. His last girlfriend of two years left him to save the wildlife in Arizona. Nick thought she might have been the one for him, but he was unwilling to move to Arizona and she didn't ask him to move with her. Plenty of women threw themselves at him, but he really didn't believe in one-night stands. However, he had no problem sleeping with a woman on a first date when he knew there was going to be a second date.

"If you had a chance to sleep with Heather or Rory, who would you pick?" Ryan asked, then thanking the waitress for refilling their water glasses.

Nick thought about the two choices. This was a tough question. There was no doubt that Heather was beautiful, and her piercing green eyes caught a lot of men's attention. However, one of her best friends, Rory Andersen, who worked full time at Lexington, was just stunningly and naturally beautiful.

"I don't know," Nick answered. "That's something I don't think about since it will never happen." He emphasized the word "never" for good measure. "I don't think guys get to choose between Heather or Rory — they decide who they want to be with."

"Yeah," Ryan admitted. "But if I had to choose, I'd probably pick Rory. She's just fuckin' hot. Any heterosexual guy wants to have sex with her. Guys would bring Heather home to meet the parents."

Although Ryan and Nick have lusted over Heather and Rory, they have never been remotely close to dating or hooking up with either of them. Relationships and other obstacles prevented them from even considering becoming involved with Heather or Rory.

A few months ago, Ryan ended a nine-month relationship after finding a diamond ring catalog in her apartment. Finding the catalog didn't scare him. It was what he found inside that made him shit. His ex-girlfriend had drawn circles around the pictures of engagement rings that she liked. So, Ryan lied about "needing time to himself" and wanting to "focus on his job."

Part of Ryan felt bad about lying and ending the relationship because he had fun with his ex-girlfriend. He hadn't believed she was the type to push marriage and their relationship, but the diamond ring catalog proved otherwise. The other part of Ryan enjoyed his freedom and loved fantasizing and flirting with other women.

But now that Ryan and Nick were free to chase Heather and Rory, they had trouble "running" into them outside of work. They had heard the wild stories about Heather and Rory being the ultimate party girls, but they could never find them at the downtown bars. Even with help from Christopher who usually knew their whereabouts, Ryan and Nick couldn't seem to make a connection.

"Hello, pretty girl," Heather purred to a tall and curvaceous woman standing in the Lexington floor room, running her slender hand sensuously up the woman's back.

"Hello, sexy," the woman said huskily, boldly running her finger through Heather's hair.

"Good God, please stop," Christopher pleaded before walking away. "Your behavior is just shameless to millions of men."

The two women laughed heartily as they watched Christopher walk away and shake his head.

"I love the power we have over men, Rory," Heather said, giggling.

Vodka Four

"I know," she said, flipping her long black hair over her shoulders.

Heather met one of her best friends, Rory Andersen, in college. They had met when Rory was learning the ropes as a stripper at the Skylight Bar, a fancy and elegant strip club. The dancers boasted about being a "Skylight Girl" and learned choreographed routines and performed in sexy — not sleazy — costumes. Rory worked hard to become one of the best Skylight Girls, which meant more money in her pocket.

There was no question that Rory was naturally beautiful. Standing at almost six feet tall, Rory had long, straight, black hair that fell down her back and showcased her hourglass figure. A daily regime of facial products took care of her naturally tan skin. Her head was always held high to show off her high cheekbones and full lips. Padded bras were not needed to add to her rounded and full breasts. Perfection was usually the first word that popped into a man's mind at first glance, but Rory knew she was far from perfect.

College was put on hold because Rory didn't know what she wanted to do in life. So, instead of wasting time and money, she became a stripper because she liked the prospect of not working full time and still being wealthy. Soon after Heather was hired at Lexington, Rory started visiting her and realized she wanted to own a business (at the time, didn't matter what kind of business). She admired Wesley's work ethics and the power he wielded and decided she wanted to be in control.

So, Rory quit dancing, applied for a part-time position at Lexington, and started to study business administration and management at the local university. Wesley was so impressed with her eagerness to learn and her perfection to detail, he promoted her to night supervisor a year later.

"So, what brings you in so early?" Heather asked, glancing around the store to see a few customers talking with other sales associates.

"The Carrington ball is at the end of the month," Rory explained. "Wesley thought an extra sales associate would be helpful today. Where were you?"

"Having lunch with Christopher at China Garden Buffet."

"Doesn't winning feel good?"

"Oh yeah," Heather said, with a grin. "Guess who we ran into at the restaurant?"

"Who?"

"Ryan and Nick."

"Yeah," Rory said, raising one of her eyebrows. "How are they?"

"Apparently Nick won some money when they were in Vegas, and Ryan was cute and flirty as usual."

"Well, he's single now."

"Oh yeah, that's right," Heather exclaimed, her eyes widening a bit. "What happened?"

"I don't know the whole story," Rory said, straightening one of the racks on the floor. "But he broke up with Anya in September or October. And as far as I know, he's not dating anyone."

"I totally forgot he broke up with Anya."

"So, what are you going to do?"

"What do you mean?" Heather asked, with feigned innocence but knew full well what Rory was talking about.

"Sweetheart, don't try to pull that innocent and naïve act with me," she replied, with a smirk. "You're not that good of an actress."

Heather pretended to act offended. "Hey, I nabbed the role of the Virgin Mary twice for my church's nativity story. Twice." She held up two fingers for emphasis.

Rory didn't look impressed with Heather's acting credentials. "Did you actually audition for the role? Did you sing and dance? Did you prepare a monologue?"

"No." Heather scowled.

Vodka Four

"So, how did you land the role of the Virgin Mary?"

"The church chose me because I had long brown hair," she admitted reluctantly as Rory laughed out loud.

"So, back to my original question, Meryl Streep. What are you going to do about Ryan?"

Heather shrugged. "I don't know. My crush is harmless."

"You have the ability to do something."

"Yeah, I know," she said. "It's just that I really don't know Ryan. He's a funny guy who has commitment issues. Do I really want to pursue a guy who doesn't want to settle down?"

Rory thought about the question. While Heather wasn't against having a good time with guys, Rory knew she wanted a normal and stable relationship. "Very true. What about Nick? He's attractive and doesn't appear to have commitment issues."

"He's too shy. You know me, I like to talk. I don't think he and I would have a lot to talk about."

"But as you pointed out, you really don't know Nick or Ryan."

"Why don't you go out with one of them?" Heather asked Rory. "Why am I the one who has to choose?"

"Honey, I don't date boys. I date men. Besides, I'm not the one with a crush on them."

"It's harmless!" she exclaimed, wandering back to her desk as a customer walked in.

Heather smiled and shook her head slightly as she sat behind her desk. What she told Rory was true — she always had a harmless crush on Ryan. But now that neither of them was in a relationship, a good chance existed that something could happen. And what Rory told Heather was true — Heather could pick between Nick and Ryan. Although she didn't know Nick or Ryan's taste in women or interest in her, for the matter, Heather suspected neither would say no if she suggested meeting for a drink.

But did she really want to start dating again? Heather was content with her life. Dating someone would mess up her perfect life. She liked her routine of going home after work, feeding her cats, and watching TV or a movie for the rest of the night. Sometimes, she read a book, did laundry, ran errands, shopped for clothes, or talked to her sisters. The routine probably sounded boring to most people, but Heather liked her privacy and space. As much as she loved hanging out with her friends, she also enjoyed being by herself.

She loved filling her apartment with music and dancing while her two cats curiously watched from afar. Sometimes Heather threw on a pair of sexy high-heeled sandals, short denim shorts, and white tank top before dancing around and singing along. At these times, she felt sexy and completely free and absolutely loved her life.

If she started dating, Heather would have to give up her alone time until the relationship soured. To avoid the agonizing, and sometimes ugly, end of a relationship, maybe she shouldn't date at all. The advantages would be no alone time would be lost and she would have plenty of time for her friends, her cats, and neglected hobbies. The disadvantages would be missing being in a relationship, not holding hands, not sharing her bed, and thinking about a guy when he's not around.

Heather looked outside the store window to see a black winter cap fly by. A bashful Nick scampered after it, which was snatched from his head and thrown by Ryan, who was standing and laughing outside of Heather's view. Nick straightened up, with cap in hand, and noticed her watching him with amusement. He gave a crooked smile and waved. Heather grinned and waved back.

CHAPTER 3

Friday, January 7

Anastacia Square is the most expensive shopping center in Amery Lake and was built around Lexington as it thrived on the wealthy's taste for expensive and fine clothing. Blake Lexington, Wesley's father, saw a lucrative opportunity as his business grew. He purchased the remaining land, announced his plan to build a new shopping center, and sold store space to interested business owners.

The square was named after David and Morna Lexington's first child, Anastacia, who died two days after being born prematurely. The death of the first grandchild in the Lexington family was hard on Blake who decided to name the square in her honor.

A Saturn dealership, China Garden Buffet, a small café called Open on Mondays, Amery Lake Sports, Bellismo, an elite, established, and expensive hair salon, and Havland Diamonds, a jewelry store specializing in diamond rings, filled the surrounding store space.

About once a week, Heather had lunch with her friends, Rory; Hera Lindley, a full-time sales associate at Lexington; Catherine Mann, who worked full time at Severson Motors and part time at Lexington; and Lily Netwall, a full-time hair stylist at Bellismo. When she wasn't having lunch with them, she would dine with Christopher and some of his friends, which included Ryan and Nick. And sometimes Heather had lunch with a mix of her friends and Christopher's friends — basically, anyone who could break away from their jobs between noon and 1 p.m.

Today, Heather, Hera, Rory, Christopher, Ryan, and Nick were getting a head start at spending their paychecks, sitting at a round table by a front window.

After the waitress dropped off their food, Ryan casually asked, "So, what you are guys doing tonight?"

"We're going out," Rory replied. "We're going downtown tonight."

"Where are you guys going?" Christopher asked, munching on his French fries.

"Deep Pink. We're going dancing!"

"Hell yeah," Hera added.

Despite standing exactly at 5 feet, people knew better than to mess with Hera Lindley. Firecracker or wildcat best described her personality but not her appearance. At first glance, people see a delicate petite woman with flawless black skin and dark brown eyes. Her naturally curly black hair was usually pulled back into a smooth and tight ponytail unless Hera took the time to straighten it. Hera had a super high metabolism that gave her an excuse not to exercise her 98-pound body.

Heather and Hera became fast friends when Heather joined Lexington. Hera worked her way up from part-time sales associate to a full-time position and impressed Wesley and many customers with her creative window displays. Fashion was Hera's first love. She loved flipping through fashion magazines and had a knack for picking out flattering clothes for herself and others. She was also an expert at adding flair to old bridesmaid dresses for the Carrington ball and had brilliant ideas for the annual fashion show.

"Is Deep Pink the club that has flashback nights?" Nick asked, before biting into his double bacon cheeseburger.

"Yeah," Hera confirmed enthusiastically. "Like once a month, they have '80s night, where they play '80s music all night long. It's great."

Vodka Four

"What are you guys doing tonight?" Heather asked, biting into her bacon cheeseburger.

"Hanging out downtown," Christopher replied. "The usual."

"Hey, Heather, when is Eli coming back into town?" Ryan asked.

"I don't know," she said, shrugging her shoulders. She was a little surprised to hear Eli's name but then remembered her ex-boyfriend had worked with Ryan and Nick at the sports store before taking off to California. "I haven't talked to him in awhile."

"Eli told us some pretty wild stories about when you guys were in college," Ryan teased. "Apparently, you drank a lot and pulled a lot of pranks."

"Oh yeah?" Heather asked, as one of her brown eyebrows arched with curiosity.

"I'm trying to remember some of the stories he told us."

"Well, don't believe everything he said," she said nonchalantly. "He and I led really boring lives in college. We spent most of our time at the library."

"Yeah, I don't think he would lie to us," Ryan replied, but wondered whether or not she was telling the truth.

"Please," Heather said, waving one of her hands in the air as if dismissing the topic. "Eli has every reason to lie. Did you know he was in the science club back then? He was a guy who studied at the library to get on the dean's list every semester. Do you really think he's going to tell the guys at work that he was a geek in college? Eli graduated from college with honors. He was like in the top fifth percentile of his graduating class. With so much time spent on studying, do you really think he had time to party like a rock star?"

Ryan studied Heather's face for a second, waiting for her to crack a smile to reveal her bluff. A couple seconds passed, and absolutely nothing.

"So, you're telling us not to believe anything Eli said," Nick said, breaking the silence.

"You guys believe whatever you want," she said, holding up her hands in mock surrender. "But think about this — when you tell stories to the guys, don't you add a little something extra?"

"No," Ryan said, a little too quickly. "We tell the truth. We have no reason to lie."

Hera laughed out loud. "Guys have every reason to lie."

"What?" Christopher asked curiously. "How would you know?"

"Because I'm not stupid," she replied quickly and firmly. "Weakness is not a option for men. You guys don't want to appear weak and girly in front of each other, so you lie."

"Weak and girly?" Nick repeated in disbelief.

"Have you guys seen each other cry?" Rory jumped in, making Heather and Hera's point stronger. "Have you ever admitted you were emotionally scared about something?"

"Because we don't cry in front of each other makes us liars?" Christopher asked.

"Quit twisting my words around. Back to Heather's original point, guys exaggerate every now and then. That's what guys do."

"And how do you know?" Ryan questioned.

"Like Hera said, we're not stupid," Rory repeated. "We're women. We know stuff."

"Like men, apparently," Christopher threw in sarcastically.

"Well, we do," Heather agreed, with a casual shrug. "We know men because you guys have the tendency to act like women. And we're experts at that subject."

Everybody laughed.

"We should probably get going," Rory said, looking at her watch and then her lunch bill.

Vodka Four

After paying, everyone started walking toward their respective stores.

"Have fun tonight," Ryan said to Heather, Hera, and Rory as he and Nick walked past them.

"You too," Heather called out, waving goodbye as Christopher held Lexington's front door open.

Christopher, Hera, Rory, and Heather hung up their coats before going in separate directions. Heather sighed as she settled behind her desk and started to study the paperwork.

She was excited about going out tonight. Even though she didn't look like a 29-year-old professional working woman, Heather felt much older whenever she went to the downtown bars, which were filled with underage drinkers and college students. In fact, she hated going downtown because of the blaring music, drunk and stupid guys constantly hitting on her, and the long wait at the bar. A quiet night in her apartment with a bottle of wine and a good movie appeared way more exciting to Heather.

However, when Rory mentioned going dancing downtown, Heather immediately jumped at the idea. For one night, she could mingle with college students, deal with stupid drunk guys, and endure the long wait at the bar just so she could dance.

But the best part was that Heather would be among her friends. Although Hera was a few years younger, she enjoyed hitting the downtown bars. Rory and Lily occasionally stopped by downtown, but they preferred more adult places, such as the Skylight Bar. Because Cat felt she was too old for the younger scene, she avoided it whenever possible. But tonight, all of them were going dancing.

"Hey, what was going on at lunch?" Rory asked, taking advantage of the slower pace. Christopher and Hera were working with customers, while the other sales associates were straightening the racks.

"What do you mean?"

"Well, you basically called Eli a liar."

"Oh, that," Heather remembered. "I don't know. I just forgot Ryan and Nick worked with him when he and I were going out."

"Why didn't you want Ryan and Nick to know that you were a party girl in college? Are you ashamed you had a good time back then?"

Heather laughed and shook her head. "No, of course not. I just think it's unfair that they know more about me than I do about them. And what they know about me happened a long time ago."

"So, you don't want them to think you're a party girl?"

"I guess. Ryan just caught me off guard when he mentioned Eli's name."

"I take it you haven't talked to Eli in awhile," Rory said, glancing around the store for customers.

"No," Heather admitted. "I can't remember the last time he and I talked on the phone, and we haven't e-mailed each other in awhile."

"Ryan and Nick are going to believe whatever they want about you because they don't know you except through Eli's stories. But even without his tall tales, they're probably creating elaborate and smutty fantasies about you."

"Ew." Heather wrinkled her nose in disgust.

"Eh, don't worry about it, though. That's what boys do. Just based on a guy's appearance, women imagine him standing in front an altar and wonder if he fits in with the dream wedding. Guys do the same thing except they picture a pretty woman naked and imagine her doing kinky stuff in bed."

"Ew."

Rory chuckled and started walking toward a customer. "You'll be fine."

Heather grinned and shook her head. After being friends for more than 10 years, Rory probably knew a little something about her. Their fierce independence and similar sassy attitudes forged and maintained their friendship. Heather and Rory both believed being single and happy was way better than being in an unhappy or dramatic relationship. Neither harped on the other about finding a boyfriend — even when one of them was in a relationship.

Yes, Heather was eternally grateful for her best friends, Rory, Cat, Lily, and Hera. All of them understood the advantages of renting instead of buying a house. Who was going to pay for a new refrigerator when it broke down? Who had to mow the lawn? Who was going to fix the screen on the patio door? For renters, the answer is the landlord. For homeowners, not the landlord.

While Heather understood the advantages of owning a house, she wasn't ready for that responsibility or commitment. Her other friends — more specifically, married or engaged friends — raved about owning a house and pushed Heather to find one. They also badgered her about her social life and nudged her to settle down. While their intentions were good and pissed her off a little, Heather never understood why she didn't say, "Fuck off and leave me alone." Instead, she faked a bright smile and gave a cliché statement about love finding her when the time was right.

"Why do you do that?" Rory had asked once after Heather had attended a dinner party that had turned into an interrogation about her love life and then, finally, a pity party. "Why don't you tell them fuck off?"

"I don't know," she had said, with a sigh. "I've known them since college, and I've had good times with them."

"The operative word is had," Rory had pointed out. "You had good times with them, but now, they're making you miserable."

"I'll be fine. I'll just avoid them for awhile."

"What kind of friendship is that, Heather? Do you really want to be friends with people who are pressuring you to lead a domestic life?"

"They mean well," she had defended. "When they're not talking about my social life, I do have a good time with them."

However, the same love-committed friends didn't understand why Heather loved her independence so much. While they needed someone to accompany them somewhere, Heather didn't mind going to the movie theater, going grocery shopping, or even dining out by herself. Being alone didn't bother her.

Heather loved her life. She didn't believe a man "completed" her life and made her "happier." If anything, a good man complimented her already fantastic and complete life. However, her high school friends only saw the senior homecoming queen not married and without children.

But Heather examined her friends' relationships and domestic lives. She wasn't ready for mortgage payments, children, and PTA meetings. Well, not just yet. And while her friends boasted about being in committed relationships, Heather knew many were not perfect or painted a fairy-tale picture. In fact, she was grateful to be single whenever she saw a husband make snide remarks about his wife's weight or appearance or when a wife needed her husband's permission to do something. And Heather also questioned whether some couples would have remained together if their child had not been born before marriage.

Heather had high relationship standards, and she wasn't going to settle for anything less. Her happiness wasn't going to be compromised in any way. As much as she didn't like clichés, Heather believed "good things come to those who wait."

CHAPTER 4

"So, we're going to Deep Pink, right?" Tristan Montgomery asked Christopher as they walked through the downtown bar crowd.

"You talked to Ryan or Nick."

"Ryan called and told me about lunch," he said, staring after a beautiful busty blonde who walked past him. "Hey, what are my odds of getting into a threesome?"

"With your pretty boy looks — very high," Christopher teased his childhood best friend, but he was telling the truth.

At age 25, Tristan wasn't looking for long-term commitment. He had no problem getting laid whenever he went to the bars. He was blessed with a boyish face, baby blue eyes and natural charm that could win over any girl's parents. His blondish brown hair was usually messy or spiky, giving the appearance that Tristan had just rolled out of bed when really he spent quite a bit of time in front of the mirror perfecting the look. Despite drinking heavily on the weekends, his body was kept in top shape with rigorous workouts at a fitness club.

Tonight, Tristan looked boyishly handsome wearing jeans and an expensive navy polo shirt. Christopher had been in numerous situations where both of them would hit on the same girl, and Tristan would be the one to take her home. Christopher never minded the outcome, because he knew his best friend was irresistible to women.

Tristan and Christopher made their way through the massive crowd at Deep Pink. The employees wore deep pink tank tops or T-shirts with the club's name printed on the front. Deep Pink was dimly lit except for the strobe lights that hit the dance floor and the deep pink lighting along the walls.

Jennifer Elliott

After grabbing a couple of beers, Tristan and Christopher made their way to the side of the dance floor, looking for other friends and familiar faces.

"Hey, isn't that Heather?" Tristan shouted, nudging Christopher and pointing toward her direction on the crowded dance floor.

Christopher saw Heather dancing between two good-looking guys. For the first time, Christopher didn't see Heather as a co-worker. Instead, he saw a ridiculously hot girl seductively moving around and having a good time. Tight low-riding blue jeans highlighted Heather's long legs. A modest dark red tank top with matching ruffles running down the middle of the front hugged and covered her slender frame, showing off her naturally tan arms and shoulders. Slinky matching red platform sandals added a few inches to Heather's average height.

"She's hot!" Tristan shouted.

"Christopher! Tristan!" a guy shouted over the crowd.

They turned to see Nick and Ryan, with beer bottles in hand, walking toward them.

"Hey," Christopher greeted. "What's up?"

"Not much," Ryan said as he scanned the crowd on the dance floor. "Shit! Is that Heather?"

"Yeah," he confirmed.

"Damn, she looks good."

"I've never seen her downtown," Nick added. "I've heard the stories about her dancing on the bars and stuff, but I've never seen it."

"Last year, a bunch of people from work headed downtown to celebrate someone's birthday," Christopher recalled. "At first, Heather was quiet, but by the end of the night, she was wasted and hurled outside a bar."

"Eli said Heather and her friends were popular in college," Nick shared. "Heather and her friends could throw back vodka shots like there was no tomorrow. They were nicknamed the

Vodka Four

Vodka Girls, and members were named Vodka One, Vodka Two … I think Heather was Vodka Four."

"Was Heather ever a stripper?" Tristan asked.

"No," Nick said, laughing and shaking his head. "However, according to Eli, she had some friends who were strippers, and they taught her a few tricks."

"Wasn't Rory a stripper?" Ryan asked.

"Yeah, she was," Christopher said. "She used to work at the Skylight Bar. Yeah, I can definitely see Rory showing Heather the trick of the trade."

"According to Eli, there's one song that Heather can't resist," Nick revealed, with a mischievous grin.

Heather needed a drink. She had been dancing all night long. She missed dancing. She honestly didn't care how she looked to others when she danced. She was with her friends and having a great time. She was in her element. And she was a little drunk.

Heather didn't expect to become inebriated, but after Gil and Danny — friends of hers since college — joined the group of friends at the club, she started draining mixed vodka drinks to keep up with them. Heather had a strict policy of never turning down a free drink, and Gil and Danny had no problem leaving generous tips to a stunning blonde bartender.

As the song was winding down, Heather looked at Danny and Gil and pointed to the bar. She needed another drink. The club was crowded, hot, and sticky. They headed toward the bar when Heather heard a familiar song play. Even in her intoxicated state, Heather didn't need to hear the words to know what song was blaring loudly from the speakers. Apparently, Danny and Gil didn't need the lyrics either, as they looked at each other and then grinned at Heather.

"No," Heather said, shaking her head as she tried to walk toward the bar.

"Let's go," Gil urged, linking one of his arms through hers.

"It's show time, sweetheart," Danny agreed, linking his arm through her other arm. "Time to shake what your momma gave ya."

Heather groaned silently, as the crowd made a path for Danny and Gil carrying her to a small runway stage with a dancer's pole at the end. They gracefully hoisted Heather onto the raised platform as the crowd chanted her name.

What the hell? She thought to herself, trying to maintain her balance after being hurled into the spotlight. *How the hell does everyone know my name?*

The sober Heather would have run off and berated Danny and Gil for throwing her onto the stage. She may have attempted to kick their asses. But the drunk Heather, better known as Vodka Four during her college years, loved being the center of attention. The massive amount of vodka in her system also helped her feel comfortable being in front of hundreds of strangers.

What the hell? She thought to herself. *Rory didn't teach me stripper moves for nothing. I should make her proud.*

Just as Heather's favorite part of the song — the chorus to Alice Cooper's "Poison" — was about to start, she didn't hesitate throwing herself expertly around the stripper pole standing before her.

Christopher, Tristan, Nick, and Ryan's jaws dropped as they watched Heather slink around the pole like an experienced exotic dancer. Watching naked women parade around on a stage wasn't new to the guys. Hell, sleeping with strippers wasn't even new to Tristan and Ryan.

Staring at someone they knew from work provocatively swaying her hips and swinging seductively from a dance pole was new to them. At that moment, Ryan and Nick realized Eli's stories about Heather being a party girl in college were absolutely true.

Vodka Four

After the song ended, Heather was escorted backstage by two bouncers.

"Damn," Ryan exclaimed. "She's not bad."

"She could be mistaken for a real stripper," Nick added.

"I'd throw money at her," Tristan said.

"Need another beer?" Christopher asked, needing to stop the rampant fantasies of Heather dancing around naked in his mind.

The guys nodded, and he headed toward the bar when the deejay yelled into the microphone for the crowd's attention.

"Gentlemen, listen up, because it's time for one of you lucky bastards to shake your groove thang for all ladies in the house!" the deejay yelled as hundreds of women screamed with delight. "As the stud of the night shakes his thang, he will be auctioned off to one lucky and beautiful woman who will then personally strip him down to his skivvies. And guys, I hope you're not going commando tonight."

The crowd went wild.

"Ladies, get your money ready!"

Christopher watched the women around him focus on the deejay get ready to announce the name of the unlucky bastard who was going to be humiliated.

"I need Nicholas Reed!" the deejay yelled into the microphone. "Don't try to run, Nicholas. I know you're out there!"

Christopher looked at Nick's priceless appalled reaction as a spotlight found him in the crowd. The women yelled with excitement and approval and pushed Nick toward the stage as a catchy dance tune started playing.

As soon as Nick was on stage, a blonde bartender appeared, with a microphone in hand, and started the bid to strip him.

"Twenty dollars!" one female hollered.

"Fifty!"

Jennifer Elliott

Christopher found Ryan and Tristan who were laughing hysterically as Nick, who looked confused and uncomfortable, lamely attempted to dance seductively.

"One hundred!"

"One ten!"

"Two hundred!" a familiar voice shouted over the crowd.

"Two hundred!" the blonde bartender yelled. "Going once, going twice, SOLD!"

As Christopher, Tristan, and Ryan watched Nick wait for the victorious bidder, someone pushed through them. The guys didn't even have a chance to react to being pushed as Heather winked and smiled smugly at them before walking toward the stage.

"No way!" Ryan exclaimed, wondering how Heather knew about their plan.

Heather hopped onto the stage, gave the bartender the money, and walked over to Nick, who looked surprised and shocked.

"How are you doing, Nick?" she murmured in his ear, standing in front of him and placing one of her hands on his left hip and the other on his chest.

"OK," he managed to squeak out.

Heather gave him a wicked smile, loving her power of sexuality and being pulled back into familiar wild abandon and recklessness.

"Do you have a girlfriend at the moment?" she asked innocently, her piercing green eyes capturing his attention.

He shook his head.

"Good," she purred before grabbing the front of his T-shirt and pulling close him for a kiss.

Heather could hear the roar of the crowd as her hot mouth explored his with passion and fierce intensity. She was more than pleased when Nick responded boldly. As she continued to kiss him, Heather expertly started to remove the unbuttoned shirt he was wearing as the crowd cheered with approval.

Vodka Four

"Does this shirt have any sentimental value?" she asked, pulling back from the kiss.

Dazed, Nick shook his head. Heather swung the shirt over her head and threw it into the sea of women who hungrily fought for it.

She smiled mischievously at Nick, running her hands up inside the gray T-shirt he was wearing. Heather pulled him into another intense kiss and seductively started to pull the shirt up his well-toned body. Automatically, Nick raised both of his arms so Heather could pull the shirt over his head. After she threw the second shirt into the audience, she slightly lowered her head and licked one of Nick's nipples. The crowd screamed with approval.

Nick thought he was going to die of anticipation and desire. Heather lifted her head and pulled him in for another hungry kiss. As his tongue explored her mouth, she expertly unbuckled his belt with one hand. She slowly pulled the belt from the jeans' loops and snaked it around his neck. With one hand, she unbuttoned his jeans as the crowd hollered with excitement and anticipation.

Heather broke off the kiss, smiled innocently at a shirtless Nick who looked at her hesitantly. He didn't know what to expect next. What Christopher, Ryan, and Tristan didn't expect was for Heather to reach into Nick's jeans and tease him in front of a crowd that roared to see more. She withdrew her hand from his pants and started to walk toward the back of the stage, making Nick follow her by gently pulling on the belt still around his neck.

A number of closed doors greeted Heather and Nick as they stepped down a few stairs. A dark pink glow lit a hallway that led to an exit or the dance floor.

Heather opened a door and led Nick into a room filled with racks of clothes. The sound of the door closing made Heather turn and look silently at Nick. She knew what she wanted, but unexpected shyness and apprehension overwhelmed her.

"Hey," he said softly, his common sense slowly coming back.

"Hey," she said, staring at him and not knowing what to do for the first time that night.

Nick bent his head and softly kissed her. Heather responded to his gentle kiss, placing her hands on his hips. One of his hands slipped behind her neck while the other gently combed her hair. As the kiss became more intense, Nick pulled Heather closer and she wrapped her arms around his neck.

His hands fell to her small waist, and one of hands started to caress her soft skin underneath her tank top. When one of his fingers found her nipple, Heather broke the kiss, opened her eyes, and looked at Nick. His eyes searched her beautiful face for an answer.

Quickly and quietly, Heather broke away from him, locking the door and turning down the light in the room. She returned to him and hungrily continued the kiss. As their tongues danced, Nick slowly moved Heather to an oversized chair sitting in a corner of the room. He gently pushed her down into the chair, still kissing her. His hands lifted the dark red tank top over her head, revealing her perky and beautiful breasts — Nick's favorite part of a woman's body.

Nick broke the kiss to caress her neck with his lips while his hands gently fondled her breasts and nipples. Heather moaned with pleasure as his fingers played with her nipples, making them hard. Soon enough, Nick's fingers were replaced by his mouth and tongue.

Heather cried out with approval and arched her back as Nick's hot tongue played with her hard nipples, making her dizzy and breathless with anticipation. Her slender body gently grinded against his, satisfying some of her sexual desires.

Nick's mouth left her breasts, kissing her flat stomach and belly button. She was so hot with sexual hunger that she didn't

Vodka Four

even notice Nick unbuttoning her jeans and sliding them off her legs, leaving only her lacy thong underwear.

Nick hardened even more at the sight of Heather in her thong and wanted to take her right there, but he didn't. He wanted to enjoy and savor this moment, and he also wanted to make sure Heather received what she wanted and desired. Before tonight, Nick envied Christopher's friendship and close working relationship with Heather. Now, his jealousy disappeared, and Nick was unbelievably thrilled to be this close to her.

Kneeling before her, Nick slipped the lacy thong off and quickly committed the image to memory. Heather's head was resting against the top of the chair while the rest of her naked body was stretched out before him. Pushing her slender legs apart, Nick started to nibble at the core of her sexual desires.

"Oh God," Heather cried out with excitement. Some guys went down on her, not really knowing what to do and not giving her pleasure. Nick was not one of those guys. His mouth and tongue knew exactly what they were doing, and Heather thought she was going to explode within a few seconds.

Just when she thought her sexual needs were going to be satisfied Nick stopped. He stood up and quickly took off his jeans and boxer briefs. He bent down to kiss her while gently pulling her naked form from the chair. Holding her hand, he sat down on the chair and pulled her onto him. Heather smiled and straddled Nick.

Once again, they were kissing with intense fire. Her hands roaming his handsome face and running through his brown hair while his hands were firmly planted on her hips, feeling and guiding. As Nick's lips kissed Heather's neck and found her nipples, he slipped inside her.

"Oh God," Heather moaned as she felt him inside her and his hot mouth on her breast. She thought she was going to die.

Heather was in heaven. Her definition of fantastic sex was with a beautiful man who wasn't afraid to explore her body and, not only heightened, but satisfied her sexual needs. Her hot and naked body felt so good against his skin, and she felt so damn good. She was on fire, and Nick could not get enough of her.

She rode Nick until spasms wracked her body. She collapsed against him as he also reached his sexual peak. The sounds of their heavy breathing and faint dance music could only be heard in the low-lit room.

"You OK?" Nick finally asked as one of his hands lazily ran up and down her soft and naked back.

"Yeah," Heather said, lifting her head to look at him and pushing part of her hair out of her face. "I'm good."

"You want to get out of here?"

"Yeah."

CHAPTER 5

Saturday, January 8

Heather woke up in her bed, feeling soft kisses on her face and shoulders. Before opening her eyes, she smiled tiredly.

"Hey, beautiful," Nick said softly.

"Hey," she replied groggily.

"How are you feeling?"

"A little thirsty."

"I'll get you water," he offered, getting out of bed and walking out of the bedroom stark naked.

Heather smiled brightly, as her eyes followed Nick's fine bare ass walk out. She was happily tired, having spent the night enjoying fantastic sex with a guy who eagerly wanted to please her and made sure she was satisfied every time.

After their tryst at the club, they went back to her place. After a quick tour of her one-bedroom apartment and an introduction to her cats, Merry and Pippen, Heather and Nick closed the bedroom door to continue their sexual escapades.

Her third orgasm knocked Heather into a peaceful slumber, with Nick's arms around her. Waking up to soft kisses was not unusual. From experience, the guy was eager for another romp before leaving her place and lying about calling her. The guy made her feel special and beautiful and acted eager to see her again. Falling for the act too many times made Heather wary and somewhat ashamed for sharing her bed too quickly.

"Here you go, Willow," Nick said, walking back into the room and offering her a glass of water.

Heather sat up, grabbing her comforter to cover her body. Her interest was piqued when Nick called her "Willow." Guys usually called her "Princess," "Lucky," or "Beautiful."

"Thank you," she said gratefully as Nick climbed back into bed with her. She wanted to ask about the new nickname, but her dry and scratchy throat demanded water.

"So, I have a question," he said as she greedily drank. "Was my striptease payback for your fake stripping?"

Heather nodded.

"How did you know the guys and I played the song?"

"My other guys friends at the club denied playing the song. So, I asked a couple of people who were helping the deejay. They said four guys requested the song and slipped the deejay $20. Rory saw Tristan and Christopher walk into the bar. We figured it had to be you guys."

"You're good," Nick said, leaning in for a soft kiss. "Very clever."

"Thank you," she murmured between the kisses. "You guys deserved it."

"Why did you choose me?"

"M revenge was going to be obvious if I had all four of you on the stage. You were picked because my friends and I thought you were the shyest out of the four."

"You think I'm shy?"

Heather shrugged. "Ryan and Tristan would have enjoyed the attention. I can't even imagine Christopher going anywhere near the stage, but depending on how much he had to drink, he would have enjoyed the spotlight. I figured you'd be the least comfortable."

"Well, I'm glad you picked me."

"Really?" Heather was surprised. "Why?"

"Because if you didn't pick me, I wouldn't be here," Nick replied, nibbling on her earlobe. "I had a great time."

"Me too," she admitted, as her mind ran down a mental checklist of what guys say the morning after.

Making her feel special? Check.

"So, when am I going to see you again?"

Asking questions women want to hear? Check.

"Whenever you want to." After years of experience, Heather knew how to play the game without looking like a complete bitch.

"Good," he replied, as his kisses started to travel south.

"However," Heather hedged, lightly shaking off his lips from her collarbone. "I'm meeting some friends for lunch today, and I have plans Sunday."

Depending on how well the guy performed the night before, Heather had no problem with morning sex. Nick exceeded her expectations, but her hangover and tired body were stopping her from initiating another round. She was even too tired to play games and flirt shamelessly. She just wanted to kick him out of her place so she could grab a few more hours of sleep before meeting her friends for lunch.

"Well, I know where you work. You'll have lunch with me, right?"

"Of course."

"Good." Nick smiled.

"I hate to kick you out, but I need to run a few errands before I meet my friends," Heather lied apologetically.

"Not a problem."

Heather slipped out of bed and headed toward the bathroom to pull on a dark blue robe while Nick pulled on his boxer briefs and jeans. He smiled mischievously as he reached for his new shirts.

"Why is there a room full of clothes?" he had asked after their sexual rendezvous.

"For a couple of reasons," Heather had said, pulling on her jeans. "When drinks get thrown around in the club, special people like me and the bartenders have other clothes to change into, and for special people like you who lose their clothes during an unexpected striptease."

"I was wondering how I was going to get my shirts back."

"You won't. Your shirts have either been torn to shreds or taken home by some woman who really wished she had won the auction. Pick out whatever you want. Think of it as compensation for your humiliation in front of hundreds of people."

"What happens with the money?" he asked as he chose a T-shirt and looked for a button down shirt.

"It goes to the humane society."

"Can I ask a somewhat personal question?"

"Shoot."

"Where did you get $200?"

"From a couple of different people," Heather replied. "I had some money on me, but not enough to win. So, some friends loaned me the rest."

Heather shook her head as images of last night replayed in her mind. No doubt Ryan, Christopher, and Tristan would want to know all of the details, she thought, leaning on the kitchen counter and barely glancing at the open newspaper. *I wonder what he'll tell them.*

Nick emerged from the bedroom fully clothed, looking rugged and handsome, and Heather wondered whether she was going to regret not letting him stay a little longer.

"Hey," he said, walking between her cats, Merry and Pippen, and reaching for his black wool jacket that was thrown on the couch.

"Thanks for coming over," she said, walking him to her apartment door.

Before leaving her, Nick pulled Heather close again.

"I want to see you again," he said softly, kissing her.

He's a great kisser, she thought, responding gently. *I could get really used to this. Dammit, why does he have to be so great in bed?*

"OK," she replied between kisses. "Call me anytime."

Vodka Four

"I will."

Nick opened the door, kissed her quickly, and said, "I'll call you."

"Promise?" Heather asked, faking sweetness.

"Promise," he said, closing the door.

She desperately wanted to believe Nick was different from the men in her past. She wanted to believe he was one of the good guys. But after foolishly believing in too many men, Heather built a wall around her heart. She no longer believed in love at first sight. She didn't believe men should be given a chance to break her heart.

How many people can fit in Danny's car?

Heather was incredibly drunk. She had way too many screwdrivers and vodka shots. She was pretty sure it was against the law to turn down free drinks from attractive guys — or any guy for that matter. The innocent flirting and laughing at lame jokes was well worth not spending her own money. She started the night with $20 in her pocket, and the bill remained there for the rest of the evening.

"Vodka Four, this way," Cat yelled, pulling her in a direction. "Time to go home."

"No!" Heather screamed but not fighting Cat's firm hand. "I'm not tired."

"Shut up," someone shouted.

At the same time, Cat and Heather yelled, "Fuck you!"

"Over here, Vodka Girls," a male voice hollered. Cat and Heather followed the order and saw Rory, Eli, Danny, Gil, and some other people climbing into a blue Plymouth Sundance.

"Let's go," Eli instructed, holding the back door open and nodding for them to climb into the backseat.

"We can't fit!" Heather protested, watching Rory smush herself into the back seat with five other Vodka Girls. "Cat and I can walk home."

"We're going to Perkins," Danny explained. "Want to go?"

Heather and Cat gasped with excitement and started jumping up down with approval.

"Yah! Let's go to Perkins!" Heather cheered, waving her arms around like a cheerleader. "Yaaah Perkins!"

Eli shook his head with amusement. "Come on then. Let's go."

"We can't fit in the car!" Cat repeated Heather's earlier statement.

Vodka Four

"It's a quick drive," Danny answered impatiently as he walked to the driver's side.

"You can sit on my lap, Vodka Four," Eli offered, pointing to the passenger seat.

"Where am I going to sit?" Cat asked indignantly. "On Heather's lap?"

"I'm not a lesbian!" Heather shouted.

"Where am I going to sit?" Gil asked, ignoring Heather last statement. "Vodka One has a point."

"Thank you!" Cat screamed gratefully. "I may be uberdrunk, but I'm not stupid."

"Sssh, Vodka One," he hushed.

"Sorry," she whispered loudly and then giggled.

As Eli and Gil argued about who was going to sit in the passenger seat and Danny demanded everyone get into the car, Heather clumsily climbed onto the hood of the car.

"Let's go," she announced.

Cat tilted her head and followed suit. "I'm ready."

"Get off," Danny ordered, looking cross.

"Dan, where else are they going to sit?" Eli asked, looking over the top of the car. "Just drive really slow and don't take the main route to Perkins. We'll be fine."

"No way. What if we get caught?"

"Perkins is about a mile away. Just drive slowly."

"Let's go!" one of the Vodka Girls in the backseat screamed. "I'm hungry!"

"If I notice something suspicious I can easily push the Vodka Girls off the hood and start running," Eli offered, smirking at the idea.

Danny sighed as he got behind the wheel.

"Gil, want the hood or the passenger seat?" Eli asked.

Gil wisely chose to travel inside the car as Eli hopped on the hood with Heather and Cat. Ignoring questions about why Eli, Heather, and Cat were on the hood, Danny prayed for two things — no cops and no one gets hurt.

Out of all the people going to Perkins, Danny was the most sober one who should have thought of a better idea (such as stuffing Heather and Cat in the trunk, with the back hood open). But that brilliant idea and other solutions weren't offered until after the story was told to others or remembered by many present that night.

Heather could never retell the story, because she had no memory of what happened after bar time. As soon as Danny started driving, Heather leaned against Eli's arm and passed out.

CHAPTER 6

"So, what happened between you and Nick?" Hera asked bluntly as soon as everyone — Heather, Rory, Catherine Mann, and Lily Netwall — ordered lunch at a local restaurant. "You two disappeared after an arousing striptease."

"We had sex," Heather replied casually, knowing she couldn't hide anything from her closest friends.

"We kind of figured," Rory said. "I'm guessing you guys hightailed it to your place."

"Actually," she clarified. "I took him back to the closet to he could find new shirts, and then he and I ended up doing it."

"In the closet?" Cat asked incredulously.

At age 5, Catherine Mann stubbornly told her kindergarten teacher that her real name was Cat because no one ever called her by her real name — not even when she was in trouble. At age 29, Cat worked full time as an administrative assistant for the owner of the Saturn dealership in Anastacia Square.

"Cute" and "pretty" were the two most popular words past boyfriends used to describe the short Korean girl. Standing at five feet, Cat had long straight black hair that was never cut above her shoulders. Her dark brown eyes were always hidden behind thin black-rimmed glasses. Cat knew she was a little overweight, but she never thought she was morbidly obese. Losing 10 to 15 pounds — maybe even 20 — wouldn't hurt her.

"The closet," Heather repeated. "I don't know what the hell I was thinking. I was so drunk last night."

"Vodka Four strikes again," Cat praised, beaming with pride. "When you're drunk, you have the tendency to become a very sexual person. God knows the number of stories I can share about you when you're butt ass drunk."

Heather laughed out loud. "Thanks, Cat. Well, I blame everything on Danny and Gil because they kept buying everyone drinks. You guys know me, I'm not one to turn down free drinks."

"Hell no," Hera cheered, raising her glass.

"If I wasn't drunk, I would have never acted like a stripper and would have never had sex with Nick in the closet. I had sex in public!"

"Is the closet at Deep Pink really considered public?" Cat asked thoughtfully.

"I say no," Rory answered. "You guys were behind closed doors."

"We did at a club," Heather said, emphasizing the word "club."

"I agree with Rory," Hera joined in. "You didn't do it in public."

"It's equivalent to doing it in a hotel room," Cat said. "The hotel is a public place, but the rooms are private."

"We did it in the closet at Deep Pink," Heather repeated stubbornly.

"I've done it in the closet at Deep Pink," Rory said.

"Me too," Hera added.

"What? Really? With who?" Cat asked rapidly, beating Heather to the same questions that sprung into her mind.

"Doug," Rory replied pensively, trying to remember that particular night. "Or David."

"Byron," Hera answered, referring to her boyfriend of three years.

"The closet door has a lock," Rory informed. "No embarrassing interruptions unless one of the managers really needed to get in the closet. Besides, after a stunt like that, sex in the closet is a given."

"Really?" Heather was unaware of this rule of thumb.

Vodka Four

"Nick must've been good if you left with him," Rory said, before thanking the waitress for bringing their food to the table.

"He was fantastic," she replied in a low voice after the waitress left. "He knew what he was doing."

"Are you going to see him again?" Lily asked, before taking a bite of her salad.

One of the perks of having a close friend as a hair stylist was the discount that Lily Netwall never seemed to mind giving. Whenever Heather wanted to change her hair style or color, Lily knew exactly what she wanted and never disappointed anyone with her work. To receive the discount though, Lily works out of her one-bedroom apartment instead of her usual place of work, Bellismo.

Though both of her parents were born and raised in the United States, Lily's Latina heritage was evident in her appearance. As a child, Lily hated being the tallest girl in her class. As a teen, she hated being one of the tallest and skinniest girls in class. As a college student, she regretted eating everything in sight, gaining more than the "freshmen 15." After her freshman year ended, Lily dropped out of college, lost the weight, and cut off her long luxurious black hair as an act of rebellion against her parents.

To further distance herself from her parents in Illinois, Lily moved to Amery Lake and became a bartender at the Skylight Bar, where she met Rory. Lily was a beautiful bartender with chin length black hair, naturally dark skin, long sexy legs, and dark green eyes. During the day, Lily worked out with Rory to maintain her slim figure.

"He said he's going to call," Heather said, taking a sip of her Coke. "But I have my doubts."

"I think he will," Rory said. "I don't believe Nick is into one-night stands. He doesn't seem like that type of guy."

"We've all talked about him and Ryan, but none of us really know them," she pointed out. "We've had lunch with them in a group setting, but we've never hung out with them outside of work."

"Rory's right, though," Lily said thoughtfully. "I can't see Nick being the type of guy to lead someone on. He was in a long-term relationship for awhile."

"Do you want to see him again?" Cat asked, before taking a bite of her chicken bacon sandwich.

Heather shrugged. "I don't know. He's nice, attractive, but I never thought about dating him."

"Do you think he's a puppy, pusher, or peddler?" Hera asked.

Whenever Heather started dating a guy, she put him into one of three categories: the puppy, the pusher, or the peddler.

The puppy was the guy who followed her everywhere. They are so in awe of her beauty and dazzling personality that they truly believe they don't deserve her. "You're so beautiful," "I'm the luckiest guy ever" and "What did I do to deserve you?" are the three most common phrases Heather hears when dating a puppy. When she wants something, say like a box of tampons, the puppy is willing to fetch it and bring it back to her at his own expense. Heather, of course, attempts to offer money, but the puppy refuses.

At first, Heather loves the attention of an adoring puppy, but soon enough, the cute little pup wants all of her attention and affection. Before meeting her, the puppy was once a social guy with friends and a life, and after they start dating, he becomes completely enamored with Heather and wants to spend all of his time with her. He feels hurt and wounded when she wants to spend time with her friends or have a moment to herself. The puppy usually believes if she is out of sight, he is going to lose her and usually does when Heather starts feeling suffocated.

The pusher is a highly attractive guy who puts little effort into picking up women since they usually flock to him. He's confident and charming — two qualities that attract Heather.

Vodka Four

During the beginning stages of dating, the pusher is almost mistaken for a puppy, but the pusher understands her need for space. The first couple of weeks are filled with dining out, going to the movie theater, renting a flick, and hanging out with close friends at a low-key bar. Heather usually identifies the pusher when she becomes completely enamored with him. At this point, she has become emotionally attached and can envision a future with him.

As the relationship progresses, the pusher wants to go out more — to more bars, parties, and other social events. He is no longer content staying in and watching a movie or TV. When he goes out, he can't be alone. Heather has to be with him because he wants to show her off. At first, she labeled herself the trophy girlfriend but realized since the pusher is just as attractive — and sometimes even more — as she is. With his good looks and winning smile, the pusher brags he can have any beautiful girl on his arm.

What the pusher wants is an attractive girlfriend so he can brag about having the "perfect" relationship. He wants others to envy him. Usually, the pusher ends the relationship when Heather finally grows a backbone and says no to going out all of the time. Heather would like to end the relationship after she realizes the guy is a pusher, however, she deludes herself that things will change. She maintains the pusher can't always want to go out, but he does. Because she is smitten and wants the relationship to work, Heather stays with him and then feels foolish when he leaves.

The third category is the peddler — a guy who peddles his issues and insecurities onto Heather. She once dated a guy who grew up living in a low-income family, but she understood he didn't have the greatest childhood memories. Coming from a middle-class family, Heather considered herself far from being wealthy or spoiled. However, the guy had no problem calling her a "spoiled rich kid" whenever she bought something new.

He then launched into a dramatic story about how his single mother worked three different jobs while raising five kids.

While that particular peddler attempted to look like he came from money — nice computer and expensive watches and clothes — he had no problem bringing up his difficult childhood. When Heather started to believe she was a "spoiled rich kid," Rory pointed out what the peddler was doing and Heather then ditched him.

Peddlers have the tendency to frequently discuss past relationships, cry about their insecurities, and believe Heather should help solve their issues. She has no problem ending a relationship with a peddler. She signed on to be a girlfriend — not a therapist. Because Heather felt she had enough issues of her own, she was in no position to help others.

"He's an attractive guy," Heather said, thinking about the categories. "I can't see him being a pusher. I guess, he's probably a puppy or a peddler."

"I say puppy," Cat volunteered.

"Too early to tell," Hera said. "His true colors will show once you get to know him."

"He needs to call first," Heather pointed out. "So, what happened to everyone after I left?"

"Cat, Lily, and I stayed until bar time," Hera replied. "Then, Byron picked us up and we went to Perkin's."

"Where were you?" Heather asked, looking at Rory.

"I slept with Tristan," Rory said casually and listened to the clanking of silverware hitting plates and the nanosecond of silence that followed.

"What?" everyone at the table exclaimed.

"How in the world did that happen?" Cat asked. "When we were leaving the club, you were leaving with someone else."

"I was leaving with Nathan," Rory clarified.

"The tall hot guy?" Lily described, trying to remember more details.

Vodka Four

"Oh, he was really hot," Cat agreed enthusiastically. "He was dreamy."

"Yes, him," Rory said, with a laugh. "I was leaving with Nathan when I ran into Tristan and Christopher. Dreamy?" She stopped for a second to look at Cat, furrowing her eyebrows with amusement. "Did you just use the word dreamy? Anyway, Tristan and Christopher were hanging out with some girls. Tristan and I started talking, and Nathan became this jealous jerk. He and Tristan shared some words, then Nathan and I shared some words, and Nathan stormed off. Tristan apologized for the incident and invited me to Christopher's place for an after-party. I said no, because I didn't feel like competing for Christopher and Tristan's attention with a bunch of nitwit girls. So, Tristan insisted on driving me home."

"And?" Heather asked, arching an eyebrow with curiosity.

"We took a detour to his place before driving me home," Rory said. "We did it. We laid in bed for awhile. Did it again. And then he drove me home. End of story."

"And?" Lily needled, wanting more information.

"He was good," Rory said, shrugging her shoulders. "It was kind of weird."

"Because you know him?" Cat asked sarcastically.

"No," she answered quickly, sighing. "You guys know me, and you've seen the guys I have been with — they're men. They're older and mature, and Tristan is none of those things. He's just a kid. How old is he?"

"Twenty-three?" Lily guessed.

"He's 25," Cat corrected.

"See, he's just a kid," Rory repeated. "He's doesn't even look like a man. He looks like a typical college student — there's nothing wrong with that, but that's not my type."

"So, why did you sleep with him?" Hera asked.

"Because I was horny, and I wanted to see if the rumors about him were true," she replied honestly, tucking a segment of her long hair behind her ears. "He's good, but I wouldn't say he was fantastic."

"Are you going to see him again?" Heather asked, as the waitress cleared the plates from the table.

"Well, I'm not going to date him," Rory said. "If we end up doing it again, then fine, but I'm not going to actively pursue him. I think he knows I'm not one of those emotional girls."

"I think everyone knows that, sweetie," Lily said.

"Did he say anything about Nick and me?" Heather asked.

"He figured you guys were getting busy after you stripped Nick down," Rory replied. "Oh, by the way, he says you should quit your job at Lexington and work at Skylight."

Heather laughed, shaking her head. "I'm going to get so much shit for that."

"I asked Tristan how they knew 'Poison' was your stripper song. He said Nick and Ryan remembered the song from Eli's stories."

"Eli," Heather grumbled about her ex-boyfriend but one of her closest guy friends. "He needs to learn to keep his big mouth shut."

"Speaking of Eli, how he is doing?" Cat asked.

"He's fine. I haven't talked to him in awhile, but I know he's thinking about visiting. He just doesn't know when."

"And how do you feel about that?" Lily asked.

Heather shrugged. "I'm OK with it. I haven't seen him since he moved. It'd be good to see him again."

"What are you going to do about Nick?" Hera asked.

"Let's focus on one step at a time," Heather said. "He needs to call me first."

"OK, let's say he's called and asked you out. What are you going to do?"

"I don't know." She hated giving a definite answer when she honestly didn't know what she would do. Nick seemed

Vodka Four

like the type of guy who kept his word, but so did numerous of other guys who lied about wanting more than sex.

"Heather!" Rory exclaimed. "This isn't rocket science. I'm willing to bet Nick asks you out before you guys end up in bed again."

"You think I'm going to sleep with him again?"

"Why wouldn't you?" Cat asked. "You said he's good in bed."

"If you had the chance to sleep with him again, you wouldn't take the opportunity?" Hera added.

"If you don't sleep with him again, can I sleep with him?" Lily inquired, with a smirk.

Heather took a deep breath and thought about the questions before answering. "Yes, Nick is good in bed, but I don't want a friend with benefits. I want a relationship that's real, normal, and stable. If he's looking for a friend with benefits, then no, I probably wouldn't sleep with him again. And yes, Lily, if Nick is just interested in fucking, then you can sleep with him."

"I'm willing to bet $100 that Nick asks her out on a date," Rory announced. "They will go on a date before sleeping together again."

"They go on one date?" Cat asked, clarifying the rules of the bet.

"One date."

"Stupid people would take that bet," Lily said. "None of us are stupid."

"I think you guys are dumb for making the bet in the first place," Heather said. "You guys can't predict what Nick is going to do."

"Wanna bet?" Rory asked, with an evil grin.

"No." Heather sighed as she pulled out her debit card to pay for her lunch. She wished she had her friends' confidence in Nick, but she couldn't allow herself to hope for something more. The best way to avoid disappointment and sadness was to not have any expectations at all.

CHAPTER 7

Monday, January 10

Cat looked like she was focusing on her paperwork in her office Monday morning, but she was thinking about the weekend events.

It's not fair, she thought sadly to herself. *All Rory and Heather have to do is breathe, and men coming running toward them. I actually have to throw myself at guys. Life is so unfair.*

For as long as Cat has known Christopher, Tristan, Nick, and Ryan, she had harbored a small crush on all of them and wouldn't mind having a one-night stand with any of them. But she knew the type of girls they wanted. A short, somewhat overweight, and moderately attractive Korean girl wasn't on their lists. Cat knew she wasn't a terrible disaster — she dressed fashionably thanks to an employee discount at Lexington and picked clothes that fit her but yet hid all the wrong curves.

Cat even pulled out a credit card to replace a simple black digital watch, with a plastic wristband, after a drunk guy criticized her for wearing it.

"It makes you look cheap," he had claimed, sitting on a stool next to Rory. After work one night at Lexington, Rory and Cat went out for a few drinks at a low-key bar.

"Shut up," Cat had replied harshly. She honestly didn't care the drunk guy was hitting on Rory from the moment they walked into the bar. Men looking at her friends, and not her, was something Cat was used to and expected.

"Guys will think you're not willing to spend money when they see the cheap watch," Drunk Boy had continued. "You will never get laid."

"Fuck you," Rory had snapped. "Get the fuck away from us."

"Hey," Drunk Boy had said, shrugging and focusing his attention on Rory. "I'm just telling her the truth. She's a cute girl. She's just not going to get laid with that plastic watch."

"Fuck you," Cat and Rory had snarled at the same time.

Even though Cat knew what Drunk Boy had said wasn't true, she started looking at expensive watches the next day. After a couple of weeks of hard searching for a watch that met her standards, Cat found a $100 watch at Macy's.

"Cat, you really don't need this," Rory had said. "What the guy said was total bullshit. He was drunk and probably didn't even know what he was saying."

"But I should get a nicer watch," Cat had insisted, looking at the very pretty and hip digital watch on her small wrist. "I guess I never really thought about it until he said something."

"But a crappy little watch isn't going to stop you from getting laid."

"Rory, I know that, but it wouldn't hurt me to have a nicer watch. You have a collection of nice watches. I just want one."

Rory had looked at the Kenneth Cole digital watch on Cat's wrist. "That watch does look good on you. Remind me again why you need a digital watch."

"Digital watches are easier for me to read," Cat had explained. "I can read normal clocks and watches, but I prefer digital. I don't know why."

Cat had purchased the watch with her credit card and has loved it ever since. She felt her self-confidence increase a bit whenever people complimented it. However, Cat knew a new watch wasn't going to improve her social life.

Vodka Four

About two years have passed since Cat had been in a serious relationship. During her days of freedom, she had gone on plenty of first dates and some second dates, but none materialized into a serious relationship. She also had her share of one-night stands or "friends with benefits," hoping something more might happen.

Fortunately, Cat found solace that Heather and Lily had experienced disastrous relationships and that both weren't getting married anytime soon. Heather had a knack for picking puppies and arrogant pushers. Because Lily's dating criteria was set high, she won't date a guy who doesn't meet her standards.

Although Rory and Hera were also single, Cat knew neither was capable of having a successful relationship. Because Rory loved her independence and had issues trusting men, she had no intention of getting married. Most of her relationships failed to last more than six months. Despite being in a long-term relationship, Hera floated from one relationship to the next before falling for Byron. Although she had no problem attracting men, Hera tempted trouble, causing relationship issues.

"Hey, I heard the boss man is gone for the day," Cat heard a familiar voice say.

She looked up from the piles of papers on her desk to see Tristan sauntering into her office and plopping himself into one of the waiting chairs. He wore expensive black pants, a crisp white button down shirt and a red tie — the daily salesperson uniform. On Fridays, staff could choose to wear a gray polo shirt with the dealership's logo on the front. At first glance, Tristan looked like a spoiled rich kid, but he was only guilty of being a player.

"What's up, Tristan?" Cat asked, continuing to focus on her paperwork.

"Nothing," he said casually, stretching out his legs and yawning. "Did you have a good weekend? I saw you at Deep Pink with Heather and Rory."

"Yeah, I had a good time."

"Good girl."

"What about you?" Cat asked distractedly, not even looking at him. "What did you do this weekend?"

"I went out Friday and Saturday night," Tristan replied. "I saw you guys Friday night, and then I ran into Lily and Rory at the strip club Saturday night. I spent Sunday recovering and watching football."

"Nice."

"Have you talked to Rory lately?" Tristan asked casually, but Cat knew what he wanted. She was a little surprised Tristan wanted to know what Rory thought about their little tryst.

"We met for lunch Saturday," Cat informed him.

"Come on, Cat," he said. "You have to give me something."

"What do you want to know?" she asked, trying to hide her impatience.

"What do you know?"

"Tristan, seriously," Cat said firmly and sharply, looking at him through her glasses. "Quit beating around the fucking bush, and tell me what you want to know."

"Wow, you're cranky today," he teased awkwardly, sitting up a little straighter. "Sorry, I just wanted to know if she said anything about me."

"Tristan, how dumb are you?"

"What?" he asked, looking confused.

"How dumb are you?" Cat repeated. "Do you seriously think I'm going to tell you anything? I've known Rory a lot longer than you. Not to mention, this conversation that you and I are having right now will be retold to Rory."

"Will you re-enact it for her?"

Vodka Four

"If Byron is available and picks up your playboy mannerisms," she shot back.

"Sorry," he apologized. "I guess I wasn't thinking."

"You don't have to apologize," Cat said, suddenly wishing she didn't sound like a bitch.

"I guess I just wanted to know if I had a shot with Rory."

"What?" Cat was speechless and surprised. For as long as she has known Tristan, he has never wanted to be in a relationship because he enjoyed playing the field. Cat had never heard him talk about getting serious with anyone.

"Why is that so shocking?" Tristan asked, cocking his head slightly while studying her shocked expression.

"Because you're never in a relationship."

"I just haven't found the right woman."

"You enjoy sleeping around with as many women as you can."

"Ouch," Tristan said mockingly, covering his heart. "That hurt."

"But it's true," Cat pointed out. "What makes Rory so different that you actually want to date her? You do realize that dating sometimes leading to a relationship."

"Thanks, Dear Abby, for the sarcasm. To answer your question, she and I are alike. We don't waste time dating people if there's not chemistry. Plus, we both have really high standards about the people we sleep with."

"When was the last time you were in a relationship, Tristan?"

He opened his mouth to answer but then shut it when he realized he had to think about the question.

"Exactly," Cat said, jumping at his silence and standing up to file some papers. "Both of you love being adored by hundreds of women — for you — and men — for her. You guys enjoy the attention. Why would you guys give that up to only be adored by each other?"

Jennifer Elliott

"I like her, Cat," Tristan said truthfully. "I've always liked Rory. She's a fun girl."

"Stop," she said, closing the filing cabinet door and sitting back down at her desk. "You called Rory a girl. She's not a girl. She's not a college student — wait, yes, she's going to school. But she's not your typical college girl who fawns over guys and hopes she'll meet her soul mate while getting an education. She's a woman who knows what she wants and doesn't take any shit from anyone."

"I know."

"Do you really think a relationship between the two of you is going to work?"

"I don't know," Tristan answered, shrugging his shoulders. "I just know that I like her, and I wouldn't mind seeing her again. If something more happened, then that's great."

"You must really like her since you're acting like we're in junior high," Cat said dryly. "Do you want me to pass her a note during lunch?"

"Will you?" he asked brightly. "Write that she can't draw a 'maybe' box. She has to check yes or no."

"You're a moron."

"Come on, Cat. Help me out."

"Absolutely not. I am her friend, not yours."

"We're not friends?" Tristan asked, looking a little crushed.

"Stop looking like a wounded puppy," she said curtly. "The only time you and I talk is at work. We never see each other outside of work."

"Sometimes we have lunch together."

"During our lunch breaks, dumbass."

"I get points because it's still outside of work."

"Whatever," Cat said, rolling her eyes. "The point is you and I don't hang out outside of work. We don't meet up at bars. We don't go to the movies. We don't do anything. We're not friends."

Vodka Four

"You're a mean friend."

"I'm realistic and telling the truth."

"So, will you be my friend if I call you one night?" Tristan asked, winking at her.

"No. It takes more than one phone call to be friends with me."

"What did Rory do to pass your friendship test?"

"I've known her since college," Cat replied.

"Did you know Heather when she was in college?"

"Yes. She and I went to the same college."

"So, you can tell me about the crazy shit that Heather and Rory did back then."

Guys always wanted to hear stories about Heather and Rory. None of them wanted to hear tales about Cat, who not only witnessed everything but was also involved in the craziness of college. But, she was used to being the messenger for guys who liked her friends.

"I won't."

"Were you a Vodka Girl?" Tristan asked, taking Cat by complete surprise.

"What?"

"Were you a Vodka Girl?" he repeated.

"How did you know about that?" she questioned.

Tristan shrugged. "I've heard some stories about Heather being a Vodka Girl. I figured since you and Rory have known her since college then maybe you were a Vodka Girl."

"I was Vodka One," Cat admitted.

"How did you guys figure out who was what number?"

"Alphabetical order," she explained. "There were like 12 of us who really liked drinking vodka, whether it was straight or mixed. When we were really super drunk, we did shots of vodka. For awhile, we were known as the Vodka Girls, but it's hard to keep 12 drunk girls together. And it was also hard to get all 12 at the bars at the same time. So, we numbered off in alphabetical order."

Jennifer Elliott

"What's Rory's number?"

"Vodka 10."

"Do you still keep in touch with the other Vodka Girls?"

"Yeah," Cat said, thinking about everyone in the group. "I keep track of most of them."

"Do you still drink vodka?"

"Only when mixed. I can't drink it straight without hurling."

Tristan laughed.

"That was a long time ago," Cat said, pushing her long black hair behind her shoulders.

"That's right, you're old!"

"Shut up, Tristan."

"No," he said quickly. "What I meant is that I forget that you're 29, because you look like you're 25."

"Really?"

"Yeah, you don't look like you're 29 at all."

"Well, thanks for the compliment."

"And Heather looks like she's an underage drinker. I can't believe she's 29."

And it's back to Heather, Cat thought dryly.

"Rory looks her age," Tristan continued, as Cat furrowed her eyebrows with confusion. "She looks like an experienced woman, which is a good thing. She looks like a woman in control."

"And she is."

"She's not a flighty college girl."

"No, she's not."

"And I really like her. I like her maturity and no-nonsense attitude."

"Then ask her out, you dumbass," Cat said bluntly. "Stop being a girl, and ask her out."

"Wow, you should be a therapist," he teased, standing up. "You're customer service skills are outstanding."

She smiled.

Vodka Four

"So, you're going to tell Rory about all of this?"

"Every single word. So, my advice is you better talk to her before I do. Because during the course of my conversation with Rory, I will tell her everything that we just talked about. If you haven't talked to her by then, she knows your intentions and will more than likely shoot you down. If you talk to her before me, she doesn't know what's going on and you might have a shot at taking her out."

"Thanks for the advice, kid," he said, leaving the office.

Cat shook her head after Tristan left. Despite his playboy and wild reputation, Cat enjoyed hearing his stories about different women and parties. At work, he was always nice to her and asked how her day was going or if she had a good weekend. On the rare occasion that they went out to lunch — just the two of them — Tristan always took care of the bill.

The conversation that just ended was normal as Tristan usually wandered into Cat's office whenever the boss wasn't around and when he wasn't busy with a client. They usually discussed what movies they've recently seen or Cat listened to him talk about a "psycho" he had slept with and she offered him advice about women. Cat never held back her honest opinions or disagreeing thoughts. But she knew Tristan would never be romantically interested in her despite her occasional daydreams that had him confessing his undying and passionate love for her.

Although Rory had slept with Tristan and Heather had slept with Nick, Cat didn't hate them — she could never hate Rory and Heather. Cat never told her friends about her minor and harmless crushes on Tristan, Christopher, Ryan, and Nick. And she couldn't blame Tristan and Nick for sleeping with her friends, because even she knew they were undeniably beautiful. Something she knew she would never be.

CHAPTER 8

Thursday, January 13

Brown Street was the second shortest street — being all of two blocks long — in the city. When drivers turned onto the street from the highway, they were greeted by restaurants, stores, and parking lots dotting the first block. After driving through a four-way stop, the next block contained town homes, apartments, and a few local businesses.

Hera and her boyfriend, Byron, lived in the first set of light blue town homes that had an attached one-car garage. Hera was excited the two-bedroom two-story town home was less than five minutes away from the mall, numerous restaurants, Walmart, Target, Shopko, two grocery stores, a movie theater, and several gas stations. She frequently described the area as "it's a neighborhood that's tucked away from the main highway, but close enough to everything that you might need."

Gray two-story high apartment buildings overlook the blacktop parking lot stood next to the line of town homes. In one of the buildings, Lily lived on the first floor in a one-bedroom apartment. During the winter, she wished she could afford the apartments with garages because she hated scraping snow and ice off her car.

Next in line were tan two-story apartment buildings that faced a line of garages, where renters had to walk across blacktop for access. When residents peeked out the back apartment window, they could see the back of the garages for the next apartment building. Cat lived in the first building in a first-floor one-bedroom apartment with her cats, Harry and

Vodka Four

Sally. Heather lived in the second building on the first floor with her cats, Merry and Pippen.

After Hera moved into the neighborhood, Heather was the second to there because the landlord allowed cats. As soon as she was settled, Heather visited the local humane society and adopted two kittens — one completely gray and the other white with gray patches. She named them after her favorite characters in "Lord of the Rings."

On the other side of the street across from Cat and Heather's apartments sat more two-story town homes with attached garages — similar to Hera and Byron's. Somewhere in the middle of the town homes lived Rory with her cats, Dixie and Bianca. When Rory accompanied Heather to the humane society, she definitely did not expect to adopt two kittens herself — two adorable pure Persian kittens. As soon as Rory saw the two sister kittens sleeping together in the cage, she could not resist the charm of the little furballs. However, due to her lack of knowledge about cats and having pets in general, Rory frequently called Heather and Cat for advice.

After the last set of town homes, Brown Street ends when drivers are forced to turn right onto Rudy Street — all of one block, and therefore, the shortest street in Amery Lake.

After frequently visiting Hera and Heather in the quiet residential area, Rory left her downtown apartment. Cat soon followed after listening to her friends rave on about the neighborhood. Lastly, Lily moved into the area after getting into an argument with her roommate.

Although Heather loved living in the neighborhood, the only bars within walking distance were ones inside restaurants. While she and her friends loved going to Applebees, Olive Garden, and other restaurants that served alcohol, they enjoyed meeting at regular bars. Unfortunately, those bars were 10 miles or more away from their beloved neighborhood.

However, in a small town 10 minutes away was one of Heather's favorite places, Lucky Alley, a popular bowling alley and bar and grill. She and her friends rarely missed going to Lucky's on Thursdays because of karaoke night. Due to their constant presence, the owner (whom Rory had slept with for awhile) and various bartenders (whom had slept with Heather, Lily, or Cat) became good friends with them despite the short-lived relationships or one-night stands.

Heather didn't know why she was looking forward to seeing her friends at Lucky's after having dinner with Nick — their first official date. Because of their unexpected tryst, Heather expected an evening filled with awkward moments and sly, maybe crass, hints about another sexual fling. But if Nick wanted to sleep with her again, he didn't say anything nor act inappropriately. In fact, he was the perfect gentleman the entire night.

Nick had arrived a few minutes early for their date and opened the passenger car door and restaurant door for her. Heather was impressed Nick took charge of the restaurant selection. Among her friends or group of people, the game of "Where do you want to go for dinner?" "I don't know. Where do you want to go?" was necessary. But when a guy asks Heather out, he should plan the date and shouldn't seek her opinion. Without her input, the guy has put some thought and effort into the date — unless it was the dinner-and-a-movie standby. Picnics by the river or at a park are impressive. Dinner and bowling are inventive and different. Dinner and a visit to an art gallery show creativity.

When a guy asks Heather for her restaurant and activity selections, he is either too lazy to plan a simple date or he is eager to impress by taking her to an expensive restaurant and seeing a romantic comedy at the movie theater. Who cares about what he wants to do? Who cares about his thoughts and feelings? The puppy just wants to be around her and make her happy.

Nick took her to a local Italian restaurant known for its fantastic cuisine and expensive, but well worth, prices.

Vodka Four

After ordering, the conversation between them flowed easily. Heather loved conversations where each person could contribute something other than a one-word answer (one of her pet peeves) and where one topic easily led to another. Heather realized they had a lot in common: they both love rock music and going to concerts; they each changed their majors during college; they had an adventure streak and love to travel; they had been to Las Vegas and list it as one of their favorite cities; and they both love coffee and a bagel with cream cheese in the mornings.

Heather hoped their easygoing, one-hour phone conversation Tuesday night would flow just as easily on their date. After recovering from minor shock that Nick called her, Heather accepted his dinner invitation for Thursday night. He must have noticed some hesitation or uncertainty in her voice, because he had asked whether she had plans. After Heather explained the routine of going to Lucky's on Thursdays for karaoke, Nick insisted she couldn't skip out. He then accepted her invitation to join her after dinner and promised to invite Ryan and other friends because Heather didn't want to make him feel like an outsider. The more the merrier was one of her favorite mottos.

As soon as Heather stepped inside the bowling alley, she heard a painfully out-of-tune version of *Living on a prayer* by Bon Jovi sung by one of the many bar staples, Eddie. Although he knew he couldn't carry a tune, his love for music was too strong to keep him from singing.

"Heather!" Cat exclaimed, raising her drink in the air when she saw Heather and Nick approach several high-top round tables littered with drinking glasses.

Heather smiled as she saw her friends, Hera, and her boyfriend, Byron, Rory, Cat, and Lily talking and laughing with Ryan, Christopher, Tristan, and some other guys from the sports store.

"Do you want something to drink?" Nick asked.

"Amaretto sour, please," she replied.

"What no vodka?"

"Uh, not tonight. I have to work in the morning."

Nick shook his head. "That's too bad. I was kind of hoping for another striptease tonight."

Heather smiled tightly as he walked toward the bar. The first sly hint of the night proved he expected sex after the date. She should have known better to think that Nick wanted something more than sex. *Sleeping with guys when uber-drunk not a good way to meet future husband,* Heather mentally checked off.

"What's going on?" Rory asked lowly, keeping an eye on Nick. "You look a little pissed."

"I think Nick is expecting another wild night like Friday," she answered slowly, trying to control her rising anger. "I'm here to have a good time, but I don't need to be stinkin' drunk."

"Don't kill me for saying this, but give the guy a break."

"What?" Rory's statement took Heather by complete surprise.

"He doesn't know you," she clarified gently. "He only knows you as Vodka Four from Eli's stories and Friday night. Not to mention, this is the first official date."

"Yeah, I guess so," Heather agreed, with a sigh.

"Time will tell whether or not Nick is about ass or a relationship. Personally, I can't see Nick chasing ass."

"I can't see it either," she admitted. "Hey, how is Tristan acting around you tonight?"

"He's totally looking to get laid again," Rory answered. "He's playing it cool, not monopolizing my time, but yet dropping obvious hints he wants to have sex."

"And?"

"Of course, we'll do it, but I'm telling him that I don't want to date him. I can't imagine dating a kid."

Vodka Four

"Well, good luck with everything," Heather said, with a grin.

Rory coughed shortly to signal that Nick was heading back to the table.

"So, Nick," Rory said, with a sweet smile. "Do you sing?"

"Only when I'm tanked," he replied. "I've been known to sing a little bit of Journey, Billy Joel, Green Day, or Linkin Park."

"Really?" His eclectic karaoke choices interested Heather.

"So, you have to be drunk in order to sing?" Rory asked, not even bothering to hide her disapproval.

"Don't you?"

Heather and Rory shook their heads. "We like to sing," Heather said, shrugging. "We're not the greatest singers in the world, but everybody at Lucky's really doesn't care about that."

"What do you guys sing?"

"*I'm only happy when it rains* by Garbage," Heather answered. "Although I don't like country, I like to sing a couple of songs by Shania Twain and the Dixie Chicks."

"Anything by Cher," Rory replied.

"Heather!" Cat called from a nearby table. "Are you singing?"

"Only if you are," she shot back, with a wink.

Although Cat doesn't have a problem singing along in a car, she adamantly refuses to sing in public. She claims to have a terrible singing voice and is afraid people will boo her when they hear her sing. Even though Rory and Heather insist no one would do that, Cat declines to sing karaoke.

"So, are you going to sing?" Nick asked, gently nudging Heather's arm.

"I will if you will," she said slyly.

He returned her smile. "Deal."

"What are you going to sing?" she asked, writing down her selections on a piece of paper.

"It's a surprise," Nick replied smugly, flipping through the songbook.

After Nick submitted their song selections, they joined Rory and Christopher's conversation.

"So, you think you know us, eh?" Rory asked doubtfully, looking at him. "Please enlighten us with your thoughts."

"Well, I do work closely with four of you," he pointed out, pausing to take a swig from his beer bottle. "But Lily cuts my hair and drops by the store frequently. So, yeah, I think I know you guys."

"I think this is the first time that we've all hung around each other outside of work," Cat observed, as Rory and Lily nodded in agreement.

"Still doesn't mean that I don't know you."

"Fine," Rory said, with a dramatic sigh. "Tell us what you know."

"OK," Christopher said, shrugging. "You're the tough one," he said, looking at Rory.

"You're the smart one," he pointed to Cat.

"You're the beautiful one," he looked at Heather.

"You're the quiet one," he said to Lily.

"You're the fun one," he told Hera.

"I'm quiet?" Lily exclaimed loudly. "What the fuck? Seriously?"

"I'm beautiful?" Heather questioned, not looking pleased with his one-word description. "Why do they get descriptions about their personality, and mine is about my appearance? Do you think I'm dumb?"

Christopher looked a little uncomfortable as Lily and Heather glared at him.

"I'm quiet?" Lily yelled, causing several heads to turn in their direction. "Seriously?"

Vodka Four

"Why didn't I get a description describing my personality?" Heather asked again. "I'm smart, dammit!"

"You think Cat is the smart one of the group?" Rory joined in. "Really? I think I'm smarter than her."

"What?" Cat whipped her head in Rory's direction. "You think you're smarter than I am? Who was the one who named all 51 states?"

"I only forgot Utah and Vermont!"

"And who constantly beats you in Scrabble and backgammon?"

"You're so competitive," Rory pointed out.

"Said the pot to the kettle."

"I'm OK with being the fun one," Hera said, holding up her hands in mock surrender and looking at Christopher. "Because I am the fun one."

"Quiet my ass," Lily snapped as Cat and Rory continued to argue in the background. "You don't know us at all."

"Beautiful my ass," Heather threw in. "That word doesn't describe my personality. Yeah, you really nailed all of us, Christopher."

"Way to go, Milly," Tristan said, with a smirk. "You really do know them."

"Shut up," Christopher groused as the five friends continued to badger him about his one-word descriptions.

"Nick Reed, you're next!" yelled the karaoke deejay.

Cat and Rory quit arguing and Lily and Heather stop badgering Christopher, much to his relief, to cheer on Nick, who headed toward the small raised platform.

"This song is dedicated to that special someone in my life," Nick said into the microphone, looking at Heather as Hera, Rory, Lily, and Cat "ooohed" and "aaahed" like idiots.

Heather started to blush furiously. *His special someone? Already? He had to be absolutely insane,* she thought.

"This song is for you, Wells," he said, pointing to Ryan and laughing as the music to *Uptown Girl* by Billy Joel started playing.

Ryan smirked and flipped Nick off while Heather and everyone else laughed hysterically. Heather was relieved that his dedication was a joke. Despite the sly hint earlier, she was having a good time and wouldn't mind seeing him again.

Rory was right, she thought as she watched Nick sing. *He really doesn't know me that well. But yet he's willing to sing sober in front of me and my friends. That has to say something.*

Heather was impressed. Nick didn't even need to look at the monitor to help him sing. She glanced around the bar and saw everyone clapping, dancing, and singing along.

The audience cheered as the song came to an end, and Heather clapped and whistled loudly. Nick took a bow before stepping off the makeshift stage and high-fiving Ryan, Christopher, and Tristan. Heather cheered again when the karaoke deejay called Rory's name.

"How did dinner go?" Lily asked, looking over at Nick, who was talking to Ryan and his other friends.

"I had a nice time," she admitted. "He took me to Victoria's, which you know is my favorite restaurant. He ordered a bottle of wine, and we just talked about different stuff throughout dinner. It was really nice."

"Are you going to see him again?"

"I wouldn't say no to a second date," Heather said thoughtfully. "Oh, by the way, is Ben here?"

"God, no!" Lily exclaimed in horror. "I'm assuming he can't escape from Jessica."

"He's such a moron," she said, referring to one of the bartenders, who claims to be totally in love with Lily, but is engaged to a selfish, spoiled, and controlling woman named Jessica.

"I agree. He's such a nice guy who doesn't deserve to be with someone so evil."

Vodka Four

Heather chuckled.

"You know, Ben's one of my closest friends, but the guy is a complete idiot. I don't understand why he won't break off the engagement."

"I can't believe he proposed to her in the first place."

"Oh, the proposal wasn't real," Lily confided. "Jessica gave him an ultimatum. If he didn't propose to her by last Christmas, she was going to leave him. She totally told him how he was going to propose to her."

"Wow. That's sad."

"Tell me about it. I don't understand why he caved. He should've let her walk away."

"Especially when he's so in love with you," Heather added.

"That's the thing I don't get!" Lily exclaimed. "If I'm the love of his freakin' life, then why hasn't he dumped to her to be with me?"

"Um, because you don't love him?"

"But what if I did? What if I told Ben that I loved him? Would he have the balls to dump Jessica?"

"Uh, yeah," Heather said, with a hint of sarcasm. "But he knows you don't love him. So, why should he break up with Jessica?"

"Because she's evil! I know it. You know it. And he knows it!"

"And this is why he's a moron."

"Not going to argue with that," Lily agreed, clapping loudly as Rory finished singing *If I Could Turn Back Time*.

"I had a nice time tonight," Heather said demurely as they stood in front of her apartment door. "Thank you for dinner."

"Not a problem," he replied. "I had a great time tonight. Thanks for inviting me to karaoke night. We should do that again."

Jennifer Elliott

"I'm there every Thursday night."

Heather was playing coy, waiting for Nick to invite himself inside. She had no intention of sleeping with Nick tonight. But what were his intentions? Was he looking for a "friend with benefits?" Or did he want something more?

"What are you doing this weekend?" Nick asked.

"Absolutely nothing," she answered, with a smile.

"I'll call you tomorrow, and we'll make plans."

"Sounds good." Heather was giddy. He wanted to see her again.

She didn't move an inch when Nick leaned in to kiss her good night. As soon as his mouth found hers, Heather wanted to drag him inside and have wild passionate sex. At that moment, she didn't care about his intentions as his lips softly kissed hers. The intimate kiss filled her with excitement, hope, and anticipation and left her wanting so much more.

"Good night, Heather," he said, breaking the kiss.

"Good night," she answered softly as she let herself into her apartment.

CHAPTER 9

Friday, January 14

The next afternoon at Lexington, Heather was at her desk, shuffling through paperwork, while Christopher, Rory, Hera, and other sales associates were straightening the floor area and waiting for their appointments to arrive. For some odd reason, the store was empty except for the sales associates, giving them a chance to catch their breath and prepare for the next wave of customers.

As Heather worked, she heard her cell phone vibrate inside her desk. Cell phone use in front of a customer was strictly prohibited. However, Wesley knew family emergencies were bound to happen and requested that cell phones be on vibrate during business hours.

Heather quietly grabbed her phone and saw she received a text message from Lily. She quickly read the message and smiled brightly.

"Hey, Christopher," she said, with a little amusement in her voice.

"What?" he asked, not looking up from his work.

"Can we see the tux you're going to wear to the Carrington ball?"

"What?" he asked again, this time looking up with a surprised look.

"You're going to the ball?" Rory and Hera asked together, who looked at each other and then laughed.

"Who are you going with?" Hera asked sweetly.

"I'm sure Heather will tell you," he replied curtly, focusing his attention on the clothing rack he was straightening.

"Magdala," Heather sang out. "He's going with Magdala."

"Why in the world are you going to the ball with Magdala?" Rory asked. "Did you lose a bet or something?"

Magdala Parker, who worked as a full-time hair stylist at Bellismo, had a reputation of being desperately in love with the idea of being in love. At first look, Magdala was naturally adorable and wholesome, whose appearance alluded fun and excitement. However, that image was a deception once people are lured into a dull or boring conversation. Most people who want to see a movie pick a recent or popular film. Magdala, on the other hand, loved to watch super dramatic foreign films with subtitles and then analyze it for deeper meanings.

At parties or other social gatherings, Magdala attempted to engage anyone in an intellectual conversation. "How do you feel about the current contingency of today's mass communication industry?" she once had asked Heather, who had no idea what Magdala was saying. The use of big words, such as "contingency" and "communication," can sometimes leave Heather a bit baffled. Luckily, Hera simply pulled Heather away from the conversation before she even attempted to answer, leaving Magdala a little miffed.

Through trial and error, most guys who have worked in Anastacia Square know not to get involved with Magdala because after the first date — in her mind — a full-fledged relationship has started. Lily and other co-workers at Bellismo have frequently comforted a crying Magdala after being gently or brutally dumped. Because of the frequency of heartbreaks, her co-workers systematically played "Paper Rock Scissors" to decide who got to comfort her.

Despite her issues, Magdala had a good heart, which made it impossible to hate her, according to Lily. She also had a good rapport with her clients and was one of the best stylists at the salon, which helps her tremendously from being fired.

Vodka Four

"Do you like her?" Hera asked, with a devious grin. "Does she like you?"

"Is her roommate paying you?" Rory badgered.

"Is this a dare?" Heather joined in cheerfully.

"You guys are terrible," Christopher said, shaking his head.

"No, seriously," Heather said, trying not to smile at the thought of Christopher attending the ball with Magdala. First, she had trouble even picturing Christopher at the ball. Second, she had more issues imagining Christopher at the ball with Magdala. "Why are you going to the ball with Magdala?"

He shrugged his shoulders, "Apparently, she and Brooke received invitations, and Brooke and her boyfriend are going. Magdala asked me to go with her." Brooke was Magdala's best friend and roommate.

"And you said yes?" Rory exclaimed. "Christopher! Seriously, what in the world possessed you to say yes?"

"You couldn't think of an excuse?" Heather asked and then said sarcastically, "You're going to have a fun and exciting night! Make sure you brush up on your current events."

"You were drunk!" Hera answered loudly, finally realizing the answer.

Christopher loudly shushed her, looking around the store to make sure other employees or Wesley didn't hear the last statement.

"You were drunk," she repeated, her brown eyes dancing with excitement. "You were probably so drunk that you don't even remember saying yes."

"How did you know?" he asked, looking surprised that Hera knew the truth.

"Because I know you," she said, with a smile. "You've told us a lot of stories about being so drunk that you either black out or don't remember stuff."

Jennifer Elliott

"Just don't tell her, OK?" he asked politely. "I don't want to hurt her feelings."

"You're going to have to her hurt feelings if you want to avoid being in a relationship with her," Heather pointed out. "Her stories are legendary."

"Legendary?" Rory said thoughtfully. "Really? You think so? I don't think that's the right word."

"Infamous?" Heather guessed.

"Oh, I like that word!" Hera chipped in gleefully. "She's infamous."

"Mmmm," Rory disagreed. "I don't think that's the right word either."

"Notorious!" Heather exclaimed.

"Oooh, I think that's it," Rory said, winking at her. "That's the perfect word."

"You guys are terrible," Christopher said, shaking his head.

"At least we're not going to the ball with Magdala," Rory shot back cheerfully. "You're going to have a real fun night."

"I will when I see you guys there," he countered, with a devious grin.

"What?" she asked, stopping her train of thought about Christopher and Magdala and the Carrington ball. "What is that supposed to mean?"

"I'm just saying that I'm not the only one who is going to the ball."

"You said 'you guys,' " Hera said carefully, thinking about what he said. "Which means you're going to see more than one of us at the ball."

Christopher just shrugged, not saying another word.

"Tristan is going to ask me, and Nick is going to ask Heather," Rory figured out.

"What?" Heather exclaimed. How the hell did she get involved? "How do you know?"

Vodka Four

"It's kind of obvious," Rory said, walking over to Heather's desk as a customer walked through the store doors.

"I think you should go," Hera said, following Rory and glancing at Christopher greeting his customer. "It might be fun."

Heather sighed loudly. "What if I don't want to go?"

Why in the world would Nick invite her to the Carrington ball? She has been on exactly one date with him. The ball was for married couples who looked forward to indulging themselves for one night out of the year. The ball was a relationship milestone for committed couples to achieve. The ball was for guys who wanted to impress their dates by spending an extraordinary amount of money. The ball was not for two people who had slept together and then gone on one date.

Even if Heather accepted the invitation, what would make Nick believe she could find the appropriate dress and accessories in less than two weeks? Most women needed at least six months to pick the perfect dress, find the perfect accessories, and then lose the necessary amount of weight to look perfectly stunning.

"Why not?" Hera asked. "Nick's a good guy who isn't going to make an ass out of himself."

"True," Heather admitted. "But isn't it a little late to be thinking about going to the ball? Most people needs months to plan everything."

"What do you have to plan?" Rory countered. "You have a dress. You have a guy. I'm assuming Nick got the tickets from work. What else do you need to plan?"

"Come on," Hera coaxed. "It'll be fun. Maybe I can convince Byron to go."

"How are you going to get an invitation?" Heather wondered.

"Besides Wesley, no one from the store wanted to go to the ball," Hera disclosed. "I don't know who else he'd give the extra tickets to."

"I'm not going with Tristan," Rory pointed out, shaking her long black tresses. "Sorry, but I'm not going with him."

"Why not?" Heather demanded. "If I'm going, you're going."

"Um, one, this isn't an 'all for one and one for all' thing," Rory clarified, with a smirk. "Two, I have no desire to go with Tristan. Three, I have no desire to go to the ball at all."

"Why don't you want to go with him?" Hera asked curiously.

"Can you guys honestly see me having fun with Tristan at the ball?"

Hera and Heather each made a mental picture before they both shook their heads. Tristan was good enough for sex, meeting at a bar with other friends, and the occasional dinner date. Rory had no intention of being mistaken of being in a relationship with him.

"Besides, I've been to the ball before," she continued. "I think you guys should go. You'll have fun. Come on, think about it."

"I don't know," Heather said doubtfully. "What are Nick and I going to do at the ball?"

"There's plenty of things to do," Rory informed her. "You'll have Hera and Byron to keep you guys company. There's dancing. There's drinking. There's touring the Carrington House. There's making fun of the women who are wearing very inappropriate dresses."

"Don't you want to get dressed up and look like a princess?" Hera asked.

"Do I look like I'm 6?" Heather shot back.

"It sounds like fun," she confessed. "Rory sold me on making fun of other women's dresses. It'll be fun to watch all the rich people. Come on, we'll sit on a bench and make fun of them."

Heather giggled.

Vodka Four

"You would look stunning," Rory offered. "Just think of all the great sex that you and Nick will have that night. You will be irresistible."

"Shut up."

"You can wear the shimmery silver dress that you wore at your sister's wedding. That's definitely elegant enough for the ball," Hera pointed out. "You have the shoes. You have the accessories. All you need is a good man. Oh wait, you have him, too."

Heather smiled at Hera's valid points. The more her two friends encouraged her to go, the more she could see herself having a good time with Nick. If he wanted to spend a ton of money, who was she to say no?

"You two are incorrigible," she said, with a sigh. "You're right. You're right. Going to the ball with Nick might be fun."

Hera squealed with delight, clapping her hands.

"What the hell was that?" Rory asked, raising an eyebrow at Hera's behavior. "Are you OK?"

"I'm just so excited," she declared, bouncing up and down. "I've never been to the ball, and I now have a great excuse to go! I'm so excited. I gotta go find Wesley."

"What if Byron doesn't want to go?" Heather asked.

"Oh, he's going. He has no choice."

Heather and Rory laughed. Hera shot off to the back of the store to find Wesley as Rory turned to greet a customer. Heather smiled at the image of Nick in a tuxedo. *God, he looks really hot in my imagination,* she thought. And for the first time, Heather really wanted to go to the Carrington ball.

Stupid Hera. Stupid Rory, Heather thought anxiously to herself later that night. She was sitting across the restaurant table from Nick, who was babbling on and on about his day at work. *When is he going to invite me to the ball,* she wondered impatiently. *If he doesn't ask me, I'm blaming Hera and Rory for getting my hopes up only to have them crushed to a million pieces. I have stupid friends.*

After Hera and Rory convinced Heather to attend the ball, Nick stopped by Lexington to invite her to dinner that night. While they were chatting for a few minutes, Hera and Rory took full advantage of the time, acting like complete morons behind Nick's back. After bouncing around like two cheerleaders high on meth, they resorted to making inappropriate sexual gestures. Although Nick knew Hera and Rory were up to no good, he could never catch them in the act. As soon as he turned to look at them, they were straightening the nearby clothing racks.

Heather figured dinner would be the perfect setting for Nick to invite her to the ball. Although a million questions were still floating in her mind, she was ready to happily accept his invitation. If he ever got around to inviting her to the damn thing.

"So, I have something to ask you," he said nervously, snapping Heather back into reality.

"Um, OK," she said, pretending to look serious but jumping for joy inside. *And Rory said I'm not a good actress ... what does she know?*

"I know this is going to sound odd," Nick said slowly. "I don't want to scare you with this, but ... "

"What is it?" Heather asked, with fake concern. *The local theater company could definitely use my gift for acting.*

"I have two invitations to the ball, and I was wondering if you want to go."

Ask your questions now! Heather's mind screamed at her. *But act cool. Be cool.*

"Um, I don't want to freak you out," she said slowly. "While I'm having a great time with you, don't you think the ball is for couples?"

Vodka Four

"Yes!" he exclaimed, looking relieved and sitting back in his chair. "I'm having a great time with you, and I don't want to rush anything."

"Nothing says rushing like an invitation to the ball," Heather teased, with a hint of sarcasm.

"I know. But here's the deal, I have two invitations and I've already made arrangements — you know, a room at the Carrington House, the limo, dinner reservations at Traditions. I've already paid for the room and limo, and if I cancel now, I lose money."

"When did you make these arrangements?" she asked suspiciously.

Nick looked down at his dinner, not answering immediately.

Heather chuckled. "Nick, when did you make these arrangements?"

"About a year ago," he admitted, looking sheepishly at her. "My ex-girlfriend, Samantha, really wanted to go to the ball. I made the arrangements, and I was going to surprise her. But then we broke up, and she moved to Arizona."

Heather did her best to contain her relief, joy, and excitement that Nick planned to take his ex-girlfriend to the ball. She completely understood why he was inviting her. If money was going to be lost, she would have done the same thing.

"I understand," she said honestly, with a smile.

"I tried to convince some of my friends to buy the package, but no one wanted to go."

"So, what convinced you to ask me?"

"Ryan mentioned it, but I didn't think it was a good idea. I think the ball is a relationship milestone that couples try to achieve."

Heather smiled as her heart melted a bit.

"But I really don't want to lose money," he said sheepishly.

Jennifer Elliott

"Doesn't the hotel and limo service have a waiting list?" she asked.

"Yeah, but because the ball is a few weeks away, I'm unable to cancel without losing money. Apparently, it takes extra effort to look at a waiting list."

Heather chuckled.

"Why didn't you cancel everything after you and Samantha broke up?" she questioned.

"I didn't think about it," Nick admitted. "I forgot about the ball until I received reminders at the beginning of the year."

"I completely understand."

"I know I'm totally springing this on you at the last minute, but if you need anything, let me know."

Heather was touched that Nick felt a little guilty admitting she was his second choice — or only choice. Although she was tempted to snag a new pair of shoes from his offer, she knew he already had invested enough money and would have felt guilty for taking advantage of his kindness. Even though their second date was still in progress, Heather was starting to believe that maybe Rory was right — maybe Nick was a guy good after all. And maybe her friends weren't so stupid either.

CHAPTER 10

Thursday, January 20

Heather usually brought her lunch to work and sat in the break room, reading a magazine or book or chatting her co-workers. Today, however, she had to run a few errands during her hour-long lunch break because she had a date with Nick after work.

Heather was driving back to work when she heard a terrible Top 40 song on the radio. As she leaned over a bit to change the radio station, her Saturn Vue lightly hit the curb, causing her front right tire to blow.

"Shit!" Heather cursed, as she pulled over to the side of the road. *This is the last thing I need right now.*

After turning on her emergency lights, she climbed out to survey the damage. Due to the winter weather and Heather remembering the last time she changed a tire was when her father showed her, she wisely decided not to attempt the mechanical feat.

"Rory?" she asked, after climbing back into her Vue and whipping out her cell phone.

"Yeah, what's up?"

"I have a flat right now."

"That sucks," Rory commented. "Where are you?"

"On Janesville Street near Franklin Middle School. I was running a few errands on my lunch break."

"I'll call Cat. She'll get someone from the dealership to help you."

"I didn't think to call Cat," Heather said, slapping her forehead with her hand. "I'm such an idiot in emergency situations. I swear I lose all of my common sense."

"Don't worry about it," Rory said, chuckling. "I'll call Cat."

"Thanks, Rory. I should call Wesley and let him know what's going on."

"Talk to you later."

After Heather talked to Wesley, who offered his help after listening to her explain the emergency situation, Rory called again.

"What's up?"

"I thought I'd keep you company until the tow truck came," Rory said. "So, how did you manage to get a flat tire?"

"I was changing the radio station," Heather explained.

"And that distracted you from driving?"

"Shut up."

"What song was playing?"

"A Hilary Duff song," Heather replied.

"Since when did The Rock start playing Hilary Duff?" Rory wondered, referring to a popular radio station that played alternative and hard rock music.

"The Rock was playing Nickelback, and you know I can't stand most of their songs. I was listening to Z93 before they started playing Hilary," Heather clarified. "Like you should say anything anyhow. This coming from a woman who has all of Celine Dion's CDs."

"Hey," Rory said shortly. "Don't make fun of Celine. You know how much I love her."

"I'm just saying you shouldn't judge that I might secretly like Hilary."

"Celine has been around a lot longer than Hilary, and Celine is 10 times a better singer. I'm not ashamed that I love Celine, whereas you secretly love Hilary."

Vodka Four

"I don't love Hilary," Heather argued, with a smile.

"Oh, I think do," Rory teased, chuckling. "So, I have a question for you."

"Shoot."

"Why didn't you call Nick to help you out?"

"I don't know," Heather said, realizing Nick had never entered her mind. "I didn't think about him. I called you because I knew you weren't at work."

"I could have been at school."

"But you weren't."

"So, why didn't you call Nick?" Rory asked again.

"One, I didn't think about it," Heather said carefully, thinking about her reasons. "Two, I'm a complete spaz in emergency situations. Come on, I didn't even think to call Cat. Three, even if I had thought about Nick, he couldn't have helped me because he's at work."

"I think he could've been able to take off to help you."

"What are you getting at, Rory?"

"I'm just surprised that you didn't call Nick to help you."

"Would you call Tristan if you had a flat?" Heather challenged.

"Good Lord, no," Rory answered quickly. "But Tristan and I aren't in a relationship."

"Nick and I aren't in a relationship."

"Yes, you are."

"No, we're not," Heather snapped, trying to keep calm. "He and I are dating. There's a huge difference between dating and being in a relationship."

"But you and Nick are definitely heading toward being in a relationship."

"Bullshit," she shrieked. "If I don't know what's going on, there's no way you know."

"Oh, I'm going to disagree with you, sweetie. How many times have you talked and seen Nick this week?" Rory asked, but didn't give Heather a chance to answer. "And correct me if I'm wrong, but didn't he spend the entire weekend at your place?"

"That doesn't mean anything."

"Why are you not admitting the obvious? You've been down this road before, Heather. Why don't you just admit that you like him?"

"I like having sex with him." Which was totally true as Heather thought about the passionate weekend that involved a lot of nakedness, numerous orgasms, and long conversations about anything.

"Bullshit!" Rory shrieked. "You're using sex to hide your real feelings!"

"Am not!"

"You are too. You don't want to admit that you like Nick, because you're afraid of being hurt."

"Why are you on my back about this?" Heather asked defiantly. "Nick and I haven't even been seeing each other for two weeks. I don't think I should be relying on him right now. And since when am I not allowed to rely on my friends?"

Rory chuckled. "You know you can always count on us. I'm just saying that I think it's OK to rely on Nick."

"Thanks for the advice, Dear Abby," Heather said sarcastically, waving to Cat who had jumped out of the tow truck that had parked in front of her Vue. "I gotta go. Cat's here."

Rory was right, Heather decided when she returned to work. *Why didn't I think about calling Nick to help?*

Whenever she was involved in a minor emergency, Rory, Cat, Hera, and Lily were the first people she called for help. After some thought, Heather knew Nick would have helped her with the flat tire. He was the type of guy who would drop what he was doing to help a friend or someone he was dating.

Although Heather didn't want to admit it, she and Nick were heading toward the relationship zone. She just wanted to

Vodka Four

enter it cautiously and carefully. Rushing into a relationship and saying, "I love you" after a few weeks had always resulted in heartbreak and pain. Now, Heather was old enough to learn from her mistakes to avoid being caught in the same vicious cycle. Maybe this time around, slow and steady would win the race.

"You OK?" Rory asked, as Heather straightened her desk before leaving work.

"Yeah," she admitted. "Everything you said was true. Except that I honestly didn't think about calling Nick to help. I guess I'm used to depending on you guys."

"That's fine," Rory said reassuringly. "I have no problem with that. I just don't want to see you shutting Nick out. I think he's a good guy."

"So far so good."

"I just don't want you to turn into a cold heartless bitch like me."

"Oh, Rory," Heather said, sighing. "You do have a heart. Unfortunately, it is surrounded by ice."

"You're a good girl who wants love and romance."

"And you're a bad girl who just wants to be spanked."

"Hell, yeah," Rory said, with a smile. "Even though I'm supporting you to pursue a healthy relationship, I will kick Nick's ass if he ever hurts you. But until then, I don't want you to miss out on something good."

"Awww, Rory," Heather sighed and started walking toward the back, with her purse and coat on her arm, when the part-time administrative assistant entered the main floor. "I think this is a Kodak moment."

"Shut up," she said abruptly, walking with Heather. "I think Nick is good for you."

"I'm having a great time with him so far."

"He's more than a good time, and you know it," Rory clarified. "You have a good chance that this could turn into a healthy and stable relationship. And you need that right now,

Heather. You've been in so many shitty relationships that you've just accepted and expected messy endings even before anything has even started."

"That is so not true," Heather protested, standing by the exit door.

"You didn't even give Nick the benefit of the doubt when you guys first slept together. You kicked him out of your apartment, thinking he was another player. Not even for a second did you think Nick was a good guy."

Dammit! Why is Rory right all of the freakin' time? Heather thought to herself.

"You need to let Nick in here," Rory said seriously while placing her hand over Heather's heart. Heather tried to hide a smile, but burst into laughter.

"Now, that was a Kodak moment," Rory laughed with her.

Operation: When Black Cats Fly

Heather's heart beat furiously. She looked at Rory and Cat and wondered whether they could sense the adrenaline running through her. They looked so calm, crouching behind the big bushes on campus and staring into the darkness. Talking or even hand gestures were forbidden during this part of the mission.

A soft whistle sounded, and Cat bolted from her place, with a large black panther lawn ornament tucked underneath her arm. A few seconds later, another soft whistle flew through the darkness, and Rory took off running, holding a large plastic eagle.

Heather wiped her sweaty hands on her jeans as she waited for the third whistle. Her heart continued to pound as she quickly glanced around her surroundings for campus security, drunken stragglers, or unsuspecting witnesses. What if she got caught? Serious consequences of her actions slowly entered her mind. Could she be expelled? Suspended? Could she go to jail? If so, for how long? For what seemed like an eternity, Heather decided something had gone wrong.

Finally, the third whistle softly sounded, and Heather sprinted off, with a large plastic cardinal in her arms. She didn't even bother to breathe or gasp for air when she reached her destination. Thoughts of being in the clink kept her adrenaline pumping. Eli quickly and quietly turned the plastic cardinal upside down, showing its feet bound with rope and a latch. Heather surveyed the undisturbed premises, waiting for him to finish the job.

"Let's go," he said, taking off. Heather chased him as fast as she could into the dark night.

The next morning, someone at the technical college, the state university, and the Lutheran university noticed the schools' mascots were missing. After locating and retrieving the plastic animals, college officials then decided to use nuts, bolts, wire and other reinforcements to prevent future kidnappings.

Jennifer Elliott

But before that decision was made, students, staff, and visitors at the Lutheran university saw each mascot dangling from the three flagpoles (one for the university flag, the state flag, and the American flag). The Lutheran university's mascot — the panther — was poised for action on the middle and highest flag pole while the eagle and the cardinal were dangling upside down by their feet on the lower side poles.

Due to the brilliant scheme that would be talked about for generations, Lutheran university officials also placed locks on all three flagpoles.

CHAPTER 11

Crap, crap, crap, Heather thought frantically as she ran into her apartment and avoided tripping over her cats who were meowing and following her for attention. As she was pulling off her work clothes, all the things she needed to do before Nick arrived raced through her mind.

All of the clothes in the bathroom and her bedroom needed to be thrown in her walk-in closet. The living room and kitchen area were adequately clean. What else did she need to do? She needed to call her nephews, Colin and Bennett, and wish them a happy birthday. She also needed to feed her cats, refresh the water bowl, and scoop out the litter box.

The doorbell rang just as Heather walked into her closet to drop a pile of clothes and pick an outfit for the date.

"Shit," Heather muttered as she grabbed her robe from the bathroom and headed toward the front door.

"Hey, Willow," Nick greeted with a smile and then quickly glanced at her robe. "Nice outfit. Am I allowed to open my gift now?" He teased, reaching for the robe's belt.

"No," she flirted, tightening the belt around her waist and keeping a firm grip on it. The lacy, black pushup bra and matching thong underneath the robe would be off in a second if she allowed him a peek inside.

"I'm sorry, but I'm running late," Heather explained, closing the front door and heading toward her bedroom. "But Rory and I ended up talking for awhile after work."

"It's OK," Nick said, gently rubbing her shoulders. "Don't worry. I'm in no hurry."

"Thanks for being so understanding, but I'm hungry. I need food."

"I'll watch some TV and play with your cats," he said, returning to the living room and turning on the TV before sitting down on the couch.

"Merry and Pippen won't be interested in you unless you feed them," Heather called from her closet. "I haven't had a chance to feed them or scoop their litter box. And I still need to call my nephews to wish them a happy birthday."

"I'm in no hurry, Willow. Get dressed and call your nephews."

"Are you sure?"

"Call your nephews and talk for awhile. We'll go to dinner and catch the late-night movie. Not a big deal."

I am so lucky, Heather thought to herself as she selected a thin black sweater with a deep V-neck.

As she walked to the bathroom to refresh her hair and makeup, she noticed Nick was in the kitchen, spooning canned cat food onto a small white plate for Merry and Pippen, who were meowing at his feet.

"What are you doing?"

"Feeding your cats," Nick said, looking up at her. "You said your cats needed to be fed. So, I'm feeding them."

"You don't have to do that."

"I know," he said, putting the ceramic plate on the kitchen floor, where her cats were looking at him intently. "You're running a little late, and I thought I'd help. I've seen you feed them before, so I know where everything is."

"You are too sweet," Heather said, with a smile. She was surprised and touched that Nick was offering his help. No guy has ever taken the initiative to feed her cats.

"Don't tell the guys, OK? It'll ruin my street cred."

Heather chuckled as she stepped into the bathroom to retouch her makeup and hair.

"Heather, where's the pooper scooper for the litter box?" Nick called out from another walk-in closet that contained

Merry and Pippen's water and dry food dishes, litter box, and other cat supplies.

"Why?"

"So, I can scoop the litter box."

"Nick, you don't have to do that," Heather called out from the bathroom as she did her makeup. "Seriously, you've done enough."

"Let me help you, Heather. I don't mind. I know how to scoop cat crap. My mom had billions of cats when I was growing up."

"It's in the white trash can by the litter boxes."

Heather smiled as she brushed her hair. She heard Nick talk to Merry and Pippen while scooping their litter boxes.

"Seriously, guys," Nick muttered to the curious cats, sitting next to him. "Why do you guys have to crap so much? Oh, dude! That's nasty. Ugh. What's up with that? Heather, something's wrong with your cats."

Heather chuckled as she continued to listen to Nick grumble. "Hey, what are you doing? Pippen, don't take a dump right now. Come on, man. That's so not cool."

Heather returned to her bedroom and picked up her cell phone to call her nephews, Colin and Bennett, who turned 4. With her phone next to her ear, she walked into the living room and kitchen area to see Nick double bagging a plastic bag full of cat pooh. Heather pointed to the front door, and Nick hurled the plastic bag outside.

"I love you, too, Colin," she said cheerfully. "Happy birthday, sweetie. Hey, Trish. So, am I the coolest aunt ever? Wait, what did Sarah buy them?"

She smiled at Nick, who was thoroughly washing his hands at the kitchen sink.

"OK, Trish," Heather said, standing behind Nick at the sink. "I'll talk to you later. Hug the boys for me."

She snapped the phone shut, circled her arms around his waist, and hugged him tightly.

Jennifer Elliott

"Thank you. You're an amazing man."

"I know," Nick teased, reaching for a towel hanging on the oven handle. "Sometimes I even amaze myself with my amazing talents."

Heather giggled as she buried her face in his back and tightened her grip.

"Hey," he said, turning around and putting his arms around her. "Don't be afraid to ask me for help. I'm here for you."

I've heard that before, Heather thought dryly.

"Really?" she said instead, looking at him.

"Really. You can count on me."

Heather knew better than to count on a man she didn't know. When she fell for the "you can trust me" line, the guy disappeared and she had learn to rely herself again. If she relied on herself, then she couldn't blame anyone for her failure.

"Does this mean you'll buy me tampons?" she asked innocently.

"Sure," Nick said, shrugging his shoulders. "Everyone's going to know that they're not for me. They'll see me as the good boyfriend — or a pussy whipped boyfriend."

"Boyfriend?" Heather asked abruptly, wrinkling her forehead in concern.

Suddenly, she remembered something Rory said earlier in the day, "You and Nick are definitely heading toward being in a relationship." Heather knew the statement was true, but she didn't want to admit it to herself or anyone else.

"Well, I guess this is the part where we talk about us," Nick said softly, gently running his fingers through her hair and making her heart jump a little in the process.

"OK," she said hesitantly, not wanting to start the conversation.

"I never thought I'd be this close to you. To be honest, I didn't think I had a chance with you."

"What? Really?"

Vodka Four

"Heather, you're beautiful. There's a million guys who wouldn't hesitate to trade places with me — right here right now."

She snorted in disbelief.

"I'm serious," Nick said, cupping her chin with his fingers and forcing her to look at him. "You're sexy. You're smart. You're perfect."

The word "puppy" suddenly appeared in her mind. A puppy adored its owner despite the owner's flaws and imperfections. A puppy only saw the love, affection, and attention from its owner.

"No," Heather said firmly, shaking his fingers from her chin. "I'm not perfect. I have flaws."

"You're perfect to me."

She forced herself not to groan or roll her eyes at the cheesy line she's heard before. The last thing Heather wanted was to be placed on a pedestal. Her flaws and insecurities could easily knock her off, and what would Nick think then? Would he still think she was perfect when she became moody and bitchy?

"So, is it OK if I start calling you my girl?" Nick asked.

Heather really wanted to say no, but she couldn't bring herself to shake her head or say the word. She knew she wanted to be near Nick, but starting a relationship was too soon. Wasn't it? Their first official date was exactly one week ago. Could a relationship work just after a couple of dates and one weekend together?

"Are you sure about this?" she asked. "I know we've known each other, but we really don't know each other. Does that make sense?"

"Yeah, I get it," Nick agreed. "You and I have known each other for years, and now, we're just getting to know one another."

"Yeah, exactly."

"But I'm crazy about you. I know this seems fast, but doesn't this feel right?"

"Yeah, it does," she agreed slowly.

"I don't want to rush you," he said, sensing her hesitation. "Take all the time in the world to think about this. But I want you to know that I'm ready."

Dammit! Why is he being so understanding and patient? What kind of sick guy is he? Heather thought. However, she couldn't deny her attraction and how being with him felt … perfect.

"I'm ready," she said, looking at him. "I'm ready."

"Really?"

"Yeah."

Despite her concerns and fears, Heather didn't have the strength to say no to a puppy who was so eager and willing to scramble up the stairs of a relationship. Like Rory said, she and Nick were heading toward a relationship anyway — they just got there a little sooner than she expected and wanted.

After celebrating the start of something new in the bedroom and about an hour later, Nick and Heather finally ordered dinner at Olive Garden.

"How was your day?" Nick asked, after the waitress left.

"It was going well until I had a flat tire on my lunch break," Heather replied, sipping her delicious sangria.

"You got a flat tire?"

"Yeah, apparently lightly tapping a curb with a tire leads to a flat."

"What did you do?"

"I called Rory," she said, and then thanked the waitress for bringing their salad and breadsticks to the table. "She called Cat, and Cat and a mechanic from Saturn picked me up."

"Why didn't you call me?" Nick asked. "I would've helped you."

Vodka Four

"I honestly didn't think about calling you," Heather said, shrugging her shoulders. "Whenever I'm in trouble, which isn't very often by the way, I always call one of my friends."

"You should've called me."

"No, I didn't."

"What?" Nick asked, surprised by Heather's short, quick, and firm response.

"I don't need to call a guy whenever I need help. That's why I'm friends with Rory, Cat, Hera, and Lily," she said teasingly, hoping to lighten up the conversation.

"You know I would've helped you today."

"I know, but Rory and Cat helped me."

"Will you call me next time you need something?" Nick asked, realizing Heather wasn't going to apologize for not calling him.

"If I think about you," she replied honestly.

"Well, you should learn to think about me."

Heather reminded herself to breathe before replying. His chauvinistic view was starting to piss her off.

"Look, Nick, I'm not a silly or helpless girlfriend who needs to call her big, strong boyfriend every time something goes wrong. I'm capable of handling my own problems."

"I can tell," he grumbled.

"Just because we're in a relationship now doesn't mean you're my go-to guy."

"I should be."

"No, you shouldn't," Heather argued, desperately trying to keep the irritation and frustration out of her tone. "I've known my friends a lot longer than I've known you, and I know I can depend on them."

"So, you think I'm undependable?"

She sighed. "I didn't say that. I know if I call you, you would help me in a heartbeat."

"So, what's the problem?" Nick asked, a little exasperated.

"I honestly didn't think of you when I got the flat."

He was desperately trying to understand Heather's logic and need for independence. His last girlfriend, Samantha, always needed his help and started crying within seconds when things weren't going her way. But Nick liked being needed. Despite her constant need for attention and assistance, he was there and willing to help.

Nick didn't expect Heather to be the exact opposite of Samantha. And he's always known Heather to be in a relationship with someone, leading him to believe she didn't like to be alone. But the more time he spent with her, the more he realized how different she was from all of his ex-girlfriends. Heather didn't want to spend all of her free time with him. Running errands or going grocery shopping by herself didn't bother her — in fact, Nick noted, she craved her "me time."

That characteristic alone drew him closer to her. Since their hookup at the club, Nick enjoyed spending time with Heather and wanted to learn more about her life. The idea of being in a relationship didn't freak him out. Nick believed Heather was the perfect girlfriend — a girlfriend who was beautiful, intelligent, and thoughtful, with an insatiable sexual appetite. Knowing he wanted to be near her didn't scare him, but her fierce independence and stubbornness took him by surprise.

"Are you OK?" Heather asked, as numerous questions popped into her mind. Was this their first fight? Why was she such a pansy? She should've said no about starting a relationship. She should've made him wait. He was willing to wait.

Dammit, she thought. *What the hell is wrong with me? Just because he's a nice guy doesn't mean I need to be his girlfriend right now. Whatever happened to taking this slow?*

Already a few hours into their official relationship, and they were squabbling over a trivial issue.

Vodka Four

"Yeah, I'm fine," Nick said, with a weak smile. "I just assumed all girls relied on their boyfriends."

"Hey," she said, softening a bit. "One, we're just getting to know each other. I know you would've help me, but I didn't think I had the right to ask you. Two, you weren't my boyfriend when I got the flat."

"You're right," he agreed. "I just figured since you relied on Eli and other guys, you would rely on me."

"I've known Eli since college. He and I were really good friends before we started dating. And by the time he and I started a relationship, I wasn't afraid to depend on him because I trusted him."

"You can trust me."

"I know, but I just need some time to realize that," Heather said, reaching across the table to squeeze his hand.

"You have all the time in the world."

CHAPTER 12

Saturday, January 22

One week before the Carrington winter ball, Heather met with Rory, Lily, Hera, and Cat for lunch at Open on Monday before heading to work.

Heather rarely had to work on Saturday, but Lexington was busy in the days before the ball. Hera normally worked the daytime hours during the week, and when necessary, she picked up a Saturday shift. Although Cat worked full time at the Saturn dealership, she worked part time at Lexington, usually a couple nights during the week and occasional Saturdays. The extra money came in handy when she needed to buy a new car or when her renters insurance was due.

"So, has Tristan said anything to you?" Rory asked Cat, as soon as the waitress left the table with their orders.

Cat shook her long black hair, "No. He hasn't said anything."

"What happened?" Hera asked, taking a sip of water.

"He's mad that I won't go to the ball with him," Rory explained. "And because he threw a hissy fit, I ended our sexual escapade."

"What did he say?" Lily asked.

"He just shrugged it off as if it's no big deal. I'm thankful he didn't cry like a baby."

"You know that's just a front, right?" Cat inquired.

"Of course," Rory answered. "He was saving face. He wasn't going to beg for a second chance when he had a playboy reputation to maintain."

"At least he didn't call you a whore," Hera pointed out.

Vodka Four

"You know, I think I'd rather be called a whore and other names than have the guy break down and bawl like a girl," she said thoughtfully.

"Really? Why?" Heather asked.

"Well, when a guy gets angry and upset over being dumped, he thinks he can hurt me by calling me names. Name-calling has never really bothered me. But the more important thing to remember is the guy leaves angry, swearing me off forever. A guy who cries will beg and plead for another chance and will try to stick around, hoping I'll change my mind. He'll call and 'accidentally' run into me somewhere. A guy who cries is a nuisance."

"Interesting logic," Lily said.

"I did hear something interesting about Tristan last night," Cat mentioned slyly. "Kristen Hartley came into the store, bragging she was going to the ball with Tristan."

"What?" Hera exclaimed. "Are you serious?"

"Yup," she said, nodding.

"Kristen Hartley is a dumb slut," Lily said, shaking her head. "I'm surprised she still has a job."

"I know," Cat said, with a sigh. "Despite her stupidity, she manages to meet her sales quota. She should thank her big rack for that."

A full-time sales associate at the Saturn dealership, Kristen Hartley has the reputation of pursuing unavailable men. At age 30, she had not achieved her two most important goals — marriage and babies. Her single status frustrated her and made her desperate.

At work, Cat hated listening to Kristen brag about all of the men who wanted to be with her, but Cat knew men just wanted to sleep with her — not a relationship. However, men's obvious sexual interest gave Kristen a conceited and shrewd attitude.

While none of the five friends didn't care for Kristen, Lily particularly didn't like her because she attempted to snag a guy

Lily was dating. When Brady Kerr came to the salon on his lunch break from Amery Lake Sports, Lily was the only hair stylist available to take a walk-in client. After one fabulous haircut and an engaging conversation, she and Brady quietly started dating. They loved hanging out at one of Brady's favorite sports bars a couple times during the week.

On one particular occasion, Lily turned down an invite to meet Brady and his friends at the bar because she had to work the early shift the next day. Lily's absence gave Kristen an opportunity to hit on Brady at the bar. Despite her best efforts, Brady's eye never wandered. However, this didn't stop Kristen from saying something to Lily a couple days later.

"Did Brady tell you what happened over the weekend?" Kristen has asked, after "accidentally" running into Lily and Cat in the square.

"He just met some friends for drinks," Lily had said, somewhat amused at Kristen's behavior. Her beauty sleep that night was interrupted because Brady needed to complain about Kristen "being all over him" and acting "like a desperate hussy."

"He was so drunk," Kristen had recalled, laughing. "He's so funny! He was dancing with so many girls that night."

"Sounds like Brady," Lily had agreed brightly. Her voice dripped with obvious sarcasm, making Cat snicker. Both Lily and Cat knew that no dancing ever happened at a sports bar.

"You're very lucky," Kristen had gushed. "He's so hot."

Unfortunately, Kristen's poor attempt at stealing Brady was not an isolated incident. However, her desperate antics amused Brady and Lily, and they did nothing to stop her. When Kristen realized Brady wasn't going to stray, she made a very unfortunate move to snag the guy Rory was seeing at that time. Rory had no problem publicly humiliating Kristen for the lame attempt, and since then, Kristen had kept her distance from Cat and Rory and knew better than to talk to Lily, Hera, and Heather.

Vodka Four

Although Lily and Brady were smitten with each other, their relationship ended after a few months when he accepted a job offer in Milwaukee.

"Yeah, she's an idiot," Heather agreed, remembering the numerous times Kristen had shopped at Lexington and threw herself at Christopher. "Of course, Tristan asked her. She's a sure thing."

"Wow, a guy really can't get more desperate than that," Rory said, shaking her head. "Tristan's a nice guy, but apparently, he has poor taste in rebound girls."

"I agree," Lily concurred, and then thanked the waitress for dropping off their lunch.

"Are you guys ready for the ball?" Cat asked Heather and Hera.

"Yeah," Heather answered. "I'm just wearing my bridesmaid dress from my sister's wedding. I've already got the shoes and accessories. I'm ready to go."

"Are you guys hanging out with Christopher and Magdala and Tristan and Kristen?" Lily asked, and then smiled brightly. "Hey, that rhymes — Tristan and Kristen."

"You're a dork," Hera said, laughing.

"I don't think we're hanging out with them," Heather said thoughtfully. "Nick didn't mention anything about going specifically with them. I just know we're going with Hera and Byron."

"Hell yeah!" Hera said excitedly. "Byron and I are hitchin' a ride with them in the limo."

"So, guess who's not happy that I'm dating Nick?" Heather said smugly.

"Who?" everyone asked at the same time.

"Hope Saint James."

"I'm not surprised," Rory said, taking a bite from her salad. "She's a big fat slut, too. Hey, I'm surprised Kristen's not her best friend."

"Two man-eating women can not be true friends," Cat theorized. "They will always be competing against each other for a man's attention. Although, I'm sure Hope sees no woman as her competition."

Hope Saint James works full time at Havland Diamonds and has a reputation of sleeping with rich male customers. She knows men only want to sleep with her because of her huge rack and because of her last name — Saint James. Her family may be one of the wealthiest in the area, but they're also one of the most dysfunctional, receiving their fair share of publicity. Despite her family's notoriety, an air of snobbery and pretentiousness always surrounds Hope.

"Just because she drives a BMW, carries designer purses, and shops only at Lexington does not make her better than any of us," Hera had once said about Hope.

"You would think that someone with her family history would try to keep a low profile," Cat had said. "Instead she spends her time whoring herself to rich men."

"Remind me why she has a job?"

"Rumor has it that in order for Hope to be included in the family will, she has to have a certain amount of money that she earned on her own."

"Smart parents."

"Smart dad," Cat had corrected. "Her mother and some of her siblings give her money whenever she threatens to reveal a scandalous secret or something. How else do you think she can afford to drive a BMW and carry designer purses? Her paycheck from Havland's basically pays the rent and gives her party money."

"Very interesting."

"It's no secret that Hope hates her father. One, he made her go to college. She rebelled by taking her sweet ass time — eight years — to graduate. Two, after she graduated, he refused to let her move back home. She rebelled by moving in with some low-life of a guy. Three, he won't give her any

Vodka Four

money. At first, she rebelled by not getting a job and spending her entire savings account on parties, clothes, and whatever. When she ran out of money and realized her father wasn't going to help her, Hope then decided maybe she should get a job."

"How do you know all of this?" Hera had asked, surprised that Cat seemed to know Hope's life story.

"Word gets around," Cat had replied, shrugging. "Hope has a big fat mouth and thinks she's the victim. So, she tells her story to anyone who will listen."

Hope's hatred for her father deepened when she announced her engagement and he refused to give his blessing or his money toward the "happy celebration." A few years later, she showed off another engagement ring, and once again, her father said she would have to pay for her wedding. Since then, to spite her father, Hope whored herself to rich men.

"Ryan went to Havland's a couple of days ago to pick up something for a customer. While he was waiting, he ended up talking to Hope," Heather explained. "She confessed to Ryan that she's always had a crush on Nick."

"What?" Lily exclaimed. "Is he rich? He's not even close to being a senior citizen!"

Heather snickered with amusement. "Anyway, after Ryan told her that Nick and I are dating, she said Nick should dump me and go out with a 'real woman.' Apparently, I'm not a woman because I'm not a size 16."

"What a bitch," Cat muttered.

"I know! When Ryan told Nick what happened, he just laughed."

"You know what you should do," Rory commented, with a wicked glint in her eyes. "You and Nick should go into Havland's to pick out jewelry when Hope's working. That'll piss her off."

Heather laughed. "That's a great idea, except I think it's too soon in our relationship for him to be giving me anything with diamonds."

"Tell Nick that you want to get something really nice for your dad at Havland's, and ask him to come along," Cat suggested. "You know Nick will do whatever you say."

"He will not," Heather protested. "Besides, I can't afford anything at Havland's. Just one item alone will max out my credit card."

"Totally agree," Lily said, remembering one of her impulsive purchases at the store. "So, I know this is very last minute, but does anyone want to go to a wedding in Madison with me next weekend?"

"Can't," Heather and Hera said together.

"Ball," Hera simply explained.

"What's going on?" Rory asked, sipping her Diet Coke.

"A cousin of mine is getting married," Lily said, with a sigh. "I knew about the wedding months ago, and I was planning on skipping it. But I talked to my mother the other day, and apparently my parents expect me to be there."

"Why were you planning to skip in the first place?" Cat questioned.

"Because I don't want to go to a fancy schmancy wedding," she moaned. "My cousin and I aren't even close. I can't even remember the last time I've seen or talked to her. Not to mention, I don't want to hear my parents brag about my brother's and sister's shining achievements. They're so ashamed that I'm a hair stylist."

"That's not true," Heather protested.

"I think you're exaggerating a bit," Cat added.

"You obviously don't know my parents. I'm the black sheep of the family. Everyone in the family has 'respectable' jobs as a chemist, financial advisor, or newspaper editor. I'm a hair stylist, and my parents don't know how to deal with that."

Vodka Four

"But didn't you become a hair stylist to spite your parents?" Rory asked.

"Hey, thanks for throwing that in my face," Lily said sarcastically.

"So, your parents are making you go to this wedding?" Cat needled. "Last time I checked, you're an adult — you can do anything you want."

"My mom used good old-fashioned guilt. She said because my cousin took the time to send me a personal invitation — which I'm positive the wedding planner and the assistants worked and sent out the invitations — I would be rude to not to attend. Apparently, every time my parents step into Wisconsin, they feel obligated to see me."

"Your mom is good," Rory pointed out.

"Yeah, I know. So, I told her I'd go to the wedding, but I really don't want to go by myself. I don't want to sit at a table with my parents and my brothers and sisters and their families. I don't want to bring a guy, because I know my parents will endlessly interrogate him and I will never see the guy again. I figured if I bring one of you guys, I'll be safe from private humiliation and we can act like lesbians."

Everyone laughed.

"Oh, in that case, bring me," Rory offered cheerily. "Nothing makes parents prouder than lesbian strippers."

Lily giggled. "Are you sure? It's a very fancy wedding, where people will smile at you while thinking you're scum of the earth."

"Sounds like a good time to me."

"Thank you, Rory! The biggest loser would have been tattooed on my forehead if I went by myself."

"Not a problem," she said, looking at her lunch bill. "We'll have a good time."

"Thanks again. I owe you."

Lily smiled as she paid her lunch bill. She could think of a million other places that she would rather be instead of attending her cousin's extravagant wedding. She dreaded seeing her parents and her siblings and their disapproving looks and condescending tones. Lily could list a hundred reasons why she moved away from her parents and refused to keep in contact with anyone of them.

CHAPTER 13

Saturday, January 29

While many of the hundreds of guests attending Janessa Netwall's wedding were in awe of the lavish and expensive affair, Lily subtly counted the number of exit doors that would help with a quick and unnoticed escape. After introducing Rory to her parents and siblings, her family practically ignored Rory and threw question after question at Lily until the wedding ceremony began. Now, Lily and Rory were forced to sit with her parents, her younger brother, David, and his girlfriend, Elise, and her younger sister, Amanda, and her fiancé, Adam, at a round table at the dinner reception.

Although Lily preferred to sit anywhere else other than with her parents, she was grateful her older brother, Terence, and older sister, Natalie, were seated at nearby another table. Both of her older siblings had brought their oldest children as they were already trained to be sophisticated and judgmental snobs. The younger nieces and nephews were left at the hotel under the watchful eye of a nanny. As much as she loved children, Lily honestly didn't care for her nieces and nephews because her brother and sister spoiled them rotten, rarely disciplined them, and then expected them to display superior manners. In short, her nieces and nephews were spoiled monsters.

Where Lily and Rory sat for dinner didn't matter because Lily knew her family would interrogate her about her nonexistent social life and push her to return to college to earn a degree in a professional field. Then they would dig their sharpened claws into Rory, interrogating her and making her feel uncomfortable and unwelcome. Bringing a girlfriend to a social and family gathering was simply unacceptable, and their cold and harsh demeanor was meant to deter the girlfriend from returning to future events.

After the interrogations, Lily's family would then boast about all of their accomplishments and praise their oldest children's talents and intellect — whether it was true or not. Because what mattered most was appearance — an image of a perfect family.

For the occasion, Lily chose a conservative ankle-length red velvet dress, with spaghetti straps and a modest slit on one side that showed off her long and slender legs. But to piss off her parents just a little, a push-up bra enhanced Lily's cleavage to peek out from the straight scoop line. Small silver barrettes pulled back the sides of her shoulder length black hair. To show her family that she wasn't destitute, Lily wore a diamond tennis bracelet on her right wrist. The piece of jewelry was an impulsive purchase when she went to Havland's to offer Rory a second opinion on an item she had been eyeing.

Rory chose a tasteful knee-length, short sleeve black dress that showed off her long legs and curvy figure. The modest V-neck cut revealed just enough cleavage to attract appropriate attention. Her long black hair was parted to one side before being pulled back into a low ponytail. A few black tendrils fell across her forehead. Diamonds sparkled from her ears and wrist. As always, Rory looked radiantly beautiful, and Lily had no doubt that at least five of her male relatives would ask about her friend.

Lily looked around the gorgeously decorated huge reception hall to welcome about 500 guests who were mingling and complimenting the picture perfect wedding. A live jazz band provided upbeat background music as guests seated themselves at assigned tables. Although Lily and Rory blended in with the high society crowd, her family managed to make them feel like outcasts.

Vodka Four

"So, Rory, Lillian tells me that you work at Lexington," said Grace Netwall, Lily's mother. Standing almost six feet tall and always immaculately dressed for any occasion, Grace managed to look welcoming and powerful at the same time. Her slender figure suggested frailty and delicateness, but her sharp tongue and wit quickly shattered that first impression. As a master of disguise, Grace knew how to brilliantly hide snide remarks that most people would mistake for genuine interest.

"Yes," Rory said, with a fake bright smile. "I work part time at the store. I'm currently attending the university and studying business administration."

"What do you plan to do with a business degree?" asked Jacob Netwall, Lily's father. Standing a few inches above his wife, Jacob's appearance alluded seriousness, dominance, and power. He wore a hard and intimidating look that never softened — not even around his grandchildren, who oddly adored him. As president of a well-established bank in Illinois, business and money were his two favorite subjects to discuss.

"I'm not really sure, to be honest," Rory replied, looking directly at him. "At the moment, I think opening a business of my own looks promising."

"What kind of business?"

"I don't know," she said, shrugging. "I'm keeping my options open."

"Maybe you should open your own beauty salon," Grace suggested coolly.

"Jesus Christ," Lily muttered under her breath.

Rory smiled at Grace's sarcastic statement. "I think that's a great idea. With my business experience and Lily's talents, I believe we would be able to operate a successful business. Not to mention, beauty salons will never be a trend as long as there are clients who wish to have their appearance professionally maintained."

Lily quietly snickered.

If Grace Netwall looked pissed with Rory's last statement, she didn't show any emotion to suggest such evidence. "How do you plan to finance such a business?"

"I have a substantial savings account. My credit is good, and I should have no problem obtaining a loan."

"It takes more than good credit and money to start a business," Lily's younger brother, David, joined in. "You need to know everything about the business field."

Lily shot an evil look to her 24-year-old brother who was earning his master's degree at a Chicago university in Illinois. She didn't like watching the youngest Netwall sibling turn into their father.

"And that is why I plan on learning everything I need to know," Rory said smoothly, not missing a beat.

"Do you feel that being a non-traditional student is a disadvantage to your overall plans?" Lily's father asked.

"Fuck," Lily quietly cursed.

"I have no problem not following society's rules," Rory answered politely, which made Lily smile. "As a society, we're told to think outside of the box. We're told to make our own paths. We're told to be individuals. But yet, as soon as we think outside of the box or create a different path, we're criticized and ridiculed for not following others' standards and rules."

"You're a woman of certain age who really shouldn't be pursing an unattainable goal," David said, oblivious to Lily's stares of hatred.

Lily had to compliment Rory later about keeping her composure in front of her family. Like her mother, if Rory was pissed, she didn't display an ounce of anger.

"I didn't realize that a woman of a certain age couldn't pursue a higher education," Rory gently challenged. "I've always admired people who had an eagerness to learn. I certainly don't believe that's a disadvantage or that it should keep someone from reaching their goals."

Vodka Four

"What are your plans when you graduate?" Jacob asked.

"To be honest," Rory responded simply. "I plan to work at Lexington and learn as much as possible from Wesley Lexington. Because I'm financially stable, I don't need to work full time, which gives me time to pursue a master's degree if I so choose."

"How did you become financially wealthy?" David questioned, with curiosity.

"David," Lily hissed, glaring at him and then turning to Rory. "You don't have to answer him."

"Oh, Lily," Rory said nonchalantly. "I don't mind answering his question. In fact, I think it's natural that he would be curious how a woman of my age could be financially wealthy. David, I just made smart investments and worked hard."

Grace coughed quietly, which was the Netwall sign to change the subject. Lily was grateful for the subtle interruption, because if the conversation went further, she was ready to make a public scene — something her family avoided at all costs.

During dinner, the conversation was light and highly superficial — something Lily could tolerate. Her sister, Amanda, 27, babbled about her own wedding plans and her work as a chemist in Madison. Lily honestly didn't know what her younger sister did for a living; all she knew was Amanda graduated with a degree in science. When Amanda talked about her job, she liked to use big words to make herself look intelligent and make others feel inferior and dumb for not being able to keep up with the conversation.

What intrigued Lily and Rory was Amanda's fiancé's job as a social worker. While Adam described his work, Lily wondered how her psycho younger sister managed to snare him. How could a normal and laid back guy love her spoiled and selfish sister?

David and her father discussed financial matters before David started boasting about his career as a financial consultant and detailing the hard work about earning a master's degree in the business field — a discreet insult directed at Rory, Lily thought. Lily was less impressed with David's girlfriend, Elise, an elementary school teacher, who giggled and gushed her way through conversations.

As soon as Lily and Rory finished a piece of wedding cake, they excused themselves from the table and headed toward the restrooms.

"I am so sorry about my family," Lily apologized, as they walked through a crowd.

"Lily, don't worry about it," Rory said simply. "I was prepared for their snide remarks. I can see why you don't like your family."

"I'm so glad that you're here. Not to mention, I'm pretty impressed with your ability to keep your cool around my family. I know you, and it doesn't take much to tick you off."

"Believe me, it wasn't easy," Rory laughed. "Your family wanted to see me squirm, and I wasn't going to give them that satisfaction."

Before Lily could reply, she heard a familiar voice call her name. She turned to see one of her many aunts approach her.

"Hello, Aunt Delores," Lily greeted, with a fake brightness. "How are you?"

"I'm fine, dear," her 60-something aunt responded politely, while taking a long look at Lily and then at Rory. "How are you, my dear Lillian?"

"I'm fine," she answered. "Aunt Delores, I would like you to meet my friend, Rory Andersen. Rory, this is my aunt, Delores Ford."

"Very nice to meet you," Rory said warmly, reaching out for the woman's hand.

"Yes," Delores murmured, quickly and lightly shaking Rory's hand. "Very nice to meet you. Lillian, when will I be

Vodka Four

attending your wedding? You know you should be married before Amanda and David."

Lily bit her tongue to prevent her from saying something inappropriate as, "Keep up with the times, Aunt Delores, you freakin' loon. I'm not getting married to please my control-freak parents and selfish siblings, who honestly don't care about me anyway."

"Adam is a wonderful match for Amanda," Rory jumped in. "He's very smart and devoted to Amanda. It would be such a shame for Amanda to postpone her dream wedding to a wonderful guy."

The aunt with firmly traditional beliefs and standards looked at Rory again — more particularly glanced at Rory's hands for an engagement or wedding ring.

"What do you do, my dear?" she asked coolly.

"I work at Lexington in Amery Lake," Rory responded, with a smile.

"Mmmm, Amery Lake is a lovely city. Lexington is a very distinguished business. You should be honored to work there. Too bad Lillian is wasting her God-given talents as a hair dresser."

"Oh, Lily is definitely not wasting any of her talent, Ms. Ford," Rory said effortlessly. "Bellismo is one of the top beauty salons in the area and only hire the best hair stylists. I'm sure if there were more hours in a day, Lily would use her other talents elsewhere."

"Aunt Delores," a male voice descended upon the trio of women. "I believe your daughter is frantically looking for you."

The older woman turned to find a good-looking gentleman handsomely dressed in a navy blue suit. "Thank you, Cooper. I appreciate you finding me."

"Not a problem, Aunt Delores," Cooper replied cheerfully. "Would you like me to escort you to your daughter?"

"I may be old, Cooper Daniel Netwall," she snapped. "But I certainly do not need an babysitter."

"You can find her at her dinner table, Aunt Delores," he offered graciously, ignoring her rude tone.

Before Lily or Rory could say goodbye, Delores stalked off in search for her daughter.

"Cooper, thank you," Lily said, greatly relieved. "Thank you so much."

"Well, us black sheep have to stick together, you know," he said, with a smile as he quickly hugged her. "I saw Delores heading your way, and I know she's incapable of saying anything nice."

"You are so right. She said I needed to get married before Amanda and David, and then she said I'm wasting my God-given talents," Lily informed him. "However, Rory defended my honor with charm, wit, and grace. Cooper, this is one of my best friends, Rory Andersen. Rory, this is my favorite cousin, Cooper Netwall."

"Nice to meet you," Rory said, extending her hand.

"Nice to meet you too," he said, accepting her handshake. "The only reason why I'm Lily's favorite cousin is because I'm more of a family outcast than she is."

"So not true," Lily protested, with a grin.

"What did you do that made you the black sheep of your family?" Rory asked.

"Ah, what didn't I do?" Cooper teased as he escorted both of them to the reception bar. "Lily didn't start rebelling until she was in college, whereas I rebelled at an early age. I'm not sure why I was such a pain in the ass, but I thought making my parents frown was way more entertaining than making them smile."

"Sounds like a good reason," Rory agreed, chuckling.

"I was pretty much a juvenile delinquent growing up," Cooper continued, after ordering and paying for a round of drinks at the bar. "My parents had no idea what to do with me, because my other three siblings were perfect. After bailing my ass out of the juvenile detention center one too many times, they sent me to a residential treatment facility. A year later, I was discharged to a group home until I was 18. My parents didn't want me to return home, and once I turned 18, I could live anywhere I wanted."

Cooper's ability to share a personal story to a complete stranger surprised Rory. The way he talked about his past was casual and simple. She didn't detect any bitterness or pain in his tone nor did she feel Cooper was bragging or looking for any sympathy.

Although Rory's childhood was similar to his, her instincts told her to not share her past with people she didn't know or trust. While Cooper's honesty and openness was refreshing, Rory didn't understand how he could be so laid back when discussing his past, especially when he was still the black sheep of his family.

"Your parents didn't want you to come home?" Rory asked, looking at Cooper and then at Lily.

"Well, I was an asshole to them for the majority of my childhood," he explained, shrugging his shoulders and handing Lily and Rory their drinks. "I understood their point. After I turned 18, I decided to grow up and went to college."

"Did this make your parents happy?" Rory wondered, walking over to an empty high round table.

Cooper shook his head as he set his drink down. "They weren't thrilled that I wanted to become a guidance counselor. They pushed me to become a psychologist or psychiatrist, because then I could get my own practice and I could have 'doctor' at the beginning of my name."

"Oh, tell her about Gina," Lily said, sipping her drink. "This story is fucked up, Rory."

"If it's too personal," Rory started to say, but Cooper interrupted her, waving his hand to stop her.

"No, it's fine," he said, with a wide smile. "I have nothing to hide. Besides, even if I don't tell you, I know Lil would. The story riles her up every time she thinks about it."

Rory was intrigued. She wanted to hear more about Cooper's life, which reminded her to later ask Lily why she's never mentioned her extremely hot cousin.

"Well, if you don't mind sharing, then I don't mind listening," she said, with a grin.

"When I met my ex-wife, Gina, we eloped to Vegas," Cooper said. "My parents weren't pleased that they couldn't throw a fancy shindig like this for me. Fortunately, they really liked Gina, who is a pediatrician, and that smoothed out our relationship for about a year. But then, they expertly started needling Gina about my career choice and how she felt about being the breadwinner in the family. Soon enough, Gina turned into my parents and had numerous affairs before I found out and left her."

"Didn't your parents take your side?" Rory wanted to know.

Cooper shook his head. "Of course not. They think Gina is a saint for putting up with me. I was the asshole for not making her happy."

"Shit."

"And that is why I'm a bigger outcast than my beautiful cousin, Lily," he said, putting his arm around Lily.

"I'm surprised you were invited to the wedding," Lily joked.

"Hey, I'm still family. I may be a black sheep, but I'm still family."

"Are your parents here?" Rory asked.

"Yeah. My parents act as if nothing is wrong when it comes to social and family gatherings. But here's the part that kills me — everyone in our family knows each other's indiscretions and humiliating moments, but yet everyone pretends each family is perfect."

Vodka Four

"I know!" Lily exclaimed. "I don't understand that. We all know the dirty truth, but no one talks about it."

"Why even pretend?" Cooper asked. "Everyone sees through the façade anyway. When people leave, they're not going to talk about the wedding. They're going to gossip about who brought the most shame to this event."

"Oh, am I in the running?" Lily wondered eagerly. "Come on, I should be in the top three at least. One, I'm still single. Two, I brought a girlfriend with me. Three, I'm still a hair stylist."

Cooper and Rory laughed at Lily's reasons.

"Yeah," he said thoughtfully. "You're in the top three for sure."

"So, who else has a secure place in the top three?" Rory asked.

"Hmmmm," Cooper said, looking around the bar and peeking into the reception area. "I'm going to say our cousin Robert makes it into the top three. One, he's an alcoholic, and his family won't admit it. And he's drunk right now. Two, I think he's hitting on one of the bridesmaids. Three, there's a fifty-fifty chance he'll do something embarrassing before anyone drags him out of here."

Lily and Rory scurried to the reception entrance to watch Cousin Robert, a 30-something guy, dancing like he's on fire while blatantly staring at a bridesmaid's cleavage. Lily and Rory looked at each other before bursting in laughter.

"I think another contender is Cousin Moira," Lily said, nodding toward a 20-something woman chatting animatedly with another bridesmaid. "One, she's failing college. The university would kick her out, but her parents' huge donations to the school are preventing that from happening. Two, she's a lesbian, and her parents refuse to accept it."

"I think she's just experimenting," Cooper offered. "She just turned 21, and I think she's just exploring different avenues. Moira's been more of a follower than a leader, if you know what I mean."

"Well, it's a good day for bridesmaids," Rory pointed out.

Lily and Cooper laughed before returning to their table inside the reception bar.

"Excuse me," Lily said. "I have to find a restroom. Rory, you OK?"

"I'm fine," Rory replied.

"Be nice to her," Lily jokingly warned, before leaving Rory alone with Cooper.

"Hey, I'm always nice," he protested, with a laugh.

As Cooper stood by the bar to refill their drinks, Rory studied him. She couldn't deny that Cooper Netwall was attractive. Standing a little over six feet tall with broad shoulders, Rory believed he worked out on a regular basis as she quickly glanced over his muscular and hard frame. His brown hair was short and combed and matched his brown eyes. While his naturally tan face was handsome and seemed welcoming and inviting, Rory could easily see a glint of a bad boy in Cooper.

"So, you live in Amery Lake with Lily," he said, returning to the table with three drinks.

"Yeah, I moved there when I was 18," Rory replied. "And where do you live?"

"I live in Milwaukee. I'm in the process of starting over."

"Does your family live in the area?"

"Good lord, no. They live in St. Louis, Missouri."

"What made you choose Wisconsin?" Rory asked, intrigued to know why he intentionally chose to live in a state known for its killer winter weather.

"To piss off my parents. Nothing says lame like being a cheddarhead."

Rory laughed out loud. "How long have you lived in Wisconsin?"

"For a couple of years now," Cooper answered. "I moved to Milwaukee after filing for divorce. I honestly didn't want to be anywhere near my parents or Gina. Luckily, I found a job as a guidance counselor at a high school in Milwaukee."

"I don't remember you ever visiting Lily," Rory said thoughtfully.

"Yeah, I'm pretty bad about visiting any family," he admitted, taking a drink from his glass. "Lily and I talk every now and then. To be honest, I'm surprised she's even here. The last time I talked to her, she said she wasn't coming."

"Her mother guilt tripped her into coming," Rory explained. "I'm here for moral support."

"I suppose Jacob and Grace haven't been very nice to you."

"Not even a little."

"I imagine Lily warned you about them."

"Of course," Rory confirmed. "She's told me plenty of stories about her battles with her parents. So, I came prepared."

When Cooper smiled, Rory tried to remember the last time a man caught her interest. She tried to remember the last guy who made her act like a school girl in junior high with a secret crush.

"Thanks for ordering me another drink," Lily said, returning to the table. "Rory, ready to head back after this drink?"

"No, please don't go," Cooper begged, looking at Lily with a sad face. "You and I haven't talked all night. How about this ... we'll finish our drinks and then head out to a real bar."

"We'd love to," Rory said, with a frown. "But Lily and I were planning on driving back to Amery Lake tonight."

"Don't worry about it," he said easily. "I'll simply book you guys a room at the hotel I'm staying at."

"Coop, we can't let you do that," Lily protested.

"Please," he said. "That's why God invented credit cards. Besides, it's time that you and I seriously catch up, because the last time you and I talked, you weren't going to be here."

Lily looked at Rory, who simply shrugged her shoulders. "OK, let's get out of here."

CHAPTER 14

Sunday, January 30

At about 4 in the morning, Lily and Rory wearily climbed into separate full-size beds in their shared hotel room that Cooper had booked for them. After leaving the wedding reception without saying goodbye to anyone, the trio headed toward a bar to talk and continue drinking. When they stumbled out of the bar after last call, Lily and Rory suggested an early-morning breakfast and Cooper directed them to small all-night diner.

Snuggling under the warm comforter and sheets, Lily and Rory both sighed as they rested their heads on a mountain of pillows.

"Thanks again for coming with me," Lily said, yawning. "I don't know what I would've done if someone didn't come with me."

"I can see why you wanted someone here," Rory said, turning on her side to face Lily. "Not that I didn't believe you before or anything, but yeah, your parents are assholes."

"Yes, they are," she agreed. "The most frustrating part is I hate seeing my brothers and sisters turn into them. I don't understand how they can let our parents walk all over them and believe they're not good enough."

"Some people still have that mentality that parents know what's best for their children."

"My parents have always instilled in us that rich equals happiness and success. I just can't believe my siblings are that stupid to believe it."

"Your siblings are people pleasers. They believe if they can please as many as people as they can, those people will respect them," Rory pointed out.

"Yeah, I know. Growing up, I regret not speaking up sooner. Even as a teen, I hated being under my parents' thumbs. As a child, I wanted to please them and I did everything they asked," Lily said sadly. "But as I grew up, I realized my parents weren't nurturing or warm; they were always critical and cold. Compliments and hugs weren't handed out a lot in our house."

"I know what you mean."

"I think I was a teen when I realized my parents weren't perfect. At that time, I figured out my mom was a complete bitch and my dad was an asshole. But what could I do, really?" Lily wondered out loud. "I was a teen who was accustomed to getting everything. I was just as materialistic as them, and I didn't want to lose any of it. Then I realized none of it mattered when I went to college."

Her awkward appearance as a teen also contributed to Lily's insecurity. Her parents did nothing to comfort her or relieve her fears about being the tallest gangly girl in class. Her mother bitched about ordering special clothes for Lily, because none of the clothes in the expensive department stores quite fit her. Her father nixed the idea of Lily joining the team because he didn't want his daughter to look like a "circus freak" on the court. Her parents felt their children's out of school time was better spent volunteering for certain organizations.

"Why did you move to Amery Lake?" Rory asked.

"I don't know. After my freshman year, I just wanted to get away from parents. When my parents realized I wasn't going back to college, they stopped giving me money. I knew I couldn't afford to live in bigger cities. Honestly, the idea of living in New York or California kind of scared me. I was thinking about heading to Madison, but then I found Amery Lake and thought it was OK."

Vodka Four

"I think the glitz and glamour of the Skylight Bar intrigued you," Rory teased, referring to the strip club where they first met.

Lily laughed out loud. "You know it."

"It has to be hard to completely break away from your parents even if you live a couple of states away."

"I know this sounds mean and selfish, but I don't want to completely break away because I kind of like rebelling against my parents. I can't explain why I like being a black sheep."

"Because it makes you stand out from everyone else," Rory explained thoughtfully. "People are going to confuse your sisters or your brothers, but they won't forget who you are. You're the Netwall who defied her parents. You're the Netwall who dropped out college. You're the Netwall who became a hair stylist. A damn good one, too."

Lily smiled in the dark. "That's true, but I can see some people confusing me with Cooper. He's the other black sheep. Hey, speaking of Cooper, it's so obvious he likes you."

"Shut up."

"You shut up."

"No, you shut up," Rory laughed, feigning ignorance. "I don't know what you're talking about."

"Oh, I think you do," Lily challenged, chuckling. "I totally love Cooper. He's a great guy who makes sure everyone is having a good time. And I think he has a little crush on you."

"Shut up. I refuse to comment."

"Fine, then I'll comment. Even though Cooper and I don't talk all of the time, he and I are close. And I'm so happy that he moved to Milwaukee, starting over and leaving the shit behind him."

"I feel bad that no one supported him during his divorce," Rory admitted, tossing onto her back to stare at the ceiling. "You would think when someone cheats, people would side with the non-cheating spouse."

Jennifer Elliott

"I know!" Lily exclaimed. "I was the only person who supported him. I can't believe his parents and even Aunt fuckin' Delores blame him for the separation and Gina's wandering eye. They don't even care that he was faithful to her until the day he signed the divorce papers."

"Your family is crazy."

"You don't need to tell me. Since the divorce, I know Cooper has dated here and there, but no one has really caught his attention. Until he met you," Lily sang out happily.

"Shut up."

"Come on, Rory. Are you going to deny his attraction to you?"

"A lot of guys think I'm attractive."

"I've known you for 10 years ... "

"We've known each other for 10 years?" Rory interrupted. "Seriously? No, we haven't."

"We met when we were like 19 or 20. Do the math," Lily said. "You were just learning the ropes as a stripper when I was hired."

Lily could clearly remember her first day on the job when she saw Rory working behind the bar. Beautiful bitch immediately entered into her mind when she saw Rory making drinks for male customers, who always had their eye on one of the best bartenders in the club.

When they were introduced to each other, Rory was not the self-centered bitch that Lily had imagined. Instead, she was smart and fun and taught Lily the ropes of being a bartender. They immediately became friends and enjoyed working with each other, but they didn't become good friends once they realized they both had similar shitty childhoods. Soon after the realization, Rory then introduced Lily to Heather and Cat.

"God, you're right. We've known each other for more than 10 years."

"See, I told you so."

Vodka Four

"Ten years," Rory repeated in disbelief. "That means I've known you a third of my life."

"Hey, don't change the subject," Lily said, interrupting Rory's train of thought. "Now tell me the truth. Do you like Cooper, because I know he likes you."

"Yes, yes, yes, I like him," she wailed loudly as if she was a witness breaking down on the stand in a murder trial.

Lily laughed hysterically. "God, you're a drama queen."

"I like Cooper, but he's also in the process of starting over and lives in Milwaukee. You know that me and long-distance relationships don't work out. If I'm going to have a boyfriend, I want my man in town."

"Maybe he could move to Amery Lake," Lily suggested. "You know, Milwaukee isn't that far away. It's like what — three, four hours away?"

"I'm not going to spend eight hours of my weekend on the road."

"He could visit you."

"Then he will resent me, because I won't take the time to visit him on my free weekends."

"You could have phone sex."

"The real thing is better," Rory countered. "Face it, Lil, there is an attraction between Cooper and I, but I'm not going to do anything about it."

Lily sighed out loud as she turned onto her back. "That's too bad. I think you and Cooper would be good for each other. You guys understand each other, and the sexual tension between you two is just hot!"

Rory laughed out loud. "You're such a liar."

"Oh, just admit it. You want to jump my cousin. If he weren't my cousin, I'd totally be all over him."

Rory laughed out loud again.

"The guy is hot," Lily defended. "He's never had any problems with women, which was also frowned upon by his family."

"What do you mean?"

"Well, sneaking out of the house to have sex with older women didn't sit too well with his parents. Especially if the women were associated with his mother."

"He wasn't lying when he said he was bad boy," Rory murmured.

"Yeah, he was a bad, bad, bad boy back in the day," Lily agreed. "But he changed when he turned 18. Actually, I think he changed when he realized that his parents didn't want him at home. With a decision like that, a lot of kids would hate their parents and just get into more trouble, but with Cooper, it was never about stealing or sleeping with older women. He just wanted his 'bad boy' reputation to embarrass his family and knock his parents off the high pedestal they put themselves on."

"If things were different, I'd go out with Cooper," Rory admitted. "I had a good time tonight. Even when your family was interrogating me, because I viewed it as a challenge. And you know me, I love challenges. I kept thinking, 'Kill them with kindness,' because I knew your parents wanted to see me sweat or cry."

"That's their goal in life — to make people they don't respect squirm and uncomfortable."

"Parents aren't perfect. You and I both know that."

"No offense or anything, but your mother has to be the biggest bitch ever," Lily said, thinking about the childhood stories that Rory had shared with her. "I thought it would be impossible for someone to be a bigger bitch than my mother, but after listening to your stories, I give the title to your mother."

"No offense taken," Rory reassured. "My mom was the biggest bitch and slut to ever walk the planet."

Rory remembered her mother as an alcoholic and convincing liar. Her mother lied about Rory being a spoiled and rotten teenager. Her mother lied about trying to be the best parent she could be. Her mother lied about why Rory needed to be placed in a group home for juvenile delinquents. And her mother lied about wanting Rory to return home. Everyone, except Rory, foolishly believed her mother's lies and no one believed Rory's protests until her mother quietly slipped out of town. After social workers and other authority figures tried to track her down, they terminated parental rights and Rory became a ward of the state and resided in the group home until she turned 18.

"When was the last time you talked to your mother?" Lily asked, breaking into Rory's memory about living in a group home.

"When I was 16," she recalled, thinking back to the last conversation — or argument — that she had with her mother. "I was at the youth home when she called. We got into a huge argument, and about a week later, I learned she skipped town."

"You don't know where she is?"

"I imagine she's in Florida or California," Rory said flatly. "She hated living in Wisconsin. She and winter were not best friends."

Lily laughed softly. "Do you think you'll ever see her again?"

"I don't know. I can imagine her being on her deathbed or something and wanting to apologize for being such a shitty mother. But other than that, I don't want to see her or have her part of my life again. I honestly can't imagine her changing for the better."

"Why not?"

"Because she was a self-centered alcoholic bitch who needed to be the center of attention, especially around men. I can't see my mother having a change of heart. She would need to die first and then be reincarnated as someone who has a heart."

"What happened to your father?"

Rory didn't say anything for a moment as she tried to remember anything about her father.

"Rory?" Lily asked softly. "I'm sorry. I didn't mean to pry."

"No," she said quickly, shaking her head against the pillow. "I haven't thought about him in so long, and I don't remember much about him. According to my mother, he left us for another woman, which I don't believe for a second. I think he left us, because my mother was a skanky bitch."

"What about you?"

"I think he knew that she would win full custody. Not to mention, he probably didn't have the money to be involved in a court case."

"Have you ever thought about tracking him down?"

"I have," Rory admitted. "But if he really wanted to see me, he can track me down."

"Rory, you totally changed your name," Lily pointed out, with an exasperated sigh. "That alone is an obstacle in tracking you down."

"Smarty pants."

"That's my middle name."

"I've thought about that too, but I figured if my father really wants to see me, then he'll find me. And if I really wanted to know him, then I'll find him. But for now, I'm doing OK without him. If I need a kidney or something, then I'll track him down."

Lily giggled. "Do you have any memories of him?"

"Not many. I was 4 when he left. I remember him calling me Bertie. I think my favorite memory is him reading a book to me every night before I went to bed."

"That's sweet, Rory."

"Yeah, I know. But I also remember him and my mother fighting a lot. I don't blame him for leaving. I really don't."

Sometimes, Lily and Rory envied Cat and Heather's healthy and close relationships with their parents and siblings.

Vodka Four

Although they love the lives they lead now, Lily and Rory occasionally wondered about the "what if" questions. What if their childhoods were happy, would their present lives be the same? What if Rory's mother wasn't a cheating alcoholic, would her father still have left? What if Lily's parents showed more love, would Lily still be the black sheep in the family?

"So, what do you think Heather and Nick are doing?" Lily asked after a moment of silence.

"Probably having sex," Rory answered dully.

"Lucky bitch. I can't even remember the last time I had sex."

"I can," she said smugly.

"Bitch."

"Yes, I am."

Lily laughed out loud. "What do you think about Nick? I really haven't formed an opinion about him yet."

"I think he's a good guy, and I think he's good for Heather."

"You think so?"

"Yeah, I think so. I haven't heard anything bad about Nick, and he seems like an all-around good guy."

"Out of all the guys that Heather has dated, which guy did you like the best?"

Rory thought about the question, recalling the numerous of men Heather had dated from the time Rory first met her. Their 10-year friendship had seen many heartbreaks, tears, first dates, first kisses, arguments, bad breakups, and all types of boyfriends.

"I'm going to say Eli," she said carefully. "They were really good friends before they started dating. Eli was a really good guy."

"Yeah, I agree," Lily acknowledged. "I really liked him, too. Where is he from again?"

"He was born and raised in Minnesota, but his parents moved to California six or seven years ago."

"And Eli moved to California to be with his mother, right?"

"Yeah, she was diagnosed with breast cancer and was having trouble with treatment or something. I don't know the full details, but it was enough to make him move to California."

"That's sweet."

"Yeah, I know," Rory admitted. "But he also didn't want to leave Heather, and they pretty much knew a long-distance relationship wasn't going to work out. They didn't even want to try, because Eli didn't know how long he needed to be in California. And Heather won't move anywhere, because she doesn't want to be further away from her family."

"She had a hard time getting over him."

"Even though she won't admit it, I think she saw a future with him," Rory revealed. "You know Heather. She doesn't want to get her hopes up and then have them blown to pieces."

"Other than the night after they had sex, I really haven't talk to her about Nick. What does she think about him?"

"She really likes him, but I think she's waiting for him to lose interest in her."

"I don't think that's likely," Lily guessed, shaking her head. "Nick really seems to like her."

"Yeah, I totally agree. She's so afraid of being hurt again."

"I don't blame her though. The past couple of boyfriends were real jackasses."

"Nick's gotta be a good guy if he wanted to take Heather to the winter ball," Rory pointed out. "Do you know how much money a guy has to drop for that event?"

"I know! I'm sure Christopher gave him a discount to rent a tux at Lexington. I think Byron tried to give him some money to share the cost of renting the limo."

Vodka Four

"Don't forget about dinner at Traditions before going to the ball. People don't want to look like complete dorks by filling up on hors d'oeuvres all night long. And we all know Traditions is not cheap."

"Don't forget about renting a room for the night at the Carrington House," Lily added. "One night in the Carrington House is not cheap."

"Although Nick was planning to take his ex-girlfriend, I'm glad Ryan talked him into taking Heather. I think she's going to have a fantastic time."

"Yeah, I know," Lily agreed, yawning.

"They look good together," Rory murmured, closing her eyes. "I can't remember the last time I stayed up this late."

"Me too."

"This day turned out to be much better than I expected," she said, before falling asleep.

CHAPTER 15

Heather was deliriously happy and satisfied as she snuggled with Nick on the couch in their hotel room at the Carrington House. The comforter from the queen-sized bed covered their naked bodies, as they talked about the night while watching late night TV. The room was dark and quiet except for the muted images on TV.

"You comfortable?" Nick asked quietly, lying on his side with his head rested on a throw pillow and his arm thrown over her naked body.

"Mmmmm," she replied lazily, as she felt his body spooning her from behind. She was completely spent as her head rested near his on the same pillow.

Moments before camping out on the couch, Nick and Heather could hardly contain their sexual desire as they headed toward the hotel room when the ball ended. After entering the immaculate and exquisite suite, their dress clothes were quickly tossed to the ground and they made no effort to head to the bedroom before succumbing to their passion.

Heather smiled at the thought of them having porn star sex on the plush carpet in the Carrington House. This was the first time that Nick took control and didn't ask her what she wanted, which had made her incredibly excited. He had silently pushed her onto her back and spread her long legs apart so that his mouth and tongue had easy access to what Heather was dying for. After peaking, Heather didn't have time to recuperate as Nick pulled her up from the floor and molded her body to kneel on her hands and knees. While he drove himself inside her, Nick kept one hand on her hip for control and the other held onto her hair.

Vodka Four

After taking what he wanted, Nick collapsed onto the padded floor, taking Heather with him. For awhile, the two laid naked, with their arms and legs intertwined, breathing heavily and taking time to regain their strength. Despite their lack of energy, they nixed going to bed immediately and decided to lay on the couch for awhile.

"You OK?" Nick murmured in her ear, as his fingers danced on her flat stomach.

"Perfect," Heather replied, turning her head slightly to look at him and kiss him.

She could not think of a better word to describe her evening. Nick was the perfect escort to the Carrington ball, and she had a perfectly lovely time spending time with him and their friends. Everything was perfect.

"Mmmmm," he responded. "I aim to please."

"Thank you for tonight. I really had a great time."

"Shit," he teased. "I was hoping you'd have a really lousy time and never want to go to the ball again."

Heather giggled softly as she shifted her body to lay on her back. "Well, then you shouldn't have danced with me the whole entire night. Don't you know how much I love to dance?"

"Damn my Fred Astaire talents!"

She laughed. "Fred Astaire you are not, but you held your own."

Nick pretended to look wounded. "What? I was fantastic out there. I don't know who you were dancing with, but I could've been easily mistaken for a Broadway dancer."

Heather laughed even harder. "You're good. I won't deny that. By the way, where did you learn to dance?"

"My mom made me and my brothers take dance lessons when we were younger. She thought it might come in handy one day."

"See, she was right."

"I also took a few dance classes in college."

"To meet women?"

"That, and it was an easy phy ed credit."

Heather laughed again. "Thank you for dancing with me."

"It was my pleasure," he said, kissing her again. "I know I told you this when I picked you up, but you looked beautiful tonight."

"Thank you. Seeing you in that tux made me want to jump you right there in my apartment."

"Really? What stopped you?"

"Hera and Byron for one. They were in the limo waiting for us."

"They could've had sex in the limo while we were doing it inside," Nick teased. "See? Problem solved."

"You are so smart," Heather joked. "I am so lucky to be with a man who is so intelligent."

"Smartass," he growled, tickling her stomach and sending her into a fit of giggles.

"Stop it," she pleaded, laughing. She tried to roll off the couch, but Nick had a firm grip around her body. "Stop it."

"Tell me," Nick said lazily, after he stopped tickling her. "What was your favorite part of the ball?"

Despite her initial reservations about the ball, Heather surprisingly had a great time. The spectacular event she once avoided was indeed grand, elegant, and lavish — just as everyone told her it would be. When she wasn't dancing with Nick, they walked through the historic hotel, admiring the paintings and small statues.

They nibbled on the hors d'oeuvres and drank as much expensive champagne as they could without becoming embarrassingly drunk. They mingled with people they knew from Anastacia Square — Tristan and Kristen Hartley, Christopher and Magdala Parker, Magdala's roommate, Brooke, and her boyfriend. They peeked into the poker room to see men smoking on cigars and drinking expensive hard

Vodka Four

liquor. They sat on a bench with Hera and Byron and watched the guests milling around the party.

"I think my favorite part was dancing with you," she said, smiling at him. "I don't think I could ever get tired of dancing. I'm glad I had a partner who could keep up with me."

"What?" Nick mocked. "Please. You could hardly keep up with me. Once again, I'm Fred Astaire."

Heather laughed. "What was your favorite part, Fred?"

"The whole entire night."

"Did the ball live up to your expectations?"

"It was what I expected, but I had a good time, because I was with you."

"Aw, that's so sweet," Heather said, truly touched by his words.

"I always have a good time when I'm with you," he murmured in her ear, as his fingers slipped down from her stomach to the sensitive area between her legs.

Heather snuggled closer to him, spreading her legs a bit as his fingers lightly padded the highly aroused area. She sighed with content as he lightly applied more pressure. As a finger slipped inside her, Heather moaned and arched her back with pleasure. In one swift move, Nick shrugged off the comforter that had covered both of them and shifted his naked body to cover hers. He bent down to kiss her as his fingers continued to excite her. She hungrily accepted his mouth, wrapping her arms around his neck to pull him closer.

Nick broke off the kiss, grinned at her, and pulled his finger out of her body. With one arm propping him up, his other hand moved up her body to fondle one of her breasts. As his fingers circled her nipple, her body bucked underneath him, letting him know she wanted more. Heather smiled wickedly at him as she lifted up her leg and rested it on his right shoulder, while her hand slipped down to play with his already hardened manhood. Nick, sitting up with his left knee on the couch and his right foot anchored to the floor, softly growled with approval, as her hand was wrapped around his shaft.

Slowly kissing her shaven leg propped on his shoulder, Nick's free hand returned to her sexual core. With his fingers slowly slipping inside her again, Heather cried out, throwing her head back and letting go of his manhood. When his fingers slid out of her body, Nick slowly entered her, starting to satisfy her wants and cravings. With his arm wrapped her leg for support and control, he slowly moved his body against hers. Heather grasped his free hand and held on for the ride.

"Oh God," she cried out as her body matched his rhythm.

Nick was no longer taking his sweet time thrusting in and out of her hot body, instead his pace quickened as he felt his own explosion coming. He shook off Heather's firm grip on his hand to knead the sweet sexual spot between her legs. Heather groaned loudly, her head moving from side to side and her hands wildly grabbing at anything above her head to help her remain stable. The sight of Heather writhing wildly under his body made Nick reach his peak. Her gloriously naked body underneath his. Her beautiful naked breasts free and perfect. Her taut nipples ready to be licked. He wanted to make sure she was satisfied, but her naked form was too much as he exploded inside her. He pulled out and collapsed backwards onto the couch.

"God," he said, wiping the perspiration off his forehead with the back of his hand. "That was fucking fantastic."

"You OK?" Heather asked, not moving from her end of the couch.

"Never better."

Silently, they laid on the couch as they recovered from another mind-blowing sexual experience. Heather was truly and completely happy. Just being around him made her happy. The porn-star sex was just an added bonus.

Vodka Four

"Are you OK?" he asked, when he regained control of his breathing.

"Mmmmm," was her response.

He smiled. "Did you get what you want?"

Heather giggled. "Did you not hear me screaming?"

Nick propped himself on his elbows to look at her. *God, she looked beautiful*, he thought to himself. Her head was resting on a pillow, and she had grabbed the comforter from the floor to cover her body.

"You take care of me every time we're together," she murmured. "I was trying to get you stop after I came."

"Telling me to stop works well."

"I was screaming at you."

"Sorry," he said sheepishly, grabbing part of the comforter to cover himself. "Not sure how I tuned you out."

After talking for a few minutes more, they retired to the bedroom. They slept in until it was time to check out of the hotel. A cab took them to their apartments, dropping Heather off first. Kissing Nick goodbye and hauling her bags out of the cab, Heather headed toward her apartment.

She smiled happily as she closed the door. She was so happy. For once in a long time, she had met a guy who seemed impossibly perfect. As much as Heather tried to guard her heart and cautiously enter the relationship, she could definitely see herself falling in love with Nick.

Heather was about to strip off her dress when she heard a knock at the door. She smiled, thinking Nick returned for something. An expression of shock and surprise crossed her face as she opened the door to find someone she hadn't thought about in a long time. Standing before her, looking perfectly handsome as ever, was one of her ex-boyfriends, Eli Clearly.

Sober drivers needed

Heather was living up to her nickname again. Another night of drinking. Another night of too many screwdrivers and vodka shots with the Vodka Girls. Another night of hunger pains after bar time.

"Let's go!" she yelled to no one in particular. "I'm starved!"

"Vodka Four, we need drivers," Rory explained, with her Miata car key in hand, standing in a bar's parking lot. "We're trying to find out who's sober enough to drive to Perkins."

"Not me!" she hollered. "I'm drunk."

"The whole city knows that," Cat pointed out, giggling.

"Good Lord, Vodka Four," Eli groused. "Shut up."

"You shut up!"

"Danny can drive his car," Rory explained. "Eli's going to drive Reese's Jeep, but we need someone to drive my Miata."

"You drive!" Heather screamed with laughter, thinking it was the greatest idea ever.

"Dumbass, I'm also drunk. And I'm riding in Danny's car."

"I can drive," Cat said, with a resigning sigh. "I puked all the alcohol out of my system about an hour ago."

"Are you sure?" Rory asked uncertainly. She rarely let anyone drive her most prized possession. The red shiny Miata represented all of her hard work and dedication. "Can you even drive a stick shift?"

"Uh no," she admitted.

"I love stick!" Heather announced gleefully. "I know what to do."

"You're not driving," Rory said firmly, shaking her head. "You're drunk."

"Cat and I can talk about it," she protested. "Come on, let's go. I'm hungry."

Vodka Four

"Vodka One?" Rory asked curiously. "You OK with this?"

"Sure, why not?" Cat replied, shrugging her shoulders. "This should be fun."

"Vodka 10, let's go!" a guy from Danny's car yelled. "I'm starved."

Rory looked at the hot guy and then at the car key in her hand. She was torn. Maybe she should just shove Cat and Heather in the trunk of the Sundance. But she knew Danny would throw shit fit at that idea as he almost had a heart attack when Heather and Cat rode on the hood of his car.

She slowly handed the car key to Cat. "Be careful. You hurt my baby, I hurt you."

"All right! Cheerio!" Cat said, with a fake and terrible British accent.

As soon as Cat and Heather scrambled into Rory's red Miata, Danny and Eli drove out of the parking lot. Cat turned the ignition and looked down at the floorboard.

"So, what I am doing?" she asked, looking at Heather.

"Going to Perkins."

"I know that, numbnuts. How do I drive this car?"

Heather shrugged. "Put it in drive."

"This isn't an automatic," Cat pointed out impatiently. "This is a stick shift."

"I don't know how to drive stick."

"What?" she screeched, looking horrified and confused. "A minute ago, you just said you knew how to drive a stick shift."

"I said I love dick," Heather corrected smugly.

"You said you could show me how to drive stick!"

"No, I said we'll talk about dick."

Not even thinking, Cat slapped Heather's forehead with the back of her hand. "Whore."

"Bitch!" Heather swore, punching Cat in the shoulder. "What the fuck?"

Cat replied by punching Heather's shoulder. "Skank."

Heather leaned over to strike again, but Cat intercepted the physical abuse and hit Heather's arm.

After arriving at the restaurant and not seeing Cat and Heather, Eli drove back to the parking lot to find Heather and Cat chasing each other around the Miata while calling each other names.

Cat and Eli would later tell everyone that Cat was beating the crap out of Heather, while Heather — once again — could not defend herself as she had no memory of the "dick" conversation and fighting with Cat.

CHAPTER 16

After taking a quick shower, throwing on jeans and a sweater with a turtleneck collar and pulling her hair back in a clip, Heather met Eli down the block at the small coffee shop. Before entering, she stood in front of the glass window and watched him sitting at a small table with one hand around a large coffee mug and the other on his cell phone.

God, he looked good, Heather decided to herself. Of course, Eli always looked good, but somehow California made him look better. The West Coast sun made his Midwestern fair skin and short brown hair a little darker. His blue eyes still somehow captured her attention and made her smile. His muscular physique has always been kept in shape and hasn't changed since the move. The one feature that first captured Heather's attention was his boy-next-door face. Even on the brink of turning 30, Eli looked like a typical attractive college student with no special qualities.

But to Heather, he had many special qualities. For more than 10 years, Eli was the one guy whom she completely trusted. During their freshman year, they signed up for the same accounting class and met when the professor paired them together for a project. At the time, both were in long-distance relationships that weren't surviving too well, giving them a chance to bond over beer and mixed vodka drinks. Throughout their four years at the Lutheran university, they never dated. They hooked up occasionally during long dry spells and after nights of getting highly intoxicated, or had rebound sex after an ugly breakup.

They both decided to stay in Amery Lake after graduation, and a year later, Eli finally asked Heather out on a date. During their years of friendship, she really never thought about dating him — even when they used each other for sex. However, during the initial dating phase, Heather felt really comfortable being with Eli on a different level. Maybe because they were really good friends who could talk about anything and everything. Maybe because no subject or topic was off limits between them.

At one point in their relationship, Heather saw a future with Eli. After dating a few months, she completely fell in love with him. She firmly believed she would always fall in love with her best friend, and Eli had been one of her closest. She didn't need to date him to know pretty much everything about him. She had met his parents. She hung out with his two older brothers and younger sister. Intellectual women caught his attention and turned him on, but he had no problem casually sleeping with women who looked like Jenna Jameson. He liked to study and work hard during the week and have a great time during the weekend.

Heather had worked as a receptionist for a nursery and garden center while Eli had accepted a sales job at Amery Lake Sports. After being hit on by every male employee in the nursery, including the owner, Heather started looking for another job. Eli was the one who mentioned Lexington was looking for an administrative assistant. Then soon enough, Eli moved to California to be with his mother, who had learned she had breast cancer.

Despite having a close friendship, they both knew their relationship had come to an end. Eli needed to focus his attention on his mother, and Heather didn't want to be in a long-distance relationship. He knew better than to ask her to move with him, because he knew she couldn't tear herself away from her family. The days after he moved, Heather thought about whether or not she had made the right decision, because she just missed him terribly. Not just as a close friend, but as her boyfriend, who understood and took care of her.

Vodka Four

While Eli was conflicted about leaving Heather, she agonized about leaving her family and moving with him. If he was the great love of her life, why did she let him go? Should she have at least tried a long-distance relationship? Should she have moved out there to be with him and take care of him? Did she do the right thing by kissing him goodbye, saying she would always love him, and watching him board the plane to California? At first, the questions just bombarded her mind, but after awhile, they faded and Heather started to move on.

She and Eli kept in touch, and they managed to tango around questions such as "Are you seeing anyone?" and "Do you miss me?" At first, Heather didn't even want to know whether or not Eli was seeing anyone, because she knew the truth would hurt too damn much. So, she kept her social life private whenever she talked to him, believing he felt the same way. But in time, they both started dropping tidbits about their social lives and soon enough, they were handing out dating and relationship advice.

Since the demise of the relationship, Heather had not met any guys who even compared to Eli — except for Nick.

"Hey," Heather said, walking into the coffee shop and sitting down at the same table.

"You were quick," Eli said, flashing a brilliant smile and making her heart melt in the process. *Dammit, why did he have to look so damn good?*

"I didn't want to keep you waiting."

Kelsea's Coffee Cup, located in the beginning of Brown Street, was one of Heather's favorite places to be after a long day at work or when she's having a bad day. In addition to square tables dotting the small area, five to seven oversized padded chairs sat against the walls, making for comfortable reading.

Heather and Cat loved coming to the shop with a good book to read. They usually ordered a drink and grabbed an oversized chair for their leisurely reading. When Heather couldn't wait for her coffee fix at work, the drive through window was always opened to offer her coffee and a warm muffin.

After Eli handed Heather a large coffee mug and sat back down at the table, they just smiled and studied each other for a moment as she added sugar and cream.

"So, what brings you to Amery Lake?" Heather asked, breaking the silence.

"After the holidays, I realized it has been awhile since I've been back," he explained. "I decided to take some time off to come back for a week."

"Yeah, I remember you saying something about a visit in your last e-mail. You just didn't know when you'd come back."

"I figured now was a good time to fly out and see everyone."

"Where are you staying?"

"With Gil and Danny," Eli said, referring to his former college roommates and close friends who've known Heather, Rory, and Cat since college.

"When did you get into town?"

"Late last night."

For some reason, Heather really didn't want to tell Eli about her wonderful relationship with Nick. Nick and Ryan's questions and stories about her college days reminded Heather that they had worked with Eli.

"How's your mom?" Heather asked, wondering whether or not Danny or Gil had told Eli about her relationship with Nick.

"She's doing well," he replied. "She's still undergoing treatment, but her future looks optimistic."

"That's good."

"How are you doing?"

Vodka Four

"I've been well." *What the hell is wrong with me?* Heather thought, frantically racking her brain for another subject to discuss to cover the uncomfortable silence between them.

Why is this so hard? She wondered. *We used to talk so much that we'd argue over who got to speak first. Why is this so fucking hard?*

"Do you want to talk about the big ass elephant in the room?" Eli asked, smiling smugly at her.

Son of a bitch, he knows! Heather didn't know whether to look mortified or smile back. Despite their "no subject is off limits" policy, she felt incredibly uncomfortable telling Eli anything about her perfect relationship with Nick. If they were such close friends, why couldn't she tell him? Would he feel hurt that she was seeing someone else? Could it be possible that he still has romantic feelings for her?

"I didn't expect you to wait for me, Heather," Eli said softly, breaking the silence. "There has always been some guy in your life."

She opened her mouth to protest the last statement, but he held up his hand to stop her. "Women like you don't stay single for long. When we broke up, I knew I wasn't going to be your last boyfriend."

"It feels weird," she finally said, then feeling like a complete idiot for saying it.

"Yeah," he agreed, leaning back in the chair and stretching out his long legs. "It does feel a little weird. I don't know if it's because we were in a serious relationship, or it's because I know Nick."

Heather didn't reply, as she looked into her coffee mug.

"I have nothing against the guy as long as he treats you well," Eli continued. "I can't imagine Nick being a gigantic jackass."

She smiled at the thought.

"He was always a stand-up kind of guy," he said, remembering the times when he worked with Nick. "He and I got along."

"He's a good guy," Heather offered. "I really like him."

"He must really like you if he took you to the winter ball last night."

"Danny and Gil told you about that, too?" she asked, sighing. "I swear, those two are just like girls. They can't keep their traps shut."

Eli laughed heartily. "Come on, you know Gil and Danny. They're just looking out for you and the rest of the girls."

"Yeah, I know," Heather said dryly. "I hope they told you that Nick was initially planning to take his ex-girlfriend."

"Yeah, they told me. I remember Samantha coming in to the store a lot."

"And?" Although Heather didn't view the ex-girlfriend as threat, she wanted to know more about her. When talking about past events, her name came up every now and then, but Nick didn't share full details and Heather didn't press for more. However, if Eli wanted to fill in the blanks, she wasn't going to stop him.

"Well, she wasn't as hot as you," he said, with a wink. "She was a cute girl, but I thought she was a nightmare of a girlfriend."

"What?"

"Come on, Vodka Four. I'm sure I've bitched about her to you before."

"Refresh my memory."

Eli sighed, shaking his head. "She was so needy. Whenever she came into the store, she always needed something from Nick — money, his car, anything. When she wasn't taking something from him, she was complaining about something. That girl loved to bitch."

"Interesting."

Vodka Four

"I honestly didn't see Nick's attraction to her. I really didn't. So, I wasn't surprised that the relationship ended when she moved to Arizona."

"Hmmmm," Heather replied, thinking about the demise of Nick's last relationship. "That's very interesting. So, what about you? Have you met Malibu Barbie yet?"

Eli laughed. "No, I haven't had much time to see anyone. Between working and spending time with my family, I don't have much free time."

"So, what you are doing this week?"

"I'm pretty much visiting friends and some relatives. When I'm not doing that, I plan on snowboarding as much as possible. Never thought I'd say this, but I really miss the cold weather."

"I thought you picked up surfing."

"I have, but I really miss snowboarding. Despite being spoiled by the warm weather, I'm always going to be a Wisconsin boy."

"Before you leave, we should stroll through the campus and have dinner sometime this week," Heather suggested, sparking memories of their college years.

"Yeah, definitely," Eli agreed enthusiastically. "Gil and Danny plan on taking me to the bars or strip clubs every night of the week."

She smirked. "Shocking."

"You know you can come with us anytime," Eli invited. "Invite the rest of the girls, too. How are they doing?"

"They're good. Rory and Lily are in Madison. Lily had to go to a cousin's wedding and dragged Rory along. And Cat and Hera are the same."

"I think Friday and Saturday are the two big nights that Gil and Danny are trying to get everyone together. You and the girls available?"

"We should be," Heather said thoughtfully. "I don't think any of us have anything going on, but I'll check."

"I'm stopping by the sports store sometime this week, and I'll probably invite the guys to go out," Eli mentioned. "Is that OK?"

"Yeah," she said casually, shrugging. "That's perfectly fine with me."

However, Heather was lying. She didn't want to spend an evening equally dividing her time between Eli and Nick. Although her imagination was getting the best of her, she knew the likelihood of Eli and Nick spending an extraordinary amount of time together at the bars was slim to nil. Heather wondered whether the guys would get along, now that the boyfriend role has been reversed.

"Well, I should probably head out," Eli said, looking at his watch. "Gil and Danny want to go snowboarding today. I'll call you, OK?"

"Definitely," she said, getting up from her seat to hug him. "Call me anytime."

"I will," he said softly, pulling her close.

I miss him, she thought, wrapping her arms around his waist. *This feels so good. So damn good.*

Eli released her and quickly kissed her on the forehead before leaving. Heather sank into the chair, thinking about their conversation and his temporary return. She was in trouble. She needed help.

One mass text message and five minutes later, Cat sat down at the table, with a mug of hot chocolate. Just as Heather was going to tell Cat about Eli's return, a very tired Hera dragged herself into the shop.

"It's fuckin' cold," she grumbled, wearing jeans, a gray hooded sweatshirt and a black winter vest.

"Maybe you should try wearing a coat," Cat pointed out.

"I couldn't find it," Hera protested, pulling her hands out of the sweatshirt's sleeves. "And I live like two seconds away."

Vodka Four

"Then don't bitch," Cat said, while Hera headed toward the counter to order.

"Shut up," she grumbled, returning to the table with a mug of coffee. "This better be good. I feel like shit."

Cat and Heather simultaneously pushed back their chairs, expecting projectile vomiting.

"Hungover?" Cat asked smugly, enjoying Hera's moment of disability.

"I drank way too much last night," she admitted. "Where there's free alcohol, I'm there. And you guys know I'm going to drink until I pass out."

Cat and Heather laughed in agreement.

"So, what's going on?" Cat asked, with a concerned look.

"Eli's in town," Heather said simply.

"What?" she exclaimed while Hera spit out a sip of coffee back into the mug.

Heather repeated her statement and then relayed the conversation she had with Eli moments earlier.

"Why is Eli's return a big deal?" Hera asked.

Heather shrugged. "I don't know. I just feel weird."

"How do you feel about Eli?" Cat asked quietly.

"He's one of my best friends."

"How do you feel about him?" Cat repeated seriously, looking at Heather.

She looked down at her coffee mug, realizing exactly how she felt about Eli and why she didn't want to tell him about her relationship with Nick.

"Heather."

"I love him."

The table was enveloped in silence for a brief moment as Heather, Cat, and Hera thought about her answer.

"Fuck," Hera said, shaking her head. "No wonder Eli's return is a big fuckin' deal."

"How can I still be in love with him?" Heather asked. "Seriously, I haven't seen him for two years. Two fuckin' years."

Cat and Hera looked at each other, wondering who was going to answer the question.

"When I saw him standing outside of my apartment, everything I had felt during our relationship just flooded back to me," Heather said thoughtfully. "I spend about half an hour with him, and I realize I still love him. How long have I been with Nick? Long enough to know that I don't love him."

"So, what are you going to do?" Cat asked hesitantly.

"Fuck if I know."

Heather didn't want to be angry, but Eli's return interrupted her peaceful domestic life. A million questions ran through her mind, and she wasn't sure how to answer them.

Silence once again surrounded the table as Heather thought about her feelings for Eli and Cat and Hera mentally searched for something brilliant to say. All three were staring into their mugs, not saying anything, when Rory and Lily walked into the coffee shop.

"What the hell is going on?" Rory demanded, quickly surveying the somber mood at the table. "What the hell happened?"

Heather retold the story after Rory and Lily sat down at the table, with hot drinks in hand.

"So, what do I do?" she asked, with a sigh. "Tell me what to do."

"Nothing has really changed," Rory said tentatively. "I think you'll always love Eli because he's been part of your life for so long."

"To be honest," Lily offered. "We all kind of thought you guys would end up together. But then he moved to California."

"So, what does this mean?" Heather asked. "Do I ditch Nick and wait for Eli to come back? Should I tell Eli that I still love him?"

"Hypothetical question here," Cat volunteered. "Would you break up with Nick if Eli confessed that he still loved you?"

"Yes." A second wasn't even needed to think about the answer.

"Are you willing to wait for him?" Lily asked.

More than a second was needed for a reply. "I don't know," Heather admitted finally. "I don't know."

"If Eli still loves you, which I'm sure he does," Rory said. "Are you willing to move to California to be with him?"

"Am I coming back to Amery Lake? How long would I have to be in California?"

"You'd be there until Eli is ready to return to Wisconsin."

"No," Heather answered, shaking her head. "I can't move there for an indefinite amount of time."

"What if it was for two years?" Hera threw in.

"Then I'd stay here and wait for him. It doesn't make sense for me to move out there for two years and then return here."

"So, nothing has really changed," Rory observed. "You know Eli won't move back here, and you won't move out there. What will you accomplish if you tell Eli that you still love him? And even if he still loves you, what kind of sacrifices are you willing to make?"

Rory was right, Heather thought. *Nothing has changed between me and Eli.*

"Well, fuck," she said out loud, setting her elbows on the table and cupping her face with her hands. "What the hell am I supposed to do now?"

"How do you feel about Nick?" Lily asked.

"I like him. I really do. I have such a good time when I'm around him."

"Do you love him?" Hera asked.

Heather shook her head. "No, but I can see myself falling in love with him."

"Do you want to stop seeing him?" Cat asked.

"No?"

Everyone laughed at the timid reply.

Heather sighed out loud. "So, what do you guys think I should do?"

"Here's my advice," Rory replied. "Do nothing, because nothing has changed. When Eli left for California, you eventually moved on. You realized it would be stupid of you to wait for him when nothing was set in stone. You don't know when he's coming back, and more importantly, you don't know if he will come back. Maybe he'd rather stay in California."

"You're right," Heather said, sitting up. "You're absolutely right."

"It's because I'm smart," Rory replied smugly, taking a sip of her coffee.

"Now how do I keep Eli and Nick apart?" she asked. "I don't want them talking to each other."

Everyone chuckled with amusement.

"OK, sweetie," Lily said, with a smirk. "That's something you can't control."

"Bullshit," Heather exclaimed. "The last thing I want to do is divide my time between my boyfriend and my ex-boyfriend. This weekend is going to be a nightmare."

"You're being overdramatic," Rory pointed out. "I highly doubt Eli and Nick will be by your side the whole entire time. Not to mention, there's going to be a huge ass group of us. Eli's going to hang out with his friends, and Nick's going to hang out with his. I don't think they're going to be trading notes about you. You're not that special."

Heather responded with her middle finger.

"Just get really super drunk," Hera suggested. "Stay out on the dance floor and just get tanked."

Vodka Four

"Better said than done."

"I'll be joining you on the dance floor," Lily added. "After this weekend, I plan on getting wasted."

"Hell yeah," Rory agreed, raising her coffee mug.

"Why?" Cat asked, looking at Rory and Lily. "What happened?"

"My parents were assholes," Lily explained simply. "They interrogated me about my lack of social life before the wedding. Then they interrogated Rory about her future during the reception. But Rory gracefully held her own, and then she fell in love with my cousin, Cooper."

"What?" Cat, Hera, and Heather asked in unison, looking at Rory, who didn't seem amused.

"I didn't fall in love," Rory replied icily, shooting Lily an evil look. But Lily just giggled and shrugged. "She just introduced me to her cousin, Cooper."

"Did you guys have sex?" Hera asked bluntly.

"No," she shot back. "I didn't have sex with him."

"Aw, our little Jo is falling in love," Cat gushed dramatically. "Someone was able to peel back her 'tough guy' exterior and realize she has a heart after all."

"*Little Women*?" Lily inquired about the Jo reference.

"*Facts of Life*," Heather answered smartly, joining the fun. "Is this the very special episode where we talk about special stages of a relationship? Remember, Rory, no means no. If he doesn't understand that you're not ready, then he's not worth it."

Everyone laughed, as Rory scowled and gave Heather the finger.

"Weren't you guys supposed to come back last night?" Cat asked.

"That was the plan," Lily replied. "But Cooper persuaded us to hit the bars. He booked us a room at the hotel he was staying at."

"Well, that was very sweet of him," Hera said, with a grin. "You should have put out for him, Rory."

"Fuck you," Rory threw back quickly.

"You must really like him if you didn't have sex with him," Heather pointed out.

"Fuck you, too."

Again, everyone but Rory laughed.

"So, the weekend wasn't a total loss," Cat said, smiling at Rory, who just shot her an evil look. "But why are you guys getting drunk this weekend?"

"As if the interrogation wasn't enough, my whole entire family thinks Rory was hitting on my sister's fiancé, Adam," Lily explained, with a sigh. "They're also upset that I ditched the reception without saying something to them."

"Are you kidding me?" Heather asked, looking at Rory.

"Don't look at me," she said, holding up her hands in mock surrender. "Apparently, talking to the guy is the same thing as hitting on him. He's a social worker, and I simply asked questions about his job. I was showing an interest and making conversation."

"Good girl," Cat praised.

"My sister, Amanda, has left several messages on my phone, instructing me not to bring Rory to another family event," Lily shared. "She's such an overdramatic bitch."

"Have you tried explaining what happened?" Cat asked.

Lily shook her head. "No, because it won't do any good. My family will only listen to what they want to hear. They feel they're the victims and want an apology, and I would rather go to hell than apologize."

"You shouldn't have to apologize for anything," Heather agreed. "You guys did nothing wrong."

"I know!" Lily exclaimed. "That's why I'm going to get totally wasted this weekend. You and I will get super drunk and forget about the rest of the world."

"Hell yeah," she agreed brightly.

Vodka Four

"So, you OK?" Hera asked tiredly, standing up.

"Yeah. Thanks for coming over," Heather said.

Even after realizing she was still in love with Eli, Heather knew nothing had changed between them and she needed to continue to move on — with Nick. However, she still didn't like the idea of spending an evening with her current boyfriend and her ex-boyfriend. *Something could be done about,* Heather thought as she walked back to her apartment with Rory and Cat. As much as Heather wanted Eli to stay, she knew the sooner he left the better.

CHAPTER 17

Thursday, February 3

"Are you sure this is a good idea?" Cat asked, frowning.

"I've been looking forward to this night all week," Heather replied, looking at her reflection in the mirror and wondering whether the outfit wasn't sexy enough.

"That's my point. You've barely said anything about Nick, and your date with Eli is the highlight of your week."

"It's not a date," Heather protested, deciding the green cable knit sweater made her look like a grandma.

"You're acting like it is," Cat pointed out, shaking her head as Heather pulled the sweater over head. "What was wrong with that sweater? How many times have you changed your outfit?"

"I look like my grandma." Heather disappeared into her walk-in closet and emerged with another selection. "Come on, Cat, this is Eli. I haven't seen him since he moved. I want to look good."

"To tempt him?"

"So, he remembers me." She pulled the white v-neck sweater over her head. "I want him to remember that I was a good thing."

"I don't think he could forget if he tried," Cat said, exasperated and fell back on Heather's bed. A second later, she sat back up and watched Heather examine herself in the mirror again. "That sweater's too slutty. He's going to stare at your cleavage the entire night."

Vodka Four

"Shit, you're right. Dammit, I don't have much time." Heather pulled the sweater over her head before disappearing into her closet again. "Why are you so worried?"

"Because you still love him!"

"But I'm not going to do anything with him. I have a boyfriend, remember?"

"But you don't love him!" Cat almost shrieked. She took a deep breath to regain some composure. "You've never been flustered or anxious as a schoolgirl over Nick."

"I'm not flustered or anxious," Heather disagreed, reemerging from the closet and wearing a form-fitting red sweater with a deep cowl neck. "And you can't compare my friendship with Eli to my relationship with Nick. They're two totally different things."

"Except that you would drop Nick in a heartbeat if Eli confessed his love for you and stayed in Amery Lake. Nice sweater, by the way."

Heather knew better than to play coy or innocent with Cat. A friendship that started when they were college freshmen meant Cat knew Heather — maybe a little too well.

"Fine," Heather said, sighing. "I didn't realize how much I missed Eli — "

"And loved," Cat interrupted dryly.

"Fine, and loved Eli until he returned to town. Since he's been back, it seems like he never really moved away. And I miss that — I miss being with him. I just want to hold on to that feeling just a little longer before I start worrying about him and Nick staring each other down over the weekend."

"I still don't think it's a good idea."

"Hey, you had a 'date' with him last night, and Rory had a 'date' with him Tuesday night. This is the same thing."

"It is not, and you know it," Cat said swiftly. "Rory and I aren't in love with him. And we also have the right to spend some one-on-one time with him because we've known him just as long as you have. Not to mention, Eli's our friend, too. You weren't the only who was devastated when he left."

Confusion swept over her face as Heather turned to study Cat's serious expression. Of course, she knew Cat and Rory were among Eli's circle of friends, but she never took the time to consider how his move impacted them. Heartache, sorrow, and guilt consumed her, and she thought about little else in the months after he left. Cat and Rory didn't hesitate to console her, and not once did Heather think they needed some comfort as well.

"Heather," Cat said gently. "Rory and I had no problem taking care of you after Eli left, because you fell in love with him. You were dealing with more than just a broken heart — a good friend had also left. But he was — is — one of our good friends, too. You're not the only one who keeps in contact with him."

"You've talked to Eli since he's moved?" Heather asked slowly. "Even e-mail?"

Cat shrugged and nodded.

"I didn't know that. Why didn't you tell me?"

"I thought you knew," Cat replied.

A million questions raced through Heather's mind as a little bit of anger — and maybe jealously — started to surface. What did Cat and Eli talk about? Did they ever talk about her? And why is Cat talking to him in the first place? He's not her ex-boyfriend.

"Settle down," Cat said firmly. "Remember the time when that one guy, Jon, called me fat and ugly after I ended the fling?"

"What an asshole!" Heather exclaimed, forgetting about her minor anger. "One, he treated you like shit. Two, you're way more attractive than him. Three, he wasn't easy on the eyes at all. I never understood why you even gave him a chance. He was a real dick."

"Thanks for dragging me down that memory lane."

Vodka Four

"Well, you brought the asshole up."

"I'm trying to make a point," Cat said, with a sigh.

"Point away."

"Of course, you and the girls told me that I wasn't fat or ugly. But you guys are obligated to comfort me when a boy hurts me."

"You're not fat!" Heather squealed. "And you're not ugly!"

"Shut up, I know!" Cat screeched back, rolling her eyes. "The point is I wanted a guy's perspective. Danny and Gil weren't around for some reason, and so I called Eli. As much as I love you and the girls comforting me and threatening to castrate Jon, Eli reassured me and offered a little guy insight."

"Yeah, I remember Eli doing the same thing with me before he and I started dating."

"Sometimes, a girl needs a guy's perspective."

"How often do you keep in contact with him?" Heather asked curiously.

"We e-mail each other more than we talk. But he hasn't been good about e-mailing for awhile — he's been busy."

"Do you guys ever talk about me?"

Cat paused before answering. "In the months after he left, Eli wanted to make sure you were doing OK. And after you tell him you're seeing someone, he asks for my opinion. I've never told him anything that you've already didn't tell him."

"Does Rory keep in touch with him?"

"Not as often as I do."

Which made sense to Heather because Cat kept in touch with everybody. Whenever she needed to catch up with one of the Vodka Girls, Heather turned to Cat for information. Between two jobs and spending much of her time with Heather, Rory, Lily, and Hera, how and when Cat made time for her billions of friends Heather never knew. But then again, Cat had far superior organizational and time management skills than she would ever hope to achieve.

"OK, we've gotten way off track here," Cat said, sighing. "I just want to make sure you're not going to do anything that you might regret."

"I'll be fine," Heather reassured. "He and I are just hanging out. That's it."

"And this is the highlight of your week? How sad."

"Shut up." She went to the bathroom to refresh her makeup and brush her hair.

"Does Nick know you're going out with Eli tonight?" Cat asked, sitting on the bed with Heather's two cats.

"Yup. I told him last night."

"So, tell me about your date with Nick last night."

"There's not much to tell," Heather answered honestly, looking at herself in the mirror. "We had dinner. We talked. He took me home. End of date."

"That sounds exciting," Cat said sarcastically. "Give me more information, dammit."

"OK, here's the truth," she said, taking a deep breath and peeking her head out of the bathroom. "I think one of the reasons why I'm looking forward to tonight is Eli will soon return to California. Once he's gone, I can stop feeling guilty about my wonderful relationship with Nick."

"Why are you feeling guilty?"

Heather shrugged. "Because I know how much I mean to Eli, and for some reason, with him here, I feel like I'm betraying him by finding happiness with Nick. I know this sounds silly and stupid, but I feel like I'm breaking Eli's heart."

"You guys broke up for a reason, and that reason still remains."

"I know, but I feel like I'm hurting him. And because of that, I really don't want to be around Nick until Eli's gone. And I know I'm probably hurting Nick, but … " Heather trailed off, not knowing what to say next.

Vodka Four

"So, what happened last night?"

"Nothing. When I say nothing, I mean nothing. We briefly talked about Eli, and I reassured him that Eli and I are just friends and that he and I are hanging out tonight. Nick didn't argue."

"I can't imagine that he would."

"We dinner, and he drove me home. I kissed him good night, and I went to bed."

"By yourself?"

"This is what I'm talking about, Cat," Heather said, shaking her head. "I had no desire to have sex — or even make out — with Nick, because I keep thinking about Eli. I told Nick that I was tired and just needed a good night's rest."

"Do you think he believes you?"

"I hope so. The excuse was kind of lame."

"Don't kill me for asking this, but do you want to sleep with Eli?" Cat asked point blank.

Heather shook her head. "No, and that's the truth. I may still be in love with him, but I have no desire to sleep with him."

"I'm not sure if that's weird or a good thing," she said slowly, thinking about Heather's explanation.

"I know!" Heather exclaimed, returning to the bathroom. "And sex with Eli was fantastic. Why I don't want to sleep with him is a mystery."

"I'll see if *Unsolved Mysteries* can investigate this case."

"Ha ha, smarty-pants."

"Well, have fun tonight and be careful," Cat warned, jumping off the bed. "You know me, I can't help but worry about my friends."

"I'll be fine. You have nothing to worry about."

CHAPTER 18

Ah, crap! I'm in trouble, Heather thought as she and Eli walked through the Lutheran university campus. *Cat has every right to be worried. Dammit, why is she always right?*

Heather's night with Eli was perfect. From the moment, he smiled at her when picking her for their "date," Heather stepped back into time to when they were in love and happy — when they were together. The evening was filled with laughter, wine, stories, teasing, gossip, and more wine, and Heather wanted to stay in the moment.

Actually, she wanted more. She was tempted to tell Eli about her feelings and beg him to stay. But Heather knew she could never ask him to leave his family, especially during a medical dilemma, when she couldn't leave hers behind. While Eli would probably seriously consider staying, he ultimately would return to California, breaking her heart all over again. The best option was to keep her big mouth shut.

"There used to be a street here," Eli said thoughtfully, stopping and looking at a well-manicured lawn. "Remember? I hated driving down the street because I was afraid I'd hit someone."

"Look, there's the flag poles," Heather pointed out, with a smile. "We're legends here, you know."

"Or an urban myth. Either way, we had some really good times here. Didn't we, Vodka Four?"

"The best," she replied, tucking her arm inside his and leaning against him. Being close to him felt so good. "Did you have a nice time catching up with Cat and Rory?"

"Yeah," Eli said, starting to walk again. "I've always wondered how Cat manages to keep in touch with everyone. I'd ask about someone, and she'd have an update for me."

Vodka Four

"I know! She knows keeps tabs on all the Vodka Girls, and I have no idea what's going. Well, that's a lie — I know Emmy is married and has two kids, I think."

"Which Vodka Girl was she?"

"Vodka Two," Heather responded slowly, remembering the simple alphabetical system used to assigned nicknames.

"Want to know a secret?" Eli looked slyly at her.

"Of course."

"She and I slept together once."

"What?" Heather stopped walking and stared at him. "When?"

"Sophomore year. Springfest."

"More details please."

"All of them?" Eli asked wickedly.

"No." She scowled, tucking her scarf into her jacket to protect against the winter cold. "Just the basics."

"I don't know," he shrugged, continuing their walk. "I just remember talking to her. Next thing, I know we're making out and we're heading back to her place."

"I don't remember any of this. Where was I? More importantly, where was Cat and Rory? Because if they knew, I would've known."

"You were seeing some guy at the time and spent most of Springfest with him. Rory is always spending time with a guy, and I have no idea about Cat."

"Huh." Heather thought about the big revelation for a moment. "So, what happened the morning after? Did you ditch her? Em's a good girl!"

"I know," Eli said defensively. "And no, I didn't ditch her. I was a gentleman — well, not all the time. Honestly? She didn't want you to know."

"Me?" She stopped again. "Why didn't she want me to know?"

"Because she thought you'd be pissed at her. According to her, there's this unspoken rule about not sleeping with your girlfriend's best guy friend. Plus, she didn't want to be kicked out of the Vodka Girls."

"OK, when have we ever kicked anyone out of the Vodka Girls? And yeah, there's an unspoken rule about sleeping with a girlfriend's close guy friend. I understand her view."

"And you guys totally kicked Jessica out of the group," Eli reminded, jabbing her shoulder. "She slept with someone's boyfriend because she didn't like one of the girls."

"Oh yeah," Heather said, nodding in agreement. "I remember now. She slept with Lena's boyfriend because everyone loved Lena. Not only was she beautiful, but she was genuinely nice to everyone. Jessica hated that everyone fawned over Lena. She deserved to be kicked out."

"I remember Lena. She was hot."

"Did you sleep with her, too?" She punched him in the shoulder, letting him she didn't forget about the friendly jab.

"No," he said shortly, grabbing the cap off Heather's head. "But I wanted to."

"Bastard!" She laughed as she chased him. "Did you sleep with any other Vodka Girls?"

"Just you and Emmy. Come on, you can run faster than that!"

"Have you seen the heels on my boots?"

"Pansy."

Heather started walking, shaking her head. Eli was jogging backwards, with her cap in hand, and wearing a clever grin. Damn, he looked so good. And to her horror, Heather recognized a sexual desire awakening inside her. Earlier, she had told Cat the truth — she didn't want to sleep with Eli. But now, the good times brought back fantastic memories of them between the sheets.

"What's wrong?" He stopped jogging and waited for her.

"Nothing." She lied, shaking her head. "It's cold, and I'm out of breath."

Vodka Four

"Want to get some coffee?"

"Yeah, sounds good."

Fifteen minutes later, Heather and Eli were sitting at a table and sipping coffee inside a nearby coffee house. She was desperately trying to push the bedtime memories from her mind while staying composed and cool.

"Feel better?" Eli asked, setting down the coffee mug.

"Yeah, much," she said, with a smile. "Any other secrets you'd like to share with me tonight?"

He shook his head and chuckled.

"Other than the Emmy secret, I learned another fact about you today," Heather revealed.

"Oh yeah? What's that?"

"I didn't know you kept in contact with Cat and Rory."

"Seriously?" Eli asked, with surprise. "I figured you knew I talked to them every now and then. Where the hell have you been?"

"Hey," she said defensively. "I never thought about it."

"I consider Cat and Rory really good friends of mine. Can you really imagine me moving away and not keeping in contact with them?"

"Hey, like I said before, I never thought about it."

"I'm glad I had a chance to hang out with them. I've missed them," he admitted. "We had some really good times together."

"I'm just surprised that we never got caught pulling a prank."

"I know! Danny and Gil and I were talking about that the other night. And we pulled a lot of pranks in college."

"Which prank scared you the most?"

Eli took a minute to think about the question. Countless of pranks had been pulled during a four-year period. "Probably the mascot prank, because it was so elaborate. We had to kidnap three plastic mascots and then string them up the flag poles all in one night. I almost bailed on that one."

"Really? I would've never guessed."

"Can you imagine the consequences if we got caught? My parents would've been pissed if I was expelled or suspended."

"I think my parents would've killed me."

"Can you believe we've known each other for more than 10 years?" Eli asked, shaking his head in disbelief. "Rory reminded me of that little tidbit."

"Yeah, I know," Heather agreed, nodding. "I feel so old! We're going to turn 30 soon! Can you believe that?"

"I know. And you still don't look a day over 21."

Heather grinned, blushing a bit at the compliment.

"Some things never change," he said softly, looking at her.

Heather's heart stopped for a moment. Did he just confess that he still loved her? Oh, she wished she could pause the moment and call Cat or Rory to figure out what Eli's last statement meant. Was this the moment to tell him that she still loved him? Oh, she desperately wanted to kiss him and be closer to him. *Keep your big mouth shut!*

"Well, the campus has certainly changed," she said, leaning back in the chair and changing the intimate mood. "The new library is simply gorgeous."

"With more places to make out," Eli added, with a wink.

Heather rolled her eyes. "Are you going to share another secret with me?"

"Maybe. Maybe not."

"Come on, you know you want to tell me," she needled teasingly.

Although the tender moment had passed and didn't surface during the remainder of the night, Heather realized holding on to her past with Eli probably wasn't the greatest idea in the world. Even though he was always going to be a part of her life, she needed to say goodbye to their past.

CHAPTER 19

Friday, February 4

Something was wrong, Nick thought to himself, taking a drink from his beer bottle while watching Heather and her friends on the dance floor at Deep Pink. He and other friends stood by a table near the dancers, watching all the pretty girls and spastic guys feel the rhythm of the pulsating music.

Although Heather said nothing was wrong and acted as if nothing was wrong, Nick was still suspicious. And he blamed Eli, the dumbass ex-boyfriend, for everything. Well, sort of. Nick couldn't find a reason to hate him or even blame him for his paranoia.

In fact, Nick and Eli laughed and joked around when he stopped by the store during the week. Despite the camaraderie, Nick highly suspected Eli's temporary return had something to do with Heather's mysterious behavior.

During a dinner date during the week, Heather reassured him nothing was wrong and seemed happy to see Nick. Ever since he heard Eli was back in town, Nick feared the worst — Heather would break up with him and get back together with Eli. He knew Eli played a significant part in her life, and he was secretly relieved that her ex-boyfriend lived thousands of miles away from her. But that didn't stop the many scenarios about Heather and Eli getting back together playing through Nick's mind.

Heather was open and honest about going out with Eli the next night — they were going to have dinner and walk around the university campus. Nick trusted Heather, and he trusted Eli — to an extent. But the idea of two best friends and former lovers spending an evening together didn't exactly thrill Nick.

The temporary relief Nick felt during dinner quickly vanished when he dropped her off at her apartment. Heather claimed she was tired and just wanted to go to bed — alone. She didn't invite him in. She didn't have sex with him. They didn't even make out. She quickly kissed him goodbye before exiting his car.

The last thing Nick wanted to do was share his girlfriend with her ex-boyfriend over the weekend. Normally, he didn't have a problem with Heather hanging out with him and his guy friends, because his friends loved being around his fun and hot girlfriend. He just had a problem with Heather focusing her attention on Eli and not him.

But the problem was that Heather wasn't spending any time with Eli or Nick at Deep Pink. She was spending time with everyone else except either of them.

Yeah, something's wrong, Nick thought, still staring at Heather, who was dancing with her friends. *Something's definitely wrong.* Not that Heather normally dressed uber-slutty when going out, but her outfit of tight blue jeans and layering two fitted T-shirts wasn't her best — or skankiest. Nick was half hoping that Heather would wear a revealing but non-trashy outfit and would hang all over him in front of Eli. *Wishful thinking, Reed*, Nick told himself. *Wishful fuckin' thinking.*

"Are you pouting?" Ryan asked, standing next to him after dancing with some beautiful girls.

"Does it look like I'm pouting?" Nick snapped.

"Uh, yeah, it does." He looked at Heather who was dancing with Cat and Hera. Standing a couple feet away from them was Eli joking around with his former college roommates, Danny and Gil. "What's your problem? It's not like she's hanging all over him."

"Nothing's wrong."

Vodka Four

"OK," Ryan said, shrugging. "This could've been a Hallmark moment, but your pigheaded stubbornness and inability to communicate your emotions and feelings just ruined it."

Nick laughed out loud and shook his head. "Just look at her."

Ryan scanned the dance floor to see Heather having a good time among her friends. She was dancing, laughing, and talking to her girlfriends. She stood behind Cat and gave her a hug from behind, wrapping her arms around Cat's neck.

"I love you, Kitty Cat," Heather said drunkenly. "You're so pretty."

"And you're so drunk," Cat laughed. "Mission accomplished."

"Remember, Nick is not coming home with me tonight. Wait, I'm not even going home tonight."

"Vodka Four, we've been through this a million times," she said, appreciating the hug but trying to disentangle herself from Heather's long arms. "You're going to be super drunk — and you're doing a fantastic job, by the way."

Cat and the rest of the girls all knew about the master plan. Always the organizer and master of anticipation, Heather needed a plan for the weekend. She was going to do her best to stay away from Eli and Nick, which she hoped would avoid confrontation or jealousy. Of course, she would talk to them here and there, but she would spend the majority of the time with her girlfriends.

However, acting normal was difficult — even with Heather's superb acting skills. Tonight, she felt uncomfortable displaying any kind of affection toward Nick while Eli was around. She wasn't sure whether Nick believed the lame excuse about being tired after their dinner date. She just didn't want him to spend the night. She didn't want to have sex with him. She didn't even want to make out with him. She didn't sure why thoughts of Eli kept her from doing anything sexual with Nick.

Heather figured Nick might try to be possessive or overprotective after bar time. He would make sure she got home OK, and he would be the one to look after her. If she wasn't too drunk, Heather thought he would try to initiate sex if they went home together. So, she and Cat decided they were going to attempt to lose the guys sometime during the night.

Part one, they would stay out until bar time. Part two, if the guys were still hanging around, then they would get something to eat — preferably at an all-night restaurant, such as Perkin's or Country Kitchen, because the service is slower than Hardee's or Taco Bell. The longer the guys stayed out, the more likely they would like to go home and crash.

Part three, if the guys didn't head home after eating, then Cat or Heather would suggest going to Cat's place to watch a movie or play a game. The movie Heather would insist on watching would be *Titanic*, because she knew of no guy who wanted to watch a three-hour romantic movie about a boat sinking. At this point, Heather knew she would either fall asleep or pass out during the movie, and Cat would firmly insist that she stayed at her place while hinting they should go home.

As soon as Cat and Heather had the outline of their plan, they told Lily, Hera, and Rory, who made minor suggestions and promised to follow it over the weekend. Heather didn't like behaving a junior high student with an agenda that benefited her, but she wanted to avoid trouble and confrontation. From experience, the best way to stay out of trouble was to stay away from it.

So far, everything was going to plan as Heather was feeling the effects of the mixed vodka drinks she had been tossing back all night. She didn't need much to become completely inebriated, but she also had to maintain some control. The last

Vodka Four

thing Heather wanted to do was destroy the master plan with her sloppy drunken behavior.

As Heather disappeared into the crowd of dancers, she quickly glanced around for Eli and Nick. They were in the same vicinity as one another, but they weren't talking to each other. However, her relief was short lived and almost preferred that option when she saw Hope Saint James walking toward her boyfriend.

"Bitch!" Heather swore, narrowing her eyes. "She needs to get her grubby hands off my man."

"Hey," Cat shouted and grabbed Heather's arm. "Nick won't do anything with her, and you know it. Don't make a scene."

Heather looked at Cat and then at Nick and Hope, who were just talking and smiling. Cat was right. Nick wouldn't do anything with Hope. Not to mention, Heather knew cheating and lying weren't part of his personality. However, she didn't blame him for soaking up Hope's attention, because she had barely spent any time with him.

"Don't be a jealous and crazy girlfriend," Cat warned. "The plan will be ruined. Not to mention, the psycho act might either scare or amuse Nick. And it will either hurt or amuse Eli."

Dammit, Heather thought. *Why is Cat so fuckin' smart? And right?*

"But it's Hope Saint James," she whined.

What Heather really wanted to do was march her butt over to Nick, throw her arms around him, and kiss him passionately. Although throwing a drink at Hope would be just as satisfying.

"And Nick knows who she is. He's not going to do anything."

"Cat," Heather pleaded. "Please get her away from him. Please."

Jennifer Elliott

Cat sighed and wrinkled her face. "Vodka Four, everything will be fine."

"I don't like her, and I don't want her pushing her big boobies in my boyfriend's face."

Cat looked over at Nick and Hope, who were still talking and now were laughing. Heather had the right to be upset. If Nick was her boyfriend, Cat wouldn't want him anywhere near Hope Saint James, the uber-slut of Amery Lake. Cat knew Hope was flirting with Nick to piss off Heather.

A back story didn't exist to explain why Heather and Hope didn't like each other. Hope didn't understand why men were attracted to Heather and always thought Heather was a pouty, whiny, and skinny bitch. Heather thought Hope was an uptight snobby bitch who throws tantrums when she doesn't get her way and wears inappropriate clothes to lure men into her sick game of "which guy will piss off my daddy."

Hope Saint James was doing almost everything she could to distract Nick from finding his lame-ass girlfriend on the crowded dance floor. Just as Heather and her friends had heard stories about Hope and her dysfunctional family, Hope had heard — and maybe even started — tall tales about each of them.

Hope felt extremely sorry for Cat, who obviously didn't belong in the circle of friends. She was cute, Hope had thought, but she wasn't naturally attractive like her friends. The glasses she wore all of the time just added to geeky appearance — a major turnoff for guys.

Hope didn't like Lily's snobby and superior attitude. The somewhat attractive Latina hair stylist came from as just as dysfunctional family that Hope did, and Hope believed Lily had no right to look down on her.

Hera needed to be the center of attention of everything, Hope had thought once when she was shopping at Lexington. She had studied how Hera laughed at everything that any guy said and how she wanted any attractive guy to focus on her.

Vodka Four

Hope wasn't sure who she hated more — Heather or Rory. Rory was a smug bitch who thought the world revolved around her and flaunted her stripper experience. And Heather was a spoiled and ignorant bitch who got everything she wanted just by batting her eyelids and showing off her skinny ass.

Hope was a real woman. She was opinionated. She knew what she wanted. She didn't back down to anyone. She was proud of her full curvy figure and naturally enhanced breasts. Hope couldn't remember the last time her hair color was naturally mousy brown. Presently, her dark reddish brown and straight hair fell to her chin.

Hope currently despised Heather more than Rory because she had two highly attractive men in love with her and deserved neither of them. By the time Hope had started working in Anastacia Square, Eli had moved to California, but she had heard about the "great love story" between Eli and Heather.

With Eli back in town, Hope knew Heather and her stupid friends would hit the bars over the weekend. When she didn't see Heather near Nick at Deep Pink, Hope saw her moment of opportunity. She intentionally and literally bumped into him.

"Hey, handsome," she shouted over the blaring music.

"Hey," Nick replied, looking her in the eye before glancing down to see the ample cleavage pouring out of her blue striped blouse.

"Where's your girl?" She stood so close to him that their arms touched and noticed Nick didn't pull away.

"Somewhere on the dance floor."

Hope scanned the dance crowd and couldn't find Heather or any of her lame ass friends. However, she spotted Eli standing with some other friends a few feet away.

"How come you're not dancing?" she asked sweetly.

"I don't dance," Nick replied dully, before taking a swig from his beer bottle.

"Who's the new guy?" Hope questioned innocently, nodding in Eli's direction.

"Eli Clearly. Heather's ex-boyfriend."

Hope gleefully noted the hostility in his voice.

"So, wanna hear a joke?" she asked. Without waiting for an answer, Hope launched into a short joke and was pleased when Nick threw his head back and laughed.

As they exchanged jokes, Hope wished Heather would stomp over in a jealous rage. Hope loved nothing more than acting innocently with other women's men while the women railed at her for being a bitch and a slut, which was true. But Hope's favorite part was when men usually defended her — in their minds, she didn't do anything wrong — against the girlfriends' tirade against her.

Just as Hope was going to suggest ditching the club, Rory appeared from the dance crowd. She narrowed her eyes at Hope while tossing her black hair behind her shoulders.

"Hey, Nick," she said, grabbing his hand. "We're heading to Skylight."

"Where's Heather?" he asked, not pulling away from her.

"She's waiting for us outside the club."

Nick smiled at Hope as Rory dragged him away. "See ya later."

Hope gave a fake and bright smile before walking away to search her own group of friends. She didn't want Nick to think Rory's presence upset her. If Hope didn't know any better, she thought Nick was having a good time with her.

"Thanks for rescuing me," Nick told Rory as they maneuvered their way to the exit.

"Not a problem," Rory replied. "I can't stand that bitch. She thinks the world revolves around her."

"I can only talk to her for so long," he admitted, walking into the fresh night air. "She and I were actually have a good time, though."

Vodka Four

"You're kidding."

"Oh, I know she was hitting on me, but you caught her while she was trying to play it cool."

Rory laughed as they moved away from a crowd of people who were coming in and going out of the club. She was about to respond when she felt her small purse vibrate. She took out her cell phone and read Cat's text message.

"Let's walk," she said. "Everyone is heading to Skylight. There's so many of us, they decided not to wait."

"Sure," Nick said, shrugging and started walking.

"Besides, Lily and I rented a private room for all of us. If we get bored in the main club, we can go the private room."

"Cool."

Nick and Rory walked in silence, listening to cars driving by, other people talking or shouting at each other, and distance music pouring out from different bars.

"Having a good time?" Rory finally asked. She noticed Nick didn't look happy while watching Heather dance.

"Yeah," was his short reply.

"What's going on?"

Rory had no problem butting in on other people's lives or issues, especially when she believed one of her best friends were involved.

"Nothing's wrong," Nick said gruffly, staring straight at ahead.

"Bullshit. I don't believe that for a second."

"Believe whatever you want."

"I believe you're mad at Heather because she's not spending the whole entire evening by your side to show Eli that she's your girlfriend."

Nick stopped walking and looked at Rory, who then stopped to stare at him. Was he really that transparent?

"Nick," Rory said, with a sigh and pulled him aside so that they didn't block the sidewalk. "Heather likes you, and I know you like her. You have nothing to worry about."

Jennifer Elliott

Nick looked at the ground, not saying anything. He already felt like an idiot for being transparent. He thought he was being cool and mysterious.

"Look, there's like a thousand of us out tonight. Did you honestly believe she was going to be by your side the entire night?"

Nick shrugged.

"She's with you. Everyone, even Eli, knows that. So, why are you so worried?"

He sighed before answering. "She and I haven't known each other for very long. And I really like her."

"Here's my advice, Nick. Stop acting like a baby, and don't do anything stupid or anything that you're going to regret," Rory warned. "Heather is your girlfriend, and she's not going to do anything to screw up this relationship."

"Really?" This was the first moment since Eli's return that Nick felt relieved. Sure, Rory was bossy, demanding, and overprotective of her friends, but he trusted her to not lie to him.

"Really." Rory echoed his statement and started walking again.

They walked in silence for awhile again, with Nick replaying their conversation in his mind. Rory was right. He was acting like a baby and should stop sulking about Heather not being by his side. God, he felt like the world's biggest idiot.

"Thanks, Rory," he said, breaking the silence.

She turned her head and smiled. "Not a problem. However, if you break her heart, I will beat your senseless."

Nick chuckled. "I imagine Cat, Hera, and Lily will be right behind you."

This time, Rory laughed out loud. "Damn right."

As they continued talking, Nick felt better. However, he still couldn't wait for Eli to leave town. Then, hopefully, things will go back to normal.

CHAPTER 20

Saturday, February 5

Heather woke up suddenly to a loud pounding noise. *What the hell?* She thought to herself, rubbing her eyes and then holding her head with both of her hands. The pounding continued, and she wanted to yell but found her throat to be dry and hoarse.

Where I am? Oh God, make the noise stop! Finally, the pounding stopped, and Heather heard voices in a different room. *I'm at Cat's*, she thought, realizing she was underneath the warm comforter in Cat's full-size bed. *I'm so not moving right now.*

As she was wondering why her body felt sore and bruised, Rory, Lily, and Cat tiptoed into the bedroom.

"Hey," she said groggily, still lying in bed.

"Morning, sunshine," Rory chirped, bouncing onto the bed and making Heather groan in pain. "How are you feeling?"

"Like shit."

"You look it."

"Thanks," Heather grumbled, as Lily sat at the end of the bed and Cat laid down in the open space next to Heather. "What time is it?"

"One o'clock," Cat replied, resting her head on the pillows Heather wasn't using.

"It's a beautiful morning," Rory sang out. "The sun in shining, and it's a great day!"

"Shut the fuck up."

"How much of last night do you remember?" Lily asked, as one of Cat's cats, Harry, jumped onto the bed to check out the action.

"The last thing I remember was heading to Perkin's," Heather said, closing her eyes. "After that, I don't know what happened. Did everything go to plan?"

"Everything went to plan," Rory confirmed, petting Cat's other cat, Sally, who was walking in circles in her lap. "A whole bunch of us went out to eat at Perkin's, but everyone split when you and Cat suggested going back to her place to watch *Titanic*."

"What about Nick?"

"I told him that you were going to crash at Cat's place, and he was cool with that. He just wanted to make sure someone was going to take care of you."

"And Eli?"

No one replied to Heather's one-word question, and she opened her eyes to look at her friends. Lily, Rory, and Cat looked at each other carefully, eyeing who was going share the news.

"What?" Heather asked, breaking the uncomfortable silence. "What happened?"

"Eli didn't go to Perkin's," Rory began. "He went home with Kristen Hartley."

"What?" She sat up immediately and then wished she hadn't moved so quickly as the room began to spin. "I'm going to be sick."

Her friends and the two cats quickly scrambled off the bed as Heather rushed to the bathroom. After hurling, she found her friends sitting in the living room and plopped herself down on the floor. Sitting on the couch, Lily handed Heather a throw pillow to rest her head as she stretched out her poor sore body on the floor.

"You OK?" Cat asked, who was also lying on the carpet with one of her cats curled beside her.

Vodka Four

"I need sleep," Heather muttered, lying on her side. "Kristen Hartley. I guess she's better than Hope fuckin' Saint James. When, where, and how did that happen?"

"At Skylight," Lily answered. "Some of us were in the private room, and some of us were in the main area. Eli was in the private room most of the night. But toward the end, he was in the main area, and that's where he met up with Kristen and her group of friends."

"How do you guys know he went home with her?"

"I asked him if he was going to Perkin's, and he said he was going to hang out with Kristen," Rory replied. "On the bright side, he was really drunk and Kristen's a sure thing. Everyone knows that."

"True," Heather agreed. She was secretly surprised that she wasn't bothered with the fact that Eli had slept with Kristen Hartley. Maybe she was making progress in the "moving on" stage. Maybe he was in the "moving on" stage. "And tonight?"

"Same game plan," Lily said. "According to Danny and Gil, everyone is heading downtown again. This time around, I think a lot more people will be wasted since it's Eli's last night in town."

"Fuck, I don't want to feel like this again tomorrow morning."

Everyone laughed.

"Did I miss anything else?" Heather asked.

"Well," Rory started. "Nick was sulking at Deep Pink because you weren't hanging all over him. But he and I talked while we were walking to Skylight, and he's fine now."

"Thanks, Ror."

"Not a problem. At Skylight, he pretty much let you hang out with other people, while he stuck next to Ryan and Christopher. He had relaxed a lot after our talk."

"I remember Hope sticking her boobies in his face. God, I wanted to bitch slap her."

Everyone chuckled again.

"No offense, but Hope is 10 times bigger than you, Heather," Lily pointed out, then smiling at the thought of Heather and Hope getting into a physical fight. "I know you're scrappy and all, but her weight alone would crush you."

"Anything else I need to know about?" Heather asked.

"Tristan and I had sex," Rory offered.

"What?" Cat and Heather asked together.

"I thought that was over," Cat reminded. "What happened?"

"I don't know." Rory shrugged. "He avoided me most of the night, but after he was somewhat drunk, he started talking to me. He apologized for acting like an ass, and he and I hung out at Skylight."

"Is he still in love with you?" Heather asked groggily.

"He was never in love with me, Miss Smartypants. Now, he understands what I want, and he seems cool with it."

"Are you sure?" Cat questioned.

"Not 100 percent positive, but he's a good guy. He just likes to get his way a lot. And when he doesn't, then he throws a tantrum."

"What about him and Kristen Hartley? They went to the ball together," Heather stated, remembering seeing them at the event.

"Tristan said he was glad that Christopher went to the ball, because he probably would have killed Kristen by the end of the night."

Everyone chuckled at the thought.

"Why?" Cat asked. She had asked Tristan about the ball, and he had shrugged and had said, "Fine." She suspected something happened but didn't press him for details.

"Apparently, Kristen was making an ass out of herself," Rory explained, chuckling a bit. "Of course, Kristen wore a dress that showed off her assets."

"Shocking," Heather muttered sarcastically.

Vodka Four

"Anyway, Tristan knows a lot of people from working at the dealership and through his family. Every time, he made introductions — like a gentleman — he just said Kristen's name. He didn't say, 'This is my girlfriend, Kristen Hartley' or 'This is my date, Kristen Hartley.' He just said, 'This is Kristen Hartley.' After meeting some people, Kristen decided to introduce herself as Tristan's girlfriend. Of course, he wasn't going to make a scene in front of customers.

"After a conversation ended or whatever, Kristen then told Tristan that the guy obviously wanted her because he kept looking at her rack. Not to mention, she took full advantage of the free champagne, and when Kristen gets drunk, she's a sloppy drunk. The straps on her dress fell off her shoulders so many times that Tristan thinks everyone at the ball saw her boobs at least once."

"She wasn't wearing a bra?" Cat asked, wrinkling her nose in disgust. "Someone with those big of hooters should be wearing a bra."

"Either she has never heard of — or doesn't believe in — the power of support cups," Rory said. "My boobs are just as big as hers, and you don't see me going out into public without a bra or some really good support."

"What a dumbass," Heather mumbled.

"Yeah, Tristan was so mad at her that he didn't even sleep with her. He had rented a room at the Carrington House, but he slept on the couch. Kristen tried to put her moves on him, but he said no," Rory continued. "The next morning with Kristen having a hangover and everything, Tristan just laid into her — acting like a sloppy drunk, showing off her boobs, telling everyone she's his girlfriend. Kristen said she was just having a good time. Tristan said it was a huge mistake to her take to the ball, and of course, that didn't sit too well with her."

"I figured things didn't go too well when I noticed they weren't talking to each other at the dealership," Cat mentioned, thinking about the days after the ball. "Tristan seemed to give Kristen the stink eye whenever she was around. I asked him about the ball, and he didn't say much."

"When Kristen and her friends arrived at Skylight, she totally avoided him. The minute she saw us together, she and her group of friends went in the opposite direction."

"What about you, Lil?" Heather asked. "Did you score?"

"No," she replied, with a shitty grin. "I was too busy helping Cat take care of your ass."

"Oh, I'm so sorry," Heather murmured, groaning and closing her eyes again.

"Don't be sorry," Lily said, waving her hand in the air. "Cat and I had fun taking care of you. Didn't we, Cat?"

"Yeah, can't wait to do it again," she said sarcastically.

Heather chuckled at Cat's lack of enthusiasm. "What happened?"

"Where do I even begin? Well, you almost destroyed your brilliant plan a couple of times," Lily explained. "Because Eli wasn't around, you felt you could hang all over Nick. Let's just say that you were getting pretty frisky with him when Cat and I weren't watching you."

"What?" She opened her eyes and looked at Lily to see whether or not she was joking. "I did not."

"Oh, yes, you did," Cat confirmed.

Heather closed her eyes, hoping last night's memories would flood her mind. No memories. No recollection.

"Other than tired and sick, how are you feeling?" Rory asked, with a smirk.

"My body feels like it was run over," she admitted. "I seriously never want to move again."

"I'm sure Nick feels the same way," Lily pointed out, laughing hysterically at the memory.

"What the hell happened?"

Vodka Four

On the walk to Perkin's, Heather decided to run — at full speed. Lily, Rory, and Cat exchanged "what the fuck" looks when she took off running down the block. Because Heather's not a runner by nature — she fears people would think she's anorexic if they saw her run — she didn't get far (the platform strappy sandals she was wearing didn't help either).

After running halfway down the block, Heather threw herself on the lawn outside a senior citizen apartment complex. Nick jogged over to help her up, but Heather had other ideas and started wrestling with him on the lawn. Somehow, she managed to get Nick on his back while she straddled him. She was about to take off her shirt when Cat flew on top of her, tackling Heather to the ground. In the process of the takedown, one of Heather's knees or foot (no one knows for sure) punched Nick's precious package.

Lily, Hera, and Rory screamed with laughter as they watched Cat wrestle with Heather, who was desperately trying to get back on Nick. Byron, Ryan, Tristan, and Christopher instinctively covered their prized possessions with their hands, believing Nick's pain was contagious, while Nick was howling in pain and agony.

As soon as Rory saw an apartment light go on and a shadow heading toward the window, she quickly instructed the laughing party to separate Heather and Cat and help Nick up before the police were called to the scene.

"Oh my god!" Heather moaned in horror. "I can't believe I did that. What the hell was I thinking?"

"It was so funny," Rory said, wiping a tear away from her eye. "I can't remember the last time you did something that stupid and funny. It was fuckin' hilarious."

"When we finally got to Perkin's," Lily continued the story. "I had to sit between you and Nick, because you were still horny and wanted to ravage him. He, on the other hand, really didn't want to be around you. He lightened up a bit after the waitress had brought him an ice pack to put on his balls."

Everyone chuckled as Heather moaned, "Oh god."

"Nick and the guys went home after Perkin's."

"Someone remind me to call him later," she said, yawning. "What time did we get home?"

"Four," Lily answered, standing up from the couch and stretching. "But we didn't go to bed until seven."

"Why?"

"Because you dumbasses actually wanted to watch *Titanic* when we got back to here."

"How did I end up in Cat's bed?" Heather asked tiredly. "Sorry, Cat, for stealing your bed."

"No problem."

"Cat fell asleep on the floor while watching the movie," Lily explained. "You and I actually watched the entire movie. Watching is the wrong word. We recited the whole entire movie. I played the part of Jack, and you played Rose. It was pretty funny."

"After the movie, you crashed on Cat's bed, and I went home."

"Thanks for taking care of me," Heather said, watching Lily and Rory put their coats on before heading out.

"We thought we would drop by and check on you guys," Rory said, wrapping a scarf around her neck. "It looks like you guys need more rest."

"Mmmmm," was Heather's reply. She was so tired. She needed more sleep. Her eyes closed, and her mind drifted away.

Rory and Lily chuckled softly as they each covered Heather and Cat with a blanket and let them sleep on the floor.

Mission Impossible: Grand Canyon

"Cuz I can feel you breathe," Heather sang at the top of her lungs and totally off key. "Just watching over me, and suddenly I'm melting into you."

Even with Cat's organizational skills and a super early morning start, getting five women from Las Vegas to the Grand Canyon in Arizona was an impossible road trip. First, Hera lost her camera and the friends had to retrace their steps to locate it. The camera was found after Hera dumped out the contents of her purse, insisting it wasn't there.

Second, the in-depth tour of Hoover Dam was a complete waste of time and money. Heather couldn't even remember the dumbass who said the tour would be "cool." She would later blame Cat, who would deny the accusation.

Third, apparently five women can't synchronize when they need to go to the bathroom. Although Lily did win $50 at a slot machine during one of the many breaks. Fourth, how was anyone to know that road construction would hold up a line for more than an hour?

After lunch, everyone agreed to forget about the Grand Canyon and return to Las Vegas. Being cooped up in a car with five women was insane and seeing the majestic scenery of Mother Nature didn't seem worth the drive.

Rory was behind the wheel, hitting 100 mph during the long stretches, while Cat was in the passenger seat with a map in her lap. Lily, Heather, and Hera were scrunched in the back seat, singing and listening to the "sounds of light FM radio," according to one of the deejays.

Night had fallen, and everyone could see city lights on the horizon. They were eager to return to the hotel and do their own thing. Hera, Lily, and Rory wanted to go clubbing while Cat and

Heather just wanted to sit at the slot machines and take advantage of free drinks.

Although Heather had a few drinks at dinner, she wasn't drunk. Well, she was deliriously drunk of being trapped in a car with four other women. Their road trip was a bust. She was tired of sitting in the car. She needed to move. She needed a drink.

"Every night in my dreams, I see you, I feel you," Celine Dion sang from the radio.

"Titanic!" Heather yelled with delight, clapping her hand. "I love this movie."

"I promise I won't let go, Jack," Lily quoted from the movie. "I promise."

"I love that movie," Cat admitted. "That was a great movie."

"Love can touch us one time, and last for a lifetime," Heather sang along with Celine, putting her hand over heart.

"Are we there yet?" Hera moaned, covering her ears. "This is hell! Listening to shit music and being trapped here."

"I think we should be there in about half an hour," Rory guessed. "The lights don't seem to be that far off."

"You're here," Heather belted out, throwing one of her arms inches away from Hera's face and the other smushed against the window. "There's nothing I fear. And I know that my heart will go on."

"I love you, Jack," Lily said, making up lines that easily could have been in the movie. "I love you more, Rose." Then she made kissing noises while rubbing her two index fingers together.

"Kill me now!" Hera groaned.

Cat laughed at Lily's re-enactment and Heather's singing but then sat up when she read the sign ahead.

"Welcome to California," she read slowly, as the car passed the state line.

"Fuck!" Rory swore.

Vodka Four

"We'll stay forever this way," Heather continued to sing, not realizing they were nowhere near Las Vegas. *"You are safe in my heart, and my heart will go on and on."*

CHAPTER 21

Heather and Cat woke up in the early evening and groaned about going for a second night. Instead of getting ready, Heather really wanted to take a long hot shower, throw on her sweats, and watch a movie at her place. She was in no mood to drink again.

"I'm too old for this shit," Cat grumbled, tossing a throw pillow back onto the couch. "Just tell everyone that I don't feel well."

"Hell no!" Heather exclaimed, folding a blanket. "If I'm going out, you're going out. We're in this together."

"What are we? *The Boxcar Children*?"

"Please, no jokes. I need a hot shower to clear my head."

A few minutes later back in her apartment, hot water relieved Heather's sore and bruised body and helped clear the fuzz from her mind. However, no memories of last night's frisky behavior appeared. Heather looked in the mirror at her slender naked figure and saw numerous, but small, black and blue spots.

Was punching really necessary to sober me up or calm me down? Heather thought, with a smirk. *Was I really that out of control that Cat needed to use physical force? Or was Cat merely taking advantage of the fact that she could punch me, knowing I would have no recollection?* Heather doubted the last question in her mind, but then again Cat was pretty crafty.

After pulling on a robe, Heather sat on her bed and grabbed her cell phone. She sighed. A phone call to Nick was necessary. She was already feeling guilty about her devious plan to keep the peace, but last night's behavior was appalling.

"Hey," he greeted easily after the first ring. "How're you feeling?"

Vodka Four

"Like shit."

"That's my girl."

Heather smiled widely. "So, I hear that I should apologize for my behavior."

"Don't worry about it, Willow. Everything was really funny until I was kneed in the groin," Nick said, chuckling at the memory. "My mom was right. Everything's all fun and games until someone gets hurt."

Heather snickered. "I'm so sorry."

"Do you remember anything about last night?"

"I just remember wanting to go to Perkin's, and after that, no memories. Rory and Lily stopped by Cat's this afternoon and filled in the blanks."

"Well, everything they said was true," Nick confirmed. "You were pretty wasted."

"I am so sorry."

"Hey, don't worry about it. I had a fun time."

Heather wondered when he started having a good time last night, as she remembered Rory saying he was pouting and sulking for awhile.

"Anyway, I think we're having dinner at Buzzard Billy's tonight and then catching a movie. Do you want to meet at my place or at the restaurant?" Heather asked, grimacing at the thought of another alcohol-induced night.

"Actually, I think I'm going to bow out tonight," Nick said. "It's Eli's last night, and I want to give you guys some time together."

What? Heather almost yelped. *Huh?*

"Are you sure?" she asked uncertainly.

"I'm positive. Ryan and some other guys are coming over here to hang out."

"You know, you and Ryan are more than welcome to come out tonight."

"It's OK," he reassured her. "I know it's been awhile since you've guys seen each other, and you guys need time to catch up."

"Thank you." Heather was truly touched that Nick was thinking about her friendship with Eli. But then again, she thought, he could also be protecting his balls. "You're too good for me."

"Have a good time."

After dinner and movie, Heather, Eli, and the rest of the group headed to Ellis Cool, a cocktail lounge known for its variety of great martinis. With drinks in hand, Heather and Eli found a vacated area and sat next to each other on a red couch.

Tonight, the tension and awkwardness between them was gone, and Heather wasn't sure whether Nick's absence or her recognized feelings for Eli were contributing factors. The air between Heather and Eli pulled them back to their college years, where no subject was off limit.

"Tell me about Kristen Hartley," Heather encouraged, sipping her chocolate-flavored martini. "I know you went home with her."

"I'm not denying anything," Eli replied, with a wink.

"And?" she pushed, raising one eyebrow.

"I know you guys aren't fond of her, but she's a sure thing," he explained. "How can a guy pass that up? She's not the most subtle person in the world."

Heather laughed, because she agreed. Kristen tried to be discreet and coy, but her actions were always blatantly and painfully obvious to anyone with a pulse.

"What else?" Heather asked.

"What else do you want to know?"

"What was she like? Is she good? Are her boobs ugly? Does she want to start seeing you? Does she know it's a one-night stand? Does she know you're going out tonight? She's not coming here, is she?" Heather fired off quickly.

"I've had better, but she's not the worst. She thought if she talked like a porn star, it would turn me on, and it didn't. It actually distracted me, because she wasn't very good at it."

Heather laughed.

"Are her boobs ugly? What kind of question is that, Vodka Four? Well, they weren't the most beautiful things in the world, but they weren't ugly. They were just there. I had a good time with them."

Heather made a face. She didn't need a mental picture of Eli playing or doing anything with Kristen Hartley's breasts.

"Well, you asked," Eli pointed out, noticing her disapproving look. "Before we did anything, I told her that all I wanted was a good time. She knows I'm leaving Sunday. Yeah, she knows I'm going out again tonight, and do you see her here? I didn't invite her, but I have a feeling she'll try and track me down anyway."

"Because she's psycho."

"Because she wants a boyfriend," Eli corrected.

"Because she's desperate."

"Because she's lonely."

"She and I are the same age, and do you see me throwing myself at every guy who looks at me?" Heather asked.

"One, you are way more secure than her. Two, you are way more attractive than her, so therefore you have more choices."

"Aw, thanks."

"Before I left this morning, she wanted my number, but I took hers, saying I would call her sometime."

"Liar."

"I'm not a liar," Eli explained defensively. "I'm not telling the entire truth. She expects me to call her sometime today, and I figured I'd call her the next time I'm in town."

"I'm surprised she didn't invite herself along."

"Oh, she tried, but I told her that I wasn't sure what was going on. I mentioned Rory was in charge of everything, and she stopped asking questions."

"Nice thinking. Pulling the Rory card," Heather praised, with a grin. "Another person who can't stand Rory."

"Yeah, I know. I also think Kristen is intimidated by her."

"Well, I'm glad you used the Rory card. I didn't want her here anyway."

"I can't believe I missed the good time last night," Eli said, shaking his head.

"See, instead of getting laid, you missed a hilarious episode of Heather making an ass out of herself," she said, hoping some mental image of last night's events would appear. Still nothing.

"According to Rory, it was better than the 'riding on Danny's card hood' incident. She can't wait to share this story to everyone she knows."

"Remind me to kill her later."

Eli chuckled.

"See, this is what happens when you choose Kristen Hartley over me," Heather said grimly, shaking her head.

"Lesson learned."

However, about an hour and several martinis later, Heather and Eli spotted Kristen scanning the crowd at Ellis Cool.

"Shit," he muttered.

"Your girlfriend's here!" Heather said, faking her enthusiasm.

"Shut up."

As soon as Kristen spotted Eli, she smiled, waved, and made her way through the crowd and sat down in the open space on the couch.

Arrogant and desperate were two words that Heather thought best described Kristen. She believed men wanted to sleep with her because she was just as beautiful, but the truth

Vodka Four

was, men wanted to sleep with her because she always put out and she had huge breasts. Kristen falsely believed if an attractive guy had sex with her, then the guy was interested in starting a relationship. Apparently one-night stands and friends with benefits didn't exist in Kristen's mind, Heather had always thought.

Kristen wasn't an unattractive woman, but she wasn't about to grace women's fashion magazine covers in the near future. Unless she was a "before" picture, Rory always liked to point out smugly. Kristen had shoulder length naturally tight curly black hair that she straightened for special occasions. When she was younger and wanted to look like everyone else, Kristen tried tanning her naturally pale complexion, but she always ended up with a sunburn. With an average height, blue eyes, and a slim figure, Kristen was simply plain and ordinary looking except for her large chest that she had no problem showing off.

"Hey, baby," she purred, focusing her attention only on Eli and ignoring Heather. "I had a great time last night."

"You know Heather, right?" he asked, not acknowledging her statement and nodding in Heather's direction.

Kristen tried to hide her frustration behind a fake smile. "Hey, Heather. How's it going?"

"I'm fine," she said, with some amusement.

"Hey, where's Nick? I think he'd be a little jealous that you're monopolizing all of Eli's time."

Nice, Heather thought to herself. *Monopolizing is a big word for you, Kristen. And by the way, do you own any tank tops that don't show off your boobs?*

"He's hanging out with his friends tonight," Heather said casually. She bit her tongue to stop her from saying, "And Nick knows that Eli and I are friends, you insecure and psycho bitch."

"Hey, let's get out of here," Kristen said, returning her attention to Eli. "This place is boring. Let's go somewhere fun."

Heather was ready for battle. *Bring it, Kristen. Seriously, you don't want to mess with me tonight*, she thought. She opened her mouth to say something when an intoxicated Cat bounded over, pulling a chair from a table to sit by the uncomfortable trio.

"Hey, Eli," she said, her voice positively sparkling with excitement. "Remember the time when I beat the crap out of Heather? I was trying to drive Rory's Miata, but I didn't know how to drive a stick shift."

"And I never said I knew how to drive a stick shift!" Heather exclaimed, knowing exactly what Cat was going to say next.

"Whatever, Vodka Four! You don't even remember the incident."

Kristen shot Cat an infuriating look while Eli laughed out loud at the memory.

"I remember driving back and seeing you guys chase each other around the Miata. I nearly died of laughter."

Cat giggled.

"You guys can go to hell," Heather commented, pretending to pout. "I honestly think you guys are making this shit up."

"Just because you can't remember it doesn't mean it didn't happen," Eli said, shaking his head.

"Hey, what's going on?" Lily asked, pulling a chair over by the group. "And why is Heather sulking?"

"I'm not sulking!" she protested.

"We were just talking about Cat beating the crap out of Heather," Eli summarized. "Lil, were you there for that incident?"

Lily shook her head. "I don't think so. But I've heard the story many times. Cat, which incident was funnier? The car incident or last night's 'groin' incident?"

Vodka Four

Cat started laughing hysterically. "Oh, shit. That's too close to call, but I'm going to vote for the 'groin' incident. Last night was just fuckin' hilarious. In either story, I'm still beating the shit out of Heather."

Lily and Eli laughed, while Heather scowled and gave Cat the bird. Just as Cat was about to launch into another trip down memory lane, Kristen stormed off without saying a word.

"Finally!" Heather said exasperated. "I was wondering when she would get the hint."

"With Kristen, it's always going to take awhile," Cat explained, looking over her shoulder to see her stalk off into the crowd. "Besides, I'm sure she wanted another chance to rock Eli's world."

"Rock she did not," Eli murmured.

Everyone laughed out loud.

"You guys had perfect timing," Heather praised. "I was ready for battle."

"Timing?" Cat asked, with an incredulous look. "I saw what was going on from a mile away and saved you guys. Vodka Four, you would've been tapped after a couple of rounds. And Kristen would've made you look like an idiot when you couldn't think of another witty comeback."

"I'm hurt." She pretended to pout, crossing her arms over her chest. "A couple of rounds, Vodka One? Seriously?"

"Sorry," Lily interjected. "But I have to agree with Cat. You're good for a couple of rounds, and that's it."

Heather tried her best to look more hurt and wounded.

"Sorry, Vodka Four," Eli said, poking her in the side. "They're right. Remember the time when you … "

From the bar, Rory saw Cat, Lily, and Eli tease Heather as she waited for two fresh martinis with Hera and Byron. Rory shook her head with amusement when Kristen bumped into her, heading toward the bathroom.

"Sorry," Kristen muttered, looking over her shoulder.

As soon as she recognized Rory was the person who she accidentally bumped into, she stopped walking and whirled around to face Rory, who was taken aback at her sudden movement. "Bitch!"

"Excuse me?" Rory asked, arching a dark eyebrow. She looked at Hera and Byron to make sure she heard Kristen correctly.

"You're a bitch," Kristen spit out. "You're so pathetic."

"And you're a desperate, insecure, and overeager slut," Rory shot back, without thinking. "What the fuck is your problem?"

"You're pathetic for taking my sloppy seconds. Do you really believe Tristan really wants to be with you?"

"More than you."

"You think so?" Kristen asked angrily. "You're so insecure that you have to have any man that looks at you. If you can't have a man, then apparently no one else can, right, Rory? Is that how it works? Just because Tristan hasn't looked in your direction, I can't be with him?"

"What the hell are you talking about? You're not making any sense."

"You're deluding yourself if you think that Tristan truly cares about you."

"You're a dumbass for ever thinking I would ever take your sloppy seconds," Rory said calmly, knowing people were watching the quarrel. She knew they were hoping it would turn into a full-fledged bitch fight. "I know for a fact that you never slept with Tristan. And more importantly, you never knew that I slept with him before last night."

A look of confusion swept over Kristen's face.

Rory continued, taking advantage of the silence. "Tristan and I were sleeping together before the Carrington ball. He only asked you to go, because I turned down his invitation and

Vodka Four

he knew you would say yes. Everything that happened at the ball, Kristen, I know all about it.

"Want to know what else I know? I know he cares about me a helluva lot more than he does about you. In fact, I don't think he actually cares that much about you after the stunts you pulled at the ball. So, if there's anyone who is taking sloppy seconds, I think that would be you."

"You're a fuckin' whore," Kristen swore. "You and that anorexic bitch ... "

"I'm sorry," Rory interrupted kindly. "Anorexic bitch? Is that how you're describing one of my friends?"

"You know who I'm talking about. Heather fuckin' Kincannon. Anorexic bitch."

"She's not anorexic! She just has a high metabolism!" Hera shouted, standing behind Rory.

"She's an anorexic bitch who gets everything she wants by playing mind games. There are two guys who are desperately in love with her, and she's stringing both of them along. She likes to break hearts because it makes her feel powerful."

Rory threw her head back and started to laugh, which pissed off Kristen even more. But her laughter didn't last long, as she stared at Kristen with a serious tone in her voice.

"The next time you say anything bad about my friends, I will not hesitate to get physical with you, Kristen. In fact, I will make your pathetic life more miserable and depressing than it already is. If you say anything bad about any of them, you better make sure I'm not around to hear it."

Kristen just stood there, staring at Rory, who continued to lash out in a calm and serious manner.

"In addition to being a desperate, insecure, and overeager slut, the only reason any guy sleeps with you is because of your gigantic rack that you constantly have to show off," Rory shot out, with fire in her eyes. Kristen knew better than to say anything. "Seriously, Kristen. Guys hit on you because they know you're a sure thing."

"You're a liar," Kristen replied weakly, but Rory could see her words were sinking in. "You're just jealous."

"I will never be jealous of you," she said slowly for emphasis, inching a little closer. "Do you honestly believe that sleeping with Eli makes you better than me? Makes you better than Heather?"

Kristen opened her mouth to say something but quickly closed it when she thought about the circumstances. She knew Heather and Eli were close friends, but she didn't think Heather would ask what happened between them.

"Do you honestly believe Eli is interested in you, Kristen? Did he give you his phone number? Did he invite you along tonight? Did you believe he wasn't going to say anything to Heather or to anyone of us? Don't be stupid. Don't think that last night with Eli was something special. And don't think for a second that it's going to turn into something more."

Kristen just looked at Rory with wide and sad eyes. For a split second, Rory almost felt sorry for her, but Kristen needed a realistic look at her life. She needed to stop living in a fantasy world. Finally, Kristen walked past Rory and Hera toward the exit door.

"So, that was interesting," Hera said, noting Rory's silence. "What's up her ass?"

"I have no idea," Rory said, shrugging and then grabbing the two martinis the bartender placed near her.

"I'm disappointed that scratching and hair pulling wasn't involved," Byron said, grabbing two more martinis from the bar. "You totally could've taken her, Rory."

Rory smiled at the thought as walked toward her circle of friends.

"So, Kristen Hartley hates me and Heather," she announced, sipping her drink and handing the other to Eli, who needed a refill.

"What?" Heather asked, sighing. "What are you talking about?"

Vodka Four

"Well," Rory started. "I was ordering drinks when she ran into me, and she started tearing into me for no reason at all! Obviously, she wasn't well, because everyone knows not to mess with me. Seriously."

"What happened?" Lily asked, with curiosity.

"I'm so disappointed in you," Byron said, shaking his head after Rory and Hera finished the story. "No bitch fight. What is a night out without a fight?"

Everyone laughed out loud.

"I hate to say this," Eli said hesitantly, looking at Rory. "But that was cold, Vodka 10."

"It was the truth," Rory corrected, rolling her eyes. "You know it. I know it. Everybody knows it. Kristen needs to stop living in a dream world and face reality."

"Did you have to be so mean?"

"Like you were nice to her," Lily said sarcastically. "Not once did you attempt to include her in our conversation."

"Fine, I'm guilty of that. But at least I was trying to spare her feelings."

"By ignoring her?" Cat asked, looking a little confused.

"Fine, I see your point."

"You weren't trying to spare her feelings," she explained. "You want to make sure she was going to be available to you whenever you're horny."

"Not true!"

"Byron, back me up."

"Sorry, bro, but Vodka One's right," Byron said, apologetically. "I would've done the same thing."

"You see," Rory said, waving her almost empty martini glass in the air. "I don't have a problem being brutally honest with people. If their feelings are hurt, buck up, kiddo. The world's not going to end because you're hurt and crying. But then, there are people like you." She pointed to Eli with her drink. "You're passive aggressive. You want to get her off your back, but you don't do it in a blatantly obvious way."

"I don't want to look like a bad guy," Eli admitted. "But on the other hand, Kristen definitely knew I wasn't interested in her from the start. It's not my fault that she was hoping for something more."

"Everyone knows she wants to be in a relationship," Lily pointed out. "I think she feels like a loser because she's not married."

"That's kind of sad," Cat commented. "We're all the same age, and none of us are married. But yet we're not throwing ourselves at the first guy that looks at us."

"I know!" Heather exclaimed.

"On the bright side, Vodka Four can remember this incident," Rory said, with a smirk. "So, you guys want to talk about last night again?"

CHAPTER 22

Sunday, February 6

Heather wanted to go to bed so badly. She was tired. She was cranky. And she wanted to go to bed. That's all she wanted. She just wanted to lay her head on her pillow and fall asleep. But no, stupid Eli used a stupid guilt trip on her to have a stupid cup of coffee before he left later that morning. Stupid Eli.

As Eli ordered decaffeinated coffee, Heather tried to remember the last time she was up this late and figured this was going to ruin her sleep schedule for the next couple of days.

At bar time, everyone headed toward Perkin's for a late-night meal and then Byron and Hera invited the group to their place to play Hera's favorite game, Cranium. The game ended about 7 a.m., and as everyone was heading home, Eli persuaded Heather to have coffee at Kelsea's Coffee Cup.

"I hate you," she growled at Eli, narrowing her eyes as he set a coffee cup in front of her. Eli laughed out loud.

"Come on, Vodka Four," he said easily. The worst of it was he didn't even look tired. He appeared cheerful and refreshed. Bastard.

"I'm too old for this shit."

Eli chuckled. "Come on, we're the same age and look at how I'm doing."

"Fuck you."

"Kiss your mama with that mouth?"

Heather gave him the stink eye and flipped him off.

Eli sipped his coffee. "I had great time catching up with you and everyone else. I've really missed this place."

She smiled. "I had fun too. It seemed like we were never apart."

"Yeah, I know," he agreed. "Despite the distance and time, some things will never change between us."

"Except I hate you," she added. "You're keeping me from getting my beauty sleep, and now, Kristen freakin' Hartley hates me!"

Eli laughed again. "I am so sorry, Heather. I really am."

"You know what?" she threw out pointedly. "I don't think you are. I think you're enjoying the moment, knowing that you don't have to see her and that you're leaving me with your mess. Kristen Hartley. Eli, really?" She made a disgusted noise.

"She's a sure thing," he explained, shrugging.

"You could've been nice to her last night," Heather pointed out. "Now she hates me. Thanks a lot, you ugly bastard."

"What a potty mouth," he mocked. "I don't remember you ever having this coarse of a vocabulary."

Again, Heather flipped him off.

"So, I have to tell you something," he said seriously, looking at her with his beautiful blue eyes. Her heart started to beat faster.

"What?" she asked, meeting his gaze.

"Even before you guys started dating, I've always thought Nick was a good guy. And even now, he's still a good guy."

"Why are you telling me this? I know."

"Heather," he said gently. "You and I have been friends for more than 10 years, and I know you. Nick is in the process of getting to know you, and he knew something was wrong Friday night. He wasn't the only one."

Shit, she thought to herself. *Was I really that transparent?*

Vodka Four

"Vodka Four, I know the idea of me and Nick together in one room didn't exactly thrill you. Were you expecting a shoving match? Were you expecting us to fight over you?"

"Hey," Heather said shortly, her eyes narrowing at him. "Maybe."

Eli chuckled. "My my, someone sure thinks highly of herself. You're not that pretty, you know."

She gave him the finger again.

"Seriously, I'm a little hurt that you'd think I would sabotage your relationship."

"Eli, I didn't think that at all," Heather protested. "I just didn't want you guys getting all territorial. You've been my friend forever. Not to mention, you're one of my ex-boyfriends. I had the right to cover my bases."

"Just remember that you don't have to worry about me. Ever."

"Sorry."

"Don't be sorry," Eli said, with a smile. "Be smart. You know me."

Heather returned his smile.

"He better take care of you," he warned.

"So far so good," she said.

After finishing their coffees, Heather and Eli headed toward the parking lot to say goodbye.

"Want a ride home?" he offered.

Heather shook her head. "I think I can walk from here. Thanks for the coffee."

"Anytime, Vodka Four. Anytime," he murmured, pulling her close for a hug.

She took a deep breath as she circled her arms around his waist. She missed being close to him. She missed everything about him. She really didn't want him to leave — again.

"Be good," Eli said softly before kissing her forehead. "I'll call you sometime."

"OK," she replied, pulling back and forcing a smile. She wasn't going to cry in front of him. She didn't want him to know he was breaking her heart again.

"See you later, Vodka Four."

And then he was gone. As Heather walked to her apartment, she thought about the good times she had with Eli. She knew he was always going to be a part of her life, and she was always going to love him. But she also knew a relationship between them wouldn't work right now. She wasn't willing to sacrifice her family and friends to be with him.

She needed to move on — again. Heather was never the type of person to sit around and pine for a lost love. Nick. Heather smiled brightly. He was great guy who wanted to be with her. He was the perfect stepping stone.

CHAPTER 23

Saturday, February 12

Cat hated Valentine's Day. She couldn't remember the last time she had been with someone from the opposite sex on the stupid ass holiday. She always smiled when her mother sent her a Valentine's Day card with a $20 bill tucked inside, with a note saying, "Do something special." However, Cat usually didn't feel so lame as Heather, Rory, Lily, or Hera would also be single around this time of year.

This year, Rory invited Lily and Cat over for a slumber party on the dreaded holiday weekend. Rory stocked up on plenty of junk food and horror movies, planning to indulge and sit around in her pajamas. She didn't need to convince Lily or Cat to spend the weekend with her as Hera had plans with Byron and Heather and Nick headed to the Twin Cities after work Friday.

With a blue duffel bag over her shoulder and a pillow under her arm, Cat walked into Rory's town home.

"Hola," Rory called from the living room.

Dumping her duffel bag in an open area leading to the living room, Cat saw Rory, already decked out in baby blue flannel pajamas, sitting on the couch and watching a rerun of *Friends* on TV, with a big glass of a strawberry daiquiri in hand.

"How was work?" Rory asked, petting a gray Persian cat napping in her lap and sipping her drink.

"The same," Cat replied, heading to the kitchen to pour herself a big ass glass of her favorite fruity drink. "How did you manage to get this weekend off?"

"I traded with some people."

"I have a question," she said, sitting on the opposite end of the couch, with drink in her hand.

"Shoot."

"Why aren't you going out this weekend?"

"I don't feel like it," Rory replied, shrugging. "I don't feel like going out to the bars and watching all of the stupid couples canoodling."

"Why not go out with Tristan?"

"Because he and I aren't a couple. We're just having sex."

"He didn't push you to go out?"

"Nope. I told him that I didn't want anything from him, and he said OK."

"You're training him very well," Cat praised, sipping her daiquiri.

"I associate Valentine's Day with love," Rory explained. "I honestly don't want to spend the weekend with someone that I don't love. I'm not good at faking my feelings. Hope Saint James knows there's no love lost between us, but we tolerate each other in public. Unless she pulled a stunt like Kristen Hartley, then I have no problem publicly humiliating her."

"Oh!" Cat's eyes danced with excitement. "Speaking of Kristen Hartley! She's telling everyone at work that you assaulted her because she had slept with Eli. She said Heather's still in love with him, and you were upset because he was interested in her."

"Bullshit!"

"I know! But no one believes her. People ask me to verify her story, and I set them straight."

"That's good."

"I've got another question," Cat said, petting a second Persian cat that was sniffing her drink. "When was the last time you fell in love?"

Vodka Four

Shit, when was the last time I fell in love? Rory thought to herself, muting the TV with the remote control.

"When I was teenager," she finally said. "I was living at a youth home at the time when a new boy came to live at the house. Brent Craig. Oh, Cat, he was beautiful, and I fell in love with him instantly. He definitely looked like a rebel."

"Why was he at the youth home?"

"He had stolen his parents' car a couple of times and defied curfews a lot. He was a very bad, bad, bad, bad boy, and I loved him so much."

Cat laughed.

"I'm serious. Brent didn't care about anything or anybody. He rarely talked to anyone, and he always fought with staff. They were so afraid of him because he could get really aggressive. The police knew him by name because they were over at the house a lot to either settle him down or transport him to the juvenile detention center."

"Did he fall in love with you?"

"Yeah, once we got to know each other. I was the only girl at the youth home who didn't throw myself at him or pass him sexually suggestive notes, which by the way, he gave to staff to get the other girls in trouble." Rory chuckled at the memory, shaking her head.

"Nice."

"Yeah, he was smart. We had to hide our attraction because youth home residents weren't allowed to be romantically involved with one another. It interfered with our treatment."

"What did you guys do?" Cat asked curiously.

"Well, we were at the youth home for a reason," Rory said, with a wink. "We were two very sneaky kids. Staff don't watch the kids all of the time if you were good. If you behave well, you earn staff trust and they let you go out in the community by yourself."

"What do you do?"

"You can shop if you had any money. You can go for a walk. The point was to do well so that staff weren't watching you all of the time. The rule was you could go out in public with someone of the same sex. But a lot of the times, Brent and I were the only ones who did really well. For some stupid reason, staff trusted us to be together in public. They figured we couldn't get into trouble if we walked to the movie theater. But Brent and I were sneaky and found places to make out or have sex."

"Why am I not surprised that you guys had sex?"

"Because you know me too well, my dear Cat," Rory said wisely. "Even during group outings to the lake or park, Brent and I found ways to quickly make out. It wasn't really hard to outsmart the staff."

"Apparently not."

"Brent had home visits about once or twice each month. Fortunately, his parents lived about an hour away from the youth home. He always found a way to get back into town so that he and I could spend time together. Once, his older brother had even rented a hotel room for us after Brent gave him some money. My mother lived like 20 minutes away from the youth home. So, when I had a home visit, I found ways to get back to hang out with him. It really wasn't that hard to find ways to be together."

"Did any of the other kids at the youth home know about you and Brent?"

"A few did and then tattled on us, but once again, Brent and I were really sneaky. Whenever staff confronted us, we lied and denied the accusations. And really, staff never caught us together and so they just assumed the person who was tattling on us was trying to get us into trouble. To make sure staff didn't catch on, every now and then, Brent and I would get into a huge argument where staff had to separate us."

"You guys were really sneaky."

"Yes, we were," Rory said proudly.

"What happened next?"

"Brent was doing well at the youth home. He really didn't clean up his act ... he just got smart about his treatment program. It looked like he was doing well so that he could go home. But once he got there, he just planned on doing the same sneaky stuff."

"So, he went home?"

"Yeah, staff saw he was making progress and recommended that he be discharged."

"How did you take that?" Cat asked.

Rory shrugged. "At first, I was devastated and heartbroken, because I wouldn't see him every day. Out of all the kids that I had met at the youth home, he and I understood each other so well. He didn't desert me when he left because he would back when he had the chance. At first, it worked out well, but then my mom left town and I kind of became a mess after that. Brent tried to help, but I kind of shut down and didn't let anyone in. He and I eventually lost contact."

"So, he was your first love?"

"Yeah," Rory said, thinking about the question for a second. "Yeah, he was my first and only love."

"I might cry."

"Shut up," she said, throwing a small sofa pillow at her and causing the two cats to jump off the couch and head for cover.

Cat and Rory were watching TV when Lily joined them after getting off work. After making a drink and settling down in the wood papason chair, she convinced Rory and Cat to watch a kid movie called *Little Manhattan* before viewing Rory's movie choice, *Valentine*. The trio laughed at humorous scenes as they watched the movie about a 10-year-old kid falling in love for the first time.

"Wasn't that a great movie?" Lily asked when the movie ended. "I think it's one of the cutest movies ever."

"It was cute," Cat agreed. "And funny."

Jennifer Elliott

"Yeah," Rory added. "It was good. I liked it."

As Rory ordered pizza, Lily and Cat changed into sweatpants and T-shirts. With their drinks refilled, everyone returned to the living room to watch TV as they waited for the pizza.

"Cat, tell me about your first love," Rory said, realizing she wasn't interested in watching TV and muting the sound.

"High school boyfriend named Theo Elstad," Cat said after a moment of thought. "He was my first boyfriend."

"But was he your first love?" Lily asked, pulling a blanket over her as she curled up in the papason chair.

"What kind of first love are we talking about?" Cat asked, stretching her body out on the couch when Rory moved to the floor with some pillows. "I fell in love with Joshua Glasser when I was in third grade. Oh, he was this cute little boy with blond hair and blue eyes. I was completely in love with him."

Rory and Lily laughed.

"He was a year older than I was, and I wasn't the only girl in my class who loved him. Unfortunately for me, he liked sweet and innocent Bridget Conroy for awhile before he had eyes for little slutty Jackie Schrader."

"Can a third grader really be slutty?" Rory asked, her head resting on a couple of bed pillows and her body covered by a quilt that Cat had made for her for Christmas.

"Jackie wanted to be slutty. She was the only girl in our class who wore makeup because she had three or four older sisters."

"I would classify Josh as a childhood crush," Lily said thoughtfully.

"I fell in love with Martin Rowell when I was in seventh grade," Cat offered. "Once again, he was a year older than I was. I thought I was going to spend the rest of my life with him."

Vodka Four

"Did he know this?" Rory asked, with a little bit of amusement in her voice.

"Of course not. As always, he had a crush on someone else," Cat answered grimly. "But he and I kept in touch throughout the years. He even visited me when I was in college."

"Then why don't I remember him? You and I met when you were in college."

"I didn't introduce him to you or Heather because I was afraid you guys would steal him away from me."

Lily and Rory laughed.

"We would've done no such thing. If we knew about your feelings for him, we would've stayed away," Rory said. "Did you ever tell him that you loved him?"

"Once when he came to visit me, I told him that I had a crush on him back in junior high. He and I laughed about it, and then we started sleeping together."

"Really?" Lily inquired, her interested piqued. "What happened?"

"We basically used each other for sex. We weren't in a relationship, but of course, I was hoping that it would turn into that. I figured Martin had to care about me because we were both virgins when we had sex."

"Wait a second," Rory interrupted. "How old were you when you lost your virginity?"

"I was 21."

"Really?"

"It's not like I didn't know what sex was about," Cat clarified. "I had made out and gotten completely naked with plenty of guys before Martin and I had sex. Believe me, I wanted to have sex, but when it came time, I was so nervous. Thankfully, the guys I was with understood and didn't push the issue."

"So, Martin was 22 when he first had sex," Lily pointed out.

"He's a very religious guy," Cat explained. "He and I went to the same Lutheran school and church. He tried to wait for marriage, but his curiosity got the better of him."

"Interesting little fact about you," Rory said thoughtfully.

"Thanks. Anyway, the more Martin and I hung out together and had sex, I fell in love with him again. I really thought he and I would be perfect together, but he never saw me as anything more than just a friend. After he graduated from college, he moved to Washington, D.C., because he had some friends out there."

"Did he know that you fell in love with him again?" Lily asked.

"Yeah," Cat said, with a sigh. "I was absolutely crushed when he told me that he was moving. I then confessed that I was in love with him and begged him to give us a chance. Martin kindly and gently told me that he couldn't see us in a relationship, but that he cherished our friendship and blah blah blah."

"What a jackass," Rory muttered.

"At the time, I was obviously crushed and thought he was decent guy, but looking back, he was feeding me a line so that he didn't look like an asshole."

"He could've been telling the truth," Lily defended. "Maybe he didn't want to ruin the great friendship that you guys had."

Cat shook her head. "No. I never heard from him again. After he moved to Washington, he never called. He never wrote. Nothing."

"Jackass," Lily then muttered.

"Let's get back to Theo," Rory said. "He was your high school boyfriend?"

"Yeah." Cat nodded. "He was the first guy to ever tell me that he loved me. We were in a relationship for seven months during our senior year. We broke up after we graduated."

Vodka Four

"Did you tell him that you loved him?"

"Yeah. Theo was my first boyfriend. I had no idea what I was doing. I thought I did, but really, I had no clue."

Lily and Rory laughed.

"Was he a good boyfriend?" Lily asked.

"Yeah, I guess," Cat said, shrugging. "I really didn't know what to expect since I had never been in relationship before. We argued here and there, and I was really mad at him when he called me a 'stick in the mud.'"

"What?" Lily exclaimed. "What was that about?"

"I don't remember the whole entire conversation, but Theo and his best friend were working on some stuff. And one of Theo's projects was to help me loosen up because I was a stick in the mud."

"What a jackass," Rory muttered.

"Yeah, I know! I was really mad at him, but he used his charm and smooth talk to settle me down."

"I would have dumped his ass," Lily mumbled.

"Yeah, in hindsight, I probably should have, but then again, he was my first boyfriend and my first real relationship, so I didn't know what the hell I was doing."

"He broke up with you, didn't he?" Rory asked.

"Yup. I was crushed at first, but I got over him because I was starting college in a few months anyway."

"Your turn, Lily," Rory announced as the three sat at the table when the pizza arrived. "Who was your first love?"

"Kyle McCartney."

"Wait, that name sounds familiar," she said, thinking about the name. "Kyle McCartney. I've heard that name before."

Lily smiled and looked at Cat, waiting for Rory to realize that she knew Kyle McCartney.

"He used to work at Skylight!" Rory finally said, lighting up. "Oh, Lil, he was hot! I remember you guys being heavily involved with each other. And I mean, heavily."

Cat laughed. "OK, tell me more about Kyle!"

"I had just moved to Amery Lake after dropping out of college my freshman year," Lily remembered. "When I was hired at the bar, Kyle caught my eye. I didn't think anything would happen because I was in the process of losing weight. Not to mention, hundreds of girls threw themselves at him."

"Yeah, he was really hot," Rory agreed dreamily and looked at Cat. "Think a younger version of Denzel Washington."

"Ooooh," Cat replied, imagining a young Denzel with Lily. "So, what happened?"

"One night after work, we were cleaning up, getting super wasted in the process. He invited me over to his place where we drank some more, watched a movie, and then had sex. And he was fuckin' fantastic."

"Lucky bitch," Rory muttered before taking a bite from her pizza slice.

"Timeout," Cat said, shaking her head. "Lil, you know I love you and everything, but if Kyle was so incredibly hot, Rory, why weren't you hitting on him?"

"Because I had a dumbass boyfriend at the time," Rory replied bitterly. "Believe me, if I was single, I would've been all over Kyle."

"That's right," Lily exclaimed, remembering what happened. "You were dating the university's quarterback at the time! Yeah, he was a total moron, but he was hot! I think the only reason why you stayed with him was because he was really good in bed and he just showered you with presents."

"His parents were super filthy rich," Rory agreed. "And you're right. He was fantastic in bed, but a complete dumbass in public. Everybody loved him because he was a great quarterback. He loved spending money, and I had no problem being there when he did."

Cat and Lily smirked and shook their heads.

"So, what happened between you and Kyle?" Cat asked, sipping her drink.

Vodka Four

"Well, after we had sex, we started dating. Then after a month of dating and sleeping together, Kyle wanted to be in a committed relationship, which just made me the happiest girl in the world. I immediately fell in love with him — well, I thought it was love — because he was so kind and nice. Everything went great for the first six months. Kyle was a fantastic boyfriend who seemed to understand me."

"What happened after the six months?"

"He kind of stopped being loving and attentive and started being a jerk and an asshole. But I was so completely in love with him that I didn't care. I mean, I cared that he was turning into a jackass, but I was so determined to make the relationship work. I knew Kyle smoked pot, but he became an even bigger pothead during our relationship. I had issues with that, because instead of spending time with me, he wanted to light up with his buddies."

"What a jackass," Cat muttered.

"I remember this," Rory jumped in. "You weren't the happiest camper. I remember having the longest discussions with you about your relationship with him."

"Yeah, I remember too," Lily said, smiling. "You told me to ditch his ass, because I deserved better. Didn't I come back with, 'But I love him, Rory.' God, I was an idiot."

Rory laughed. "You were in love, Lil."

"So, what happened?" Cat asked before munching on her pizza.

"At first, I tried talking to him. He promised he would change, but he didn't. I tried to let it go, but I couldn't. Finally, I had enough of his jackass behavior and dumped him. But a week later, Kyle came crying to me, saying how much he loved me and blah blah blah. Of course, I was so in love with him that I took him back. And then for the next year and a half, he and I had a tumultuous relationship. When he started acting like a jerk, I left him. Then he begged me to come back, and because I was an idiot, I went back.

"He and I even moved in together, thinking that would help our relationship. But I think it just made everything worse. We really tried to make the relationship work, but we were so young and just made some stupid choices."

"What happened that made you not go back again?" Cat asked.

"He cheated on me," Lily said simply. "That was the final straw. I caught him in bed with some skank, and I left him. When he came crying for forgiveness, I told him that I couldn't and our relationship was finally over. He called me for a month, saying he was sorry and how much he loved me, but I knew I could never trust him again."

"What happened when you guys had to work together?"

"I quit when I found out he cheated on me. I couldn't work with him. Thankfully, Rory helped me out, letting me crash at her place for awhile. I found a piddly little job to save money."

"And at work," Rory continued. "Kyle constantly asked me questions about you and how to win you back. I hated working with him, because he was such a whiny little baby."

"Does he still work at Skylight?" Cat asked.

Rory and Lily shook their heads. "He was fired for drinking too much on the job," Rory replied. "And he was giving away too many free drinks to the women customers. After Kyle realized Lily wasn't coming back, he went through a whore phase, where he had to sleep with every woman that looked at him."

"Do you know where he's at now?"

"Last I heard, he moved to Milwaukee after he was fired," Rory said. "He had some friends out there."

"I think his family was from that area, too," Lily added.

"Well, we've loved some real winners," Cat said sarcastically, cleaning up the table.

Rory and Lily chuckled.

Vodka Four

"This is one of my favorite quotes," Rory said thoughtfully. "The most prized possession a man could ever have is a woman's heart. Or love. I think it's love. Shit, I can't remember."

Lily and Cat snickered at Rory's inability to correctly remember a quote. After cleaning up the table, they returned to the living room to watch more horror movies.

Cat was happy. She, Lily, and Rory watched movies and TV, talked about the gossip at Anastacia Square, drank strawberry daiquiris, went to bed late, and slept even later the next day.

For Cat, the weekend was perfect. She wasn't spending the "most romantic time of the year" alone in her apartment with her two cats. Most days and weekends, Cat honestly didn't have a problem with that, but for some reason, she felt like a loser when Valentine's Day rolled around. She knew she wasn't alone and knew she wasn't the only person in the world who didn't have a boyfriend.

But this year, Cat didn't need a boyfriend to make her happy. She hanging out with two of her best friends, talking and laughing. On Monday — the day she dreaded and hated so much as a single woman — her work day was made when Rory sent her a dozen yellow roses.

CHAPTER 24

Thursday, March 3

Heather was happy. She couldn't help but feel happy. A little more than two weeks had passed since the romantic Valentine's Day getaway in the Twin Cities.

To ease her guilt about still loving Eli and in an effort to move on, she had booked a room with a Jacuzzi in a hotel near the Mall of America and one of her favorites stores — Ikea. After work, she and Nick drove to the cities and grabbed dinner at a nice restaurant. The next day was spent walking around the Mall of America and Ikea, with Nick asking if Heather really needed to buy cat beds for Merry and Pippen or a soft-serve ice cream machine. Crossing her fingers, Heather hoped Nick was a fan of the Minnesota Wild when she surprised him with two tickets to the game. Her guess paid off as Nick loved the team and enjoyed attending the game later that night.

Since then, their relationship has been wonderful and peaceful. During the week, Nick gave her a couple of days to herself — either for "Heather time" or to catch up with her friends. During the weekends, they usually caught a matinee show at the movie theater and played board games or rented a movie with their friends at night. They had fallen into a nice routine that Heather liked.

The best part was Nick didn't fall into any of the three categories that Heather normally grouped guys in: the puppy, the pusher, and the peddler. He enjoyed spending time with her, but that didn't make him a puppy. He liked going out to the bars every now and then, but that didn't make him

Vodka Four

a pusher. He didn't mind discussing some of his fears and worries, but that didn't make him a peddler.

Heather couldn't believe she had been with Nick for about two months when she was flipping through the appointment book at work. February had come and gone, and March was just beginning. And for some reason, she couldn't help but include Nick in her future plans, such as weekend with her sister, Michelle, and her family who lived north of the Twin Cities. In the summer, maybe they could take an extended weekend somewhere by Amtrak.

Other than the Eli situation, their relationship was fantastic. Nick was still a wonderful and nice guy who still treated her like a princess. And the sex was still incredible.

However, Heather couldn't help but wonder how long their relationship was going to remain perfect. Her previous relationships crumbled around the two- or three-month mark. She either became annoyed with the guys for changing into a completely different person or the guys' irritating habits that she ignored at first started to drive her insane.

For awhile, Heather thought there was something wrong with her whenever a relationship failed after a few months. Maybe she wasn't the perfect girlfriend after all. Maybe she needed more patience. More she needed to be more understanding.

"There's nothing wrong with you," Rory had said after Heather's last break up.

"Then why can't I be in a relationship that lasts longer than two months?" Heather had cried. "Seriously? What's so freakin' hard about it?"

"You have to be with the right guy."

"My last three relationships lasted two months, Rory. There seriously has to be something wrong with me if I can't maintain a relationship for more than two months."

"There's nothing wrong with you. It's the dicks you date."

Rory's words gave Heather a little comfort, but deep down inside, Heather wondered whether something was wrong with her. Why couldn't she maintain a relationship for more than two months? The longest relationship she had ever been in was with Eli. As much as she didn't want to think about the many different reasons her past relationships failed, Heather wondered whether her current relationship was on the same path.

After work, she quickly cleaned her apartment before Nick dropped by with Chinese food. By the time he arrived, she had plates and silverware set out on the kitchen counter. During dinner, they shared funny stories that happened at work and made tentative weekend plans.

"What do you want to do tonight?" Nick asked as he loaded the dishwasher once they were finished with dinner.

"Not much," Heather admitted, scooping up Merry in her arms and petting him. "I feel like laying low tonight."

"I kind of feel like going out," he said slowly. "It's karaoke night at Lucky's."

"I know Cat's staying in, and Rory and Lily are working tonight. I really don't feel like going out tonight."

"Ryan and some other guys were going out later."

"Well, you can go out with the guys. I don't mind," she said casually. "I really don't mind staying home by myself."

"Why don't come out with me?"

"Because I don't feel like it."

"Why not?"

"Because I just feel like laying low," Heather repeated, becoming a little impatient with the conversation and letting go of Merry.

"You should come out for awhile," Nick insisted. "When you're ready to go, then we'll go home."

"Nick, I really don't feel like going out tonight. But you are more than welcome to hang out with your friends. I'm not keeping you from hanging out with them."

Vodka Four

"Come on. It'll be fun."

"Seriously, Nick, I don't want to go."

"God, you're boring," he sighed, and immediately wished he could take the words back when Heather's head whipped up and her piercing green eyes glared at him.

"Fuck you."

"I'm sorry, Heather. I didn't mean to say that," he apologized.

"But you did," she said angrily. "Sorry that my life bores you, Nick, but this is my life. My life doesn't depend on getting drunk on the weekends."

"Neither does mine."

"Look, my days of going downtown to get drunk and hooking up with someone are over. This might sound boring to you, but to me, this is my life."

"But what about the night we met, Heather?" Nick countered, starting to get angry himself. "Deep Pink isn't exactly a casual night with the girls."

"You don't need to remind me. Yeah, I get drunk every now and then, but I don't want to do that every single weekend. I have more important things to do."

"Like spend quality time with your cats?" Nick asked sarcastically.

"Get out," she yelled. Oh, she was pissed now! Like he should be telling her how to spend her life. "Get the fuck out of my apartment."

"What happened to the girl in Eli's stories?" he asked angrily, ignoring her last statement. "You had no problem going out and getting drunk when he was around. What? Am I not good enough to take downtown?"

"Stop being overdramatic, Nick. I hadn't seen him since he moved to frickin' California. Of course, I'm going to go out whenever he's in town."

"How many times has he seen you drunk and party like you were in a *Girls Gone Wild* video?"

Jennifer Elliott

"We were in freakin' college!" Heather shouted at him. "That's what college students do! They do their homework during the week, and party like it's spring break in Florida on the weekends."

"So, you only become Vodka Four whenever Eli's around?" he snapped. He was livid at Eli for being a significant part of her life and knowing more about her than he did. He was angry at Heather for being a different person when Eli was around.

"And while we're on the subject of Eli," Nick continued. "What the fuck was your problem during his visit?"

"What are you talking about?" Heather asked, but she knew what he was talking about. At the moment, she wasn't about to tell him the truth because he didn't even deserve to hear the truth. He was being a complete asshole.

"You and I barely saw each other when he was in town."

"He was here for only a week!"

"We didn't even have sex."

"Do we need to have sex all of the time?" Heather yelled. "Would that have made you feel better if we had sex when he was in town?"

"You weren't yourself," Nick insisted. "You said everything was fine. Rory said everything was fine, but it wasn't. I know you, Heather. I could tell something was wrong."

"Maybe you wanted something to be wrong because of your insecurities about my friendship with Eli," she shot back.

"That's fuckin' bullshit, Heather. Don't try to pin this on me. I know something was wrong."

"Nothing was wrong! I wanted to spend time with Eli because he and I have been friends for so long! What's wrong with that?"

"He's your ex-boyfriend!"

Vodka Four

"He and I were friends long before we were in a relationship," she pointed out. "Are you saying that I can't be friends with any of my ex-boyfriends?"

"I'm not saying that," he said, trying to calm down. "I'm just saying that you weren't acting like yourself that week."

"I don't know how many times I can say this, but nothing was wrong. Why don't you believe me, Nick?"

He thought about her question for a moment before answering. "We didn't have sex at all while he was here. I had a feeling you were avoiding both of us. Something was wrong."

"Do we have to have sex all of the time?" Heather asked again, starting to become defensive again. "Is that the equivalent of marking your territory? By having sex, does that mean I like you more than him?"

"Stop it," Nick said harshly. "Stop it."

"I'm not telling you this again," she said, narrowing her eyes at him. "Nothing was wrong when Eli was in town."

"I don't believe you."

"At this point, I don't care." And she truthfully didn't care. He was being a complete jackass about everything. Heather was glad that Nick didn't know the truth, because she somehow figured he throw it back at her.

"How come I never see Vodka Four?" he asked, returning to the original subject matter. "What happened to her?"

"That girl only exists in stories. I'm not in college anymore."

"Neither am I, but that doesn't stop me from having a good time."

"Good for you, Nick," Heather threw out sarcastically. "My life doesn't revolve around getting drunk and laid. My goals have changed since graduating from college."

"Like finding a job and getting two cats?"

"Fuck you." She was furious, and she really wanted to throw something at his head. Anything. One of her cats. A glass. Something. In reality, if Heather had thrown a glass at his head, it probably would've sailed passed his head and crashed into the wall behind him.

But in her fantasy, the glass hit him in the face, making him sink to the floor in pain and agony — and wouldn't she be the one to drive him to the hospital? Knowing her crappy instincts in stressful situations, Heather would frantically call 911 and then the police would come and question her. Then she'd probably get slapped with a domestic disturbance ticket or something. And Nick would probably lose an eye.

Throwing something at his head probably wasn't worth the trouble, Heather thought disgustedly.

"Where the hell is Vodka Four? I saw her once when Eli was in town," he challenged. "I've heard the wild stories about the Vodka Girls. Where the hell are they?"

"They grew up," Heather shouted. "We grew up, Nick! I'm 29 years old. God knows, I don't look like I'm 29, but I am. I was Vodka Four when I was in college. I'm not her anymore, and I don't want to be. I don't want to lead her life. This is the life I lead now. Take it or leave it."

Nick looked at her. God, she was pissed. Her green eyes were still glaring at him, and both of her hands were firmly planted on her hips. But he was pissed too. He just wanted her to go downtown with him and his friends. One night downtown wasn't going to hurt her. What did she have against having a good time among friends?

Finally, Nick coolly walked past her and slammed the door on the way out. When the door closed, Heather willed herself not to cry. The great relationship she had been confident about had finally collapsed. This was their first fight. This was their first serious fight.

Heather wondered whether Nick would come back, apologize, and say everything was going to be OK. She would feel better if he did.

Vodka Four

There's nothing wrong with my life, Heather thought to herself as she laid down on her bed. *There's nothing wrong with my life.*

Heather was too busy wiping her tears away and petting her cats to hear Hera silently open her apartment door.

I am such a bastard, Nick thought miserably to himself. He was sitting at the bar at Blue Jay Way, a popular sports bar near his house. Although he was waiting for Ryan and other friends to show, he didn't care that sat pathetically by himself and nursed a bottle of beer as several groups of friends cheered and talked during the game that played on the big screen TV in the background.

The fight with Heather was still reeling through his mind. He felt ashamed for calling her life boring, but he was still pissed that she didn't want to go out for one drink with his friends. After his third beer, Nick didn't know what to do and wasn't sure where he wanted to be.

Part of him wanted to sincerely apologize to Heather and make love to her, but the other part of him felt he need to take a stand. He wanted to see her come to him. He was tired of not being wanted or needed. Going to bed with her was his favorite part of their day because he felt loved when she curled up against him and he protectively put his arm around her.

"You look like shit," Ryan said, sliding onto an empty barstool beside Nick and throwing some money on the bar.

Nick didn't say anything.

"What happened?"

Nick sighed before telling his best friend about the fight with Heather.

"What are you going to do?" Ryan asked after Nick finished the story.

"I dunno know," he said, shrugging his shoulders.

"Want some advice?"

Nick again shrugged. At this point, he didn't feel like talking and if his best friend felt like giving him a few words of advice, then so be it.

"I've known you for a long time, buddy," Ryan began, rolling his beer bottle between his hands. "So, I'm not going to lie to you. I think Heather is the best thing that has ever happened to you. She's smart. She's funny. She's beautiful. And she's also her own person — someone who knows what she wants in life. Honestly, she doesn't need you."

"Hey, thanks for cheering me up," Nick interrupted rudely.

"Shut up and let me finish, jackass," he said, matching Nick's dark tone. "Heather doesn't need anyone to define who she is. You knew from the get-go that she's independent and tries not to depend on anyone, especially guys. The only people who she really trusts are Rory, Cat, Hera, and Lily.

"You probably already regret saying it, but you know that she doesn't lead a boring life. Heather's a fun girl, and you know it. So what if she likes to stay in every now and then? Does she always need to be with you?"

Nick didn't say anything, because he knew Ryan was right.

"I know you don't want to hear this, but I'm going to say it anyway, because it's rare that I get to throw something in your face," Ryan continued seriously. "You fucked up, buddy. And if you're going to fix this mess, you need apologize right now. You need to get off your sorry ass and buy her some flowers and chocolate. Even better, buy her a kitten. Who can resist a guy with a kitten?"

"Fuck you," he muttered, before taking another swig of his beer and thinking about what Ryan said.

"Are you seriously going to sit here and wallow?"

Nick didn't say anything. Honestly, he didn't feel like moving or talking. He just wanted to sit and drink.

Vodka Four

"Are you seriously thinking about breaking up with her?" Ryan asked, somewhat surprised at the thought of Nick ending the relationship.

Silence.

"If you're thinking about it, you have to be biggest, dumbest asshole I've ever met. Did you just hear what I said about Heather? What I said about you? About her being the best thing that has happened to you? Jesus, you've got to be kidding me."

Ryan looked at his best friend, who still didn't say a word. *What the fuck was going on?* He thought to himself. He had never seen Nick like this before. After his last girlfriend, Samantha, moved to Arizona, Nick moped around for less than a week before going out to the strip club. While Nick was understandably hurt about the breakup, he saw it coming as his ex-girlfriend talked about being closer to her friends and family.

"Well, let me know if you break up with her, because I'm going to be the first guy to ask her out," Ryan said smugly.

Nick suddenly looked at him and just glared at him. "That's not fuckin' funny," he spit out. "Keep away from her."

"Fuck you," Ryan snapped back. "Are you going fight every guy who wants to date Heather? Because you don't want to be with her, no one can? Is that what you want?"

"Fuck you," Nick muttered.

"Come on, get over yourself, buddy. Did you honestly believe your relationship with Heather was going to be fun and exciting all of the time? Sooner or later, the relationship has to settle down."

"You don't know what you're talking about."

"The fuck I don't. Heather is 29, Reed. Do you honestly believe she's not ready to settle down and not want what every woman has always dreamed about? Come on, don't be stupid. And since when you are the good-time guy? The last time I checked, you liked being in a relationship. You liked having a girlfriend."

Nick stared at the beer bottle in his hands.

"Fine, do whatever you want," Ryan said. "But keep this in mind. There are a hundred guys who want to mend her heart and tell her that you're a fuckin' bastard. She's not going to run after you. She's not going to call you. If you want her, then you need to get off your ass and fix the fuckin' problem."

"Fuck you," Nick muttered as he slid off the bar stool, throwing some money on the counter and leaving the bar.

Ryan remained, noting the blinking red light on his cell phone, indicating messages. He listened to several messages from Rory demanding to know where the hell Nick was. *Shit,* Ryan thought. *The shit has hit the fan.*

He finished his beer before heading out of the bar to catch up with Nick. Ryan knew he couldn't stop Rory from beating the shit out Nick.

Maybe she'll beat some sense into him, he thought.

CHAPTER 25

Rory was pissed. And when she was pissed, no one should stand in her way or even think about arguing with her. Luckily, she was closing Lexington early and was the last person to leave when Cat's Vue screeched to a halt in front of the store. Cat quickly had told her what had happened between Heather and Nick.

Cat was coming home when she heard shouting, and her curiosity led her to investigate. With cell phone in hand, she called Hera for help, knowing Rory and Lily were still at work, and headed toward Lexington when they saw Nick storm out of Heather's apartment and squeal off in his car.

After a quick text message to Lily telling to check on Heather after work, Cat and Rory headed downtown to look for the asshole. Cat could see the fire in Rory's eyes as they walked around the bars.

"Rory!" a male voice called out behind them. Rory and Cat turned to see Christopher and Tristan walking toward them.

"Have you seen him?" she demanded, not caring that other people were looking at them with curiosity. "Where the hell is he?"

"We haven't seen him," Tristan said, knowing better than to tell her to calm down. He had heard about her temper and knew not to cross her or make her more upset.

Rory, Cat, Tristan, and Christopher were discussing where they've been in their search for Nick when they heard a familiar, super loud, and girly laugh from across the street. Everyone looked over to see Hope Saint James stumble out of the bar, with her arm around Nick, who looked plowed.

Jennifer Elliott

"Fuckin' idiot," Rory roared, heading across the one-way street, not even looking for oncoming traffic. Cat, Tristan, and Christopher followed her, all grateful that there were no cars to dodge.

"Rory!" Hope exclaimed, with a smug grin on her face, as she saw Rory approach her. "How are you?"

She completely ignored Hope and swiftly clocked Nick in the jaw, causing him to fall to the ground.

"You fuckin' bastard," Rory yelled at him, completely ignoring the crowd of onlookers that had gathered around them. Nick was sitting on the ground, rubbing his jaw where Rory had hit him. "Her life is boring? Are you stupid?"

Rory was poised to punch him again, but Cat and Tristan had a firm grip on each of her arms. She wanted to tear him apart. She thought he was a good guy. She actually thought he was going to be good for Heather. Turns out, she was wrong.

"Fuck you," Nick spit out. "You guys think you're so great, but you're not. You're a bunch of lonely women looking to fuck over a guy because your lives are so miserable."

Cat and Rory looked at each other, completely surprised. Where the hell did that come from? What the hell was he thinking?

"Get over yourselves," he sneered, looking at Rory, Cat, and Hope, who had been looking victorious but then crestfallen when he also shot her a dirty look. "You think guys are stupid? You should look in the mirror."

"Nick," Christopher said roughly. "Let's go."

"Whatever," he said, refusing Christopher's hand as he clumsily stumbled to his feet. "For someone so beautiful and smart, her life is boring and dull."

"Fuck you," Rory and Cat snapped together. Both of them were glaring at him. And Rory was ready to deck him again, but Cat and Tristan were firmly holding her back.

Vodka Four

"You have to be the easiest person ever," Nick said, directing his hostility at Hope. She didn't understand. Inside the bar, Nick was pouring his heart out to her. She knew all about the fight and couldn't wait to tell her friends. The high and mighty Heather Kincannon had fallen off her pedestal. And now, Nick looked at her as if she was the enemy. As if she was the one who broke his heart. As if she was the one who didn't want to be with him.

"What does it take to sleep with you, Hope?" he asked angrily. "How much money does it take for some poor schmuck to fuck you? Do you really honestly believe I was going to sleep with you? How stupid are you?"

Hope was shocked. She didn't know what to say. Finally, she shook her head and regained her composure. "Fuck you, Nick," she snapped before disappearing into the crowd behind her.

Rory and Cat looked each other and then at Tristan and Christopher, who were just as surprised as they were to hear such mean words come out of Nick's mouth. Tristan and Christopher had seen Nick drunk before, but he had never been a mean drunk.

"And you." Nick glared at Cat. "You're just as boring as Heather, did you know that? You and your stupid cats. But you know what makes you worse? You're a follower. You follow them around like a pathetic and scared little child. Seriously, Cat, get a life of your own instead of living vicariously through your slutty friends."

"Nick," Tristan said sharply, gripping Rory's arm a little tighter as he felt her moving forward. "That's enough."

"The fuck it isn't. I'm so tired of them thinking they're better than everyone else. Because they're not. Just dull and stupid."

"Nick," Christopher said firmly. "Let's get outta here."

"And I should have slept with you," Nick said, looking at Rory and ignoring Christopher. "You're the good-time girl of the group, aren't you? You're the one who likes to party and open her legs to anyone?"

Before Rory could even move forward to punch him again, Cat was quicker. She let go of Rory's arm and pushed Nick with all her strength against the wall of the bar. As he was falling to the ground again, Cat kicked him in the groin. The curious crowd groaned in unison as they saw the shocked and hurt expression on Nick's face and him holding his manhood. Before Cat could do further damage, Tristan let go of Rory and grabbed Cat around the waist and pulled her back while Christopher held Rory back.

"You're a fuckin' idiot," Cat yelled, her fists punching the air. "How in the world did we think you were a good guy? You're a complete asshole. Asshole!"

Ryan pushed his way through the crowd, looked at Cat screaming at Nick, and then saw Nick crumpled against the bar's wall, not making an effort to get up.

"Let's go," Byron said firmly, coming up from behind Rory and Cat and pulling them both back from the scene. "You guys did enough damage. Let's go."

Rory and Cat didn't say anything as they continued to watch Nick sit on the ground and just blankly stare into space as Ryan crouched in front of him. Byron didn't need to say anything to Tristan and Christopher to convey that he was taking Rory and Cat back home.

Welcome to Amery Lake

Heather and Cat tried to look normal, hanging out by a wall of mailboxes at one of the state university's dormitories. Incoming freshmen and their unsuspecting parents would never know that they actually attended the Lutheran university in the college town. Thanks to their friendships with Danny and Gil, who attended the state university, Heather and Cat knew the campus like the back of their hands.

Summer had passed, and fall had quickly descended upon Amery Lake. And Heather and her friends were ready to welcome new and eager students with open arms.

Heather and Cat looked at Eli, who was manning the main entrance for new arrivals, and Danny and Gil, who were keeping an eye for intruders on the staircase.

"All clear," Eli called, surveying the outside premise.

"All clear," Gil repeated from the staircase.

Cat giggled as she and Heather went to work. Each holding a screwdriver (the tool, not the drink), they started unscrewing the small "men" and "women" name plates on the bathroom doors.

"How's it going?" Eli asked, peeking inside the entrance.

"Fine," Cat replied, pulling the "men" sign off the door. "I'm done. Heather?"

"Done," she responded, with the "women" sign and two screws in her hand, and quickly walked over to the men's bathroom door.

"Get at least one screw in, because the fourth floor door opened," Danny instructed. "Someone's coming down."

"Shit, incoming," Eli said at the same time.

"Fuck," Heather muttered, as she quickly twisted one screw in and breathed a sign of relief that the sign held in place. She looked over at Cat, who had done the same thing and returned to her post at the mailboxes.

"Hello!" Eli greeted cheerfully to a freshman and her parents who had approached the entrance.

Heather could hear him expertly directing them to the dorm front office, the place where freshmen needed to check in. Danny and Gil scrambled out of the staircase to join Heather and Cat by the mailboxes as a dorm leader emerged a few seconds later.

"Good afternoon!" the residential leader greeted cheerfully to Heather and Cat, mistaking them for freshmen. "Do you guys need help with anything?"

Heather shook her head. "We're OK. Thanks."

"Well, my name is Amy," she said brightly. "I live on the third floor of Francesca Hall. If you need anything, knock on my door."

"Thanks, Amy!" Cat replied enthusiastically, matching Amy's bouncy attitude. "We will!"

Danny and Gil quietly snickered at Cat's fake response.

Amy smiled before heading outside to personally guide the new arrival who was still chatting — flirting — with Eli. Danny and Gil shot back to the staircase, and Eli poked his head back into the entrance to give the all clear.

"Thanks, Amy! We will!" Heather mimicked Cat's response, as she went back to screwing the "women" sign on the men's bathroom door.

"Shut up," Cat muttered, tightening the last screw on the women's bathroom door. "We didn't want her to become suspicious, did we?"

"I think you missed your calling as an actress," she said, twisting the last screw in place. "Or a spy."

"Done," Cat shouted as she dropped the screwdriver into her purse.

"Done," Heather confirmed, handing over her tool to Cat.

"Let's get out of here before Amy comes back," Eli said, watching out for the dorm leader and the new freshman's return.

Vodka Four

"You know, it's really too bad that we can't stick around," Cat lamented sadly as everyone walked away from the dorm. "I really want to see people's reaction to this prank."

"I know," Heather agreed.

Returning students and staff would automatically head for the correct bathroom without looking at the sign on the door. They knew what to do and where to go. New students and their parents, however, read everything in a new environment.

Later, according to Danny and Gil who heard several stories from different people, the prank was a success. The mother of a freshman student screamed bloody murder when she opened the door to the "women's" bathroom to find a returning male student, with pants around his ankles, doing his business in the urinal. She was in such a hurry to go to the bathroom, she didn't notice the urinals when she entered a stall. While the situation was being corrected, no one was smart enough to man the doors to prevent more incidents.

According to rumors, dorm leader Amy had some serious and loud bowel issues and became highly flustered and embarrassed when she opened the stall door in the women's bathroom to find several fathers washing their hands, who thought they were in the men's bathroom.

Because of the prank, university leaders voted to paint "men" and "women" on the bathroom doors.

CHAPTER 26

Friday, March 4

Heather was sad and tired. She wanted to cry again. Her heart felt so heavy. Her heart just ached. It felt broken. Warm tears slid down her face as she turned on her side in bed.

"Hey," Cat said softly, who was in bed beside her. Her head was resting on the pillow, and her eyes were halfway closed.

Heather burst into tears.

Byron had dropped Rory and Cat off at Heather's apartment after the fight. They took turns replaying the scene to Heather, Hera, and Lily, who were all shocked and mortified by Nick's drunken statements. But none of them made excuses or defended him.

As much as Heather wanted to be left alone to cry and wallow, she was glad her friends stuck around to comfort and reassure her that she did nothing wrong. She also didn't care about completely breaking down in front of them.

Hera, Lily, and Rory headed home a little after midnight, and Cat forced Heather to leave a message for Wesley, saying she wasn't feeling well and wasn't going to be at work. Cat left a similar message on her boss' voicemail.

Heather and Cat just laid in her bed, talked, thought about the chain of events in silence, petted Merry and Pippen when they craved attention, and finally fell asleep. However, Heather didn't sleep well as she dreamt about her fight with Nick and the events that followed.

Vodka Four

Heather rolled over and reached for a tissue on her nightstand. As she blew her nose, she noticed her cell phone's blinking red light, indicating she had messages.

"You OK?" Cat asked, her head still resting on the pillow. Like Heather, she didn't get a good night's rest. Thoughts of Rory punching Nick and her pushing him ran through her mind while she slept. Cat knew Rory was going to kick his ass, but she had no idea she was going to become physically aggressive.

"I'll be fine," Heather murmured, wiping her nose and then resting her head back on the pillow, with cell phone in hand. Rory, Hera, and Lily had texted her to see how she was doing, but there were no messages from Nick.

"Anything from Nick?" Cat questioned.

Heather shook her head. "I wonder what happened after Byron dragged you and Rory home."

"I don't know."

"Thanks for making me take the day off," she said, sighing loudly. "I feel like shit."

"And you look it," Cat offered, closing her eyes.

"I know," Heather groaned. "I don't understand how this happened! One minute, he and I were so happy, and then in the next minute, he says my life is boring and wants to sleep with Rory. How fucked up is that?"

"He's an asshole."

"And he left a bar with Hope?"

Cat nodded.

"I wonder what would've happened between Nick and Hope if you guys didn't hear her witchy laugh."

Cat sighed. "I don't know."

Heather wanted to talk more, but all of a sudden she felt tired. Being sad was exhausting. She closed her eyes for a minute before falling asleep again.

Heather and Cat woke up a little after noon and talked a little bit more before Cat headed for her apartment to shower and change into fresh clothes. After taking a long hot shower, Heather wrapped herself in her bathrobe and stood in her kitchen. She looked at the place where she and Nick argued. *What the hell happened*, she thought miserably. *What the hell happened last night?*

One thing Heather knew for sure was the relationship was over. She couldn't forgive Nick for what he said about her and her friends. She also couldn't call and yell at him. She didn't want to look like a total lunatic. Heather sighed as she made toast and texted her friends back, saying she was OK. Rory texted back saying she and Cat were coming over in a few minutes.

As soon as Heather quickly changed into sweatpants and a T-shirt, Rory and Cat knocked on her apartment door and let themselves inside.

"You look better, sweetie," Rory said, with a weary smile.

"I feel a little better," Heather admitted, munching on her buttered toast as she sat on the couch with Cat.

"What's going on?" Cat asked Rory, who grabbed a stool by the counter.

"I talked to Tristan last night to find out what happened after we left. And I talked to Ryan this morning," she began. "After Byron dragged Cat and me away from the scene, the police came."

"What?" Cat and Heather asked in unison; their eyes widened with surprise.

"Apparently, some moron in the crowd called 911 when Cat was beating the shit out of Nick," Rory said, with a smirk. "The police came to find Nick wailing on Ryan."

"What?" Cat and Heather asked together again in disbelief.

"Nick was beating up Ryan?" Heather asked, shaking her head. "What happened?"

"According to Tristan, Ryan was checking on Nick, and then all of a sudden, Nick starts pounding on Ryan. Tristan,

Vodka Four

Christopher, and some other guys were in the process of tearing them apart when the police showed up. They arrested Nick for disorderly conduct."

"He's in jail?" Heather exclaimed. "Are you serious?"

"So serious," Rory replied. "He's in jail right now. Ryan refuses to bail him out, and Nick won't call his parents or other friends to help. He's in there for a few days until his initial court appearance."

"Holy shit."

"Yeah, I know! When I talked to Tristan, he said he had never seen Nick like that before. He was just as shocked as we were. This morning, I talked to Ryan, who took the day off from work to recover from the beating."

"Was he hurt badly?" Cat asked, concerned.

Rory shook her head. "He said he has a black eye and his jaw is a little sore."

"He doesn't know the reason why Nick attacked him?" Heather inquired.

"No. Ryan said he was just trying to help Nick. Numerous witnesses could confirm that Ryan was the victim, and so the police arrested Nick. Ryan thought about bailing him out but then decided Nick needed some time to cool down and think about things. Believe me, Ryan is just as shocked as we are about the whole thing. He has no idea what's going through Nick's mind."

Even Nick's best friend had never seen him act this way before, Heather thought. *Was he fooling everyone? What the hell is he thinking?*

"You OK?" Rory asked, looking at Heather.

"Yeah, I feel better," she admitted. "This sucks, because I really really liked him. I thought he was a good guy. And I think that's what sucks the most because everyone thought he was a decent guy."

"What are you going to do?" Cat questioned.

"Nothing for now," Heather said, shrugging. "I'm not chasing after him. He got himself into this mess, he can get himself out."

"Good girl," Rory praised.

"Even if he apologizes and even if he has a really good excuse, the relationship is over. I can't trust him. I can't believe the mean things he said about you two. What he said about Hope was true, but I don't care about her."

Cat and Rory nodded in agreement.

"God, this sucks!" Heather exclaimed, slouching back in the couch. "He was like the perfect boyfriend, and now, he's not. But I can live with not so perfect. I just can't live with someone being verbally abusive when things don't go his way.

"Does he really think my life is boring? What was he thinking when he said all of those mean things? What was he doing with Hope Saint James? Were they were going to have sex? Does that mean he was going to cheat on me? Or did we break up when he stormed out? I don't know the answers to any of these questions. And do I even want to know?"

"Hey, hey," Rory said, jumping off the stool and crouching down beside Heather. "Slow down, kiddo. Slow down. You don't have to know everything right now."

"I know," Heather said, sniffling a bit. "I just want a good explanation for what happened last night."

"But will it change your mind about breaking up with him?" Cat asked gently.

Heather shook her head, wiping tears from her eyes. "Nick did too much damage. I can't trust him, especially after what he said. Even if he says he didn't mean it and he was just drunk, what he said had to come from somewhere. Maybe deep down inside he really thinks that, and I can't be with someone like that."

"And that's totally understandable," Cat agreed.

Vodka Four

After talking a bit more, Rory headed to work at Lexington and Heather convinced Cat that she was OK to be by herself. She wanted to give her apartment a good scrub down. With her hair in a ponytail and her stereo blaring rock music — love songs were definitely out of the question — Heather needed a distraction.

She was in her room stripping the bed sheets off her bed. She gathered the sheets and the matching pillowcases in her arms and walked into the living room, where she saw Ryan standing in her doorway with her cats sniffing his boots. She grabbed the remote to her stereo and turned off the loud rock music.

"Hey," she said, looking at a slightly battered Ryan. He was wearing baggy jeans, a black Amery Lake Sports T-shirt underneath a black leather jacket, and a Green Bay Packer baseball cap.

"I just wanted to drop by and see how you were doing," he said awkwardly. "I knocked, but the music ..."

Heather dropped the sheets by the bathroom door. "Come in," she invited. "Don't worry about your boots."

Ryan avoided stepping on Merry and Pippen and took a seat on the couch. Heather perched on the stool that Rory had used earlier.

"Are you OK?" she asked, noticing his black eye and the tired look on his face.

He shrugged. "I've been through worse."

Heather wasn't sure what to say next, but she was touched Ryan stopped by to check on her.

"I suppose Rory told you what happened," he said, breaking the uncomfortable silence.

"Yeah," Heather confirmed. "She told me about an hour ago."

"I'm sorry, Heather," Ryan started. "I honestly don't know what Nick's thinking. I really don't. I've never seen him like this before. I was up most of the night wondering why he turned into such a bastard, and I can't give you a good explanation."

"You don't have to explain."

"I know, but I feel like I should say or do something, because he's one of my best friends."

"Ryan, it's OK."

"No, it's not. The argument you two had doesn't bother me. Couples fight. What bothers me the most was the things he said about you and your friends. I don't really think he meant any of that, Heather. He was upset, and I really didn't give him good advice."

"What?" Heather asked, cocking her side to one side. "You didn't give him good advice?"

"I met him at Blues after your fight," Ryan explained. "I told him that he made a mistake and that he should beg for your forgiveness."

"And how is that bad advice?" Heather questioned, smiling.

"I should've supported him. I was thinking about this last night, and I realized I sided with you. I told Nick that he was wrong."

"Regardless of which side you took, you spoke your mind. He's an adult with a mind of his own. He could've taken your advice or he could've done something completely different. This isn't your fault."

"I still feel bad."

"Yeah, me too," Heather admitted.

"I can't imagine how you feel right now," Ryan said, petting Merry who decided to curl up in his lap. "I know all of you hate him right now. To tell the truth, I don't even like him."

"I don't hate him. I just don't understand what happened. Yes, I'm angry and upset, but I don't hate him."

"Rory and Cat hate him."

Heather laughed. "I'm mad I missed that. I would've loved to see Cat beating the shit out of him."

Ryan smiled too and shook his head. "Little Cat attacking Nick. I was in the crowd, watching the whole thing, and I had trouble pushing my way through. I didn't catch everything he said about Hope, but I heard what he said about Rory and Cat. Then I see Cat flying at him."

Heather laughed harder at the mental image of Cat going *Crouching Tiger Hidden Dragon* style on Nick's ass.

"I expected Rory to attack him, but I never thought about Cat," Ryan said.

"I would've loved to see that."

Heather and Ryan smiled at the thought. "I can't believe Nick's in jail right now. I never would've guessed in a million years that he would be tossed in there," Heather said, shaking her head.

"Yeah," Ryan said slowly, thinking about what was said that led up to Nick being handcuffed by police. "He needs some time to cool off. He's done enough damage."

"I agree," Heather added.

"I talked to Rory this morning, and she doesn't seem scarred by what Nick said about her."

"Yeah, it takes a lot to shake Rory. I mean, she was pissed about last night, but it takes a lot to shake her confidence."

"No, I get it. Is Cat OK?"

"I think so," Heather said thoughtfully. "She and I talked a lot last night. I think she was a little hurt, but she knows it's not true."

"Good," Ryan said, sighing. "I wasn't worried about Rory as I was about Cat."

"That's sweet."

"Yeah, well, Cat's a nice girl."

Although Heather appreciated Ryan checking in and attempting to explain Nick's behavior, she wanted to talk to

Jennifer Elliott

Nick. She wanted to know what the hell he was thinking. She wanted to know what the hell was going on.

Heather finished cleaning her apartment and talked to her friends, who had organized a weekend slumber party at Rory's place. She knew their intentions were to distract her, but she couldn't help but wonder what Nick was doing or thinking. When was she going to talk to him again? Would they even need to talk? What did he think about the status of their relationship? Was it over to him?

CHAPTER 27

Friday, March 11

When Monday morning came around, Heather was refreshed and ready for work. She was a little nervous about running into Nick, but she felt prepared to see and maybe talk to him. And Heather was ready to battle Hope if the spoiled rich princess was going to open her big fat mouth if they ran into each other. She could imagine Hope wanting to flaunt the whole debacle in front of her, and then Heather would point out that Nick made some mean — but true — remarks about Hope. Hopefully, that would shut her up.

Heather almost expected Nick to call Wednesday night after she and Rory each received a beautiful bouquet of flowers at Lexington earlier that day. Both cards read, "I'm sorry. Nick." Cat had e-mailed Heather, saying she had also received flowers and a card from Nick. But he never called.

On Friday, Heather was straightening her desk at the end of her day. She was heading home to make dinner and watch a little bit of TV before she meeting the girls at a low-key bar, where the music wouldn't be blaring and they didn't have to yell at each other. After this week, a strong vodka drink sounded good to her.

After saying goodbye to Rory and Cat at the store, Heather headed toward her car in the back parking lot. When she stepped outside and headed toward her Vue, her heart raced as she saw Nick standing near it. He was waiting for her. And dammit, he looked good. He looked sexy as hell, standing there in his work clothes. He should look like crap. But he didn't.

Jennifer Elliott

"Hey," he said softly when she stopped before him.

"Hey," she replied, looking directly into his sad and beautiful eyes. *Dammit! Why do I want to kiss him? Why do I want to throw myself at him?*

"Heather," Nick began, looking tormented. "I'm so sorry. I know I said and did a lot of things to piss off a lot of people, but I'm really sorry."

Heather didn't respond. She had expected the apology. She wasn't going to say, "That's OK. Don't worry about it." He hurt her, dammit. And he hurt her friends.

"I don't know what happened," he continued, looking at the ground for a second before looking at her again. "I just wanted you to come out for a drink. When you refused, I just got angry. I know this isn't an excuse for my behavior."

Again, Heather didn't say anything, hoping her silence killed him inside.

"Can we go some place to talk?" Nick asked quietly. "Please."

She took a deep breath before answering. "Yeah. Meet me at Kelsea's."

As Heather drove to her favorite coffee house in her neighborhood, she wondered what Nick wanted to say. On a Friday night, Kelsea's was usually deserted — the perfect location to have a private talk in a public place. Heather didn't quite trust herself to be alone with Nick. Her urge to kiss him and to be held by him surprised her.

A handful of college students were scattered around the coffee house, occupying the square tables with laptops and textbooks. A couple of other people were sitting in the oversized chairs, reading books and magazines. Heather found an empty corner table as Nick ordered two coffees.

"Thanks for doing this," he said, after sitting down at the table. "How are you doing?"

Are you serious? Heather thought incredulously. *You just asked me how I'm doing? How do you think I feel, nimrod?*

Vodka Four

"What do you want?" she asked bluntly.

"Look, I fucked up," Nick began. "I've had a lot of time to think about what happened."

"You told me this at Lexington," Heather said shortly. Her patience was beginning to wear thin, and she didn't care if Nick noticed. If he continued to feed her more lame lines about fucking up, she was not going to have a problem breaking up with him and walking away.

"OK. Here's the truth, Heather." Nick took a deep breath. "I'm in love with you, and that scares the shit out of me. I've never fallen in love with anyone this fast. You and I connect. And I just fell in love with everything about you. Well, almost everything. Your independence and determination are two things that scare me.

"You see, you don't need a guy in your life to make you happy. You're not like most women I know — you're OK being single. Not once have you asked where our relationship is going and what I want. You're just happy with what we have — or had. You haven't asked for anything more, and I should've been happy with that. Hell, most guys would die if their girlfriends didn't ask those questions.

"When we were arguing about going to the bars, I realized you're capable of living without me. But I don't think I can live without you. I know that sounds cheesy and lame, but it's true. I became angry because you didn't need me. You were perfectly happy and content to stay at home by yourself. I was — am — completely in love with you, and you didn't seem like you even cared about me."

Heather opened her mouth to protest, but Nick held up his hand to stop her.

"Please let me finish this. I know you don't love me, but I know you do care about me. That night my insecurities were messing with me and just got the best of me. I'm sorry I took everything out on you. You did nothing wrong, Heather. I was the jackass. I was the asshole. I fucked everything up."

Fuuuuuuck! Heather thought frantically, trying to keep her steel composure. Nick was not going to see her crumble just because he confessed to being in love with her. Love was the furthest thing from her mind. And now, Heather couldn't bring herself to say and do everything she had thought about over the past week. *Fuckin', eh. Love changes everything.*

"I know I didn't handle our argument well," Nick said, taking advantage of Heather's moment of silence. "After running out on you and after meeting with Ryan, I should've gone back to your place and apologized. But I was mad, and I wanted to hurt you as much as you hurt me that night."

"You said my life was boring," she finally said.

"I was just trying to hurt you. You have to understand, Heather, that I'm in love with you. I want to be around you. When you want time to yourself or your friends, I get a little jealous because I want you with me. I think about you all of the time, and I wonder if you even think about me. When you got the flat tire, you didn't even think about calling me for help."

"We had just started dating, and — "

"No, you don't need to say anything," he interrupted. "I understand where you're coming from. I really do."

"What about Hope?" she asked coldly.

Nick sighed. He suddenly looked tired. "I wasn't going to sleep with her. After talking to Ryan, I wandered to different bars and got drunk in the process. Hope was at one of the bars and wouldn't leave me alone. I finally told her what happened because I was just tanked. You have to believe me, Heather, that I wasn't going to sleep with her."

"You said some really mean things about Cat and Rory."

"I know. But what I said about them came from Hope. After telling her about the argument, she started railing on you and your friends. Everything about Cat and Rory I remembered Hope saying it to me at the bar. Please believe

Vodka Four

me that I don't think Cat needs to get a life of her own, and I don't believe Rory is a whore."

Heather didn't know whether she should believe him. On one hand, the explanation sounded true. But on the other hand, was he just blaming Hope for his thoughts, knowing she wouldn't confront Hope? And if Heather did confront her, Hope would deny everything and it would turn into a game of "he said, she said."

"The flowers you sent were nice," Heather thanked.

He looked confused for a split second, and Heather thought something was wrong. "You're welcome. I just want you guys to know that I'm really sorry about everything."

"So, what do you want?" But Heather knew what he wanted. She didn't need to even ask, but she wanted to hear him say it.

Nick took a deep breath. "I know it's a long shot, but I want another chance. I know I did and said a lot of shitty things, but you have to realize that I love you. You mean everything to me, and I don't want to lose you."

Could she give him a second chance? An even better question would be: Should she give him a second chance? Yesterday, Heather was so sure the relationship needed to end despite his apologies and explanations. What she didn't expect was him saying he loved her. Now, she wasn't sure what to do.

"I don't know," Heather finally said, shaking her head. "I don't know, Nick."

"Think about what I said," he replied, tentatively reaching over to cover her hand with his. "Please think about what I said. I love you."

She wanted to pull her hand away as act of defiance, but she couldn't do it. His hand felt warm, and she desperately missed his touch. *Dammit!* Heather thought. *I had everything figured out yesterday. Why does he look so good right now? Why do I want to throw myself at him?*

Jennifer Elliott

"I'll think about it," Heather answered. "I'll call you later."

Nick stood up and hesitantly kissed her on the forehead before leaving the coffee house. *Dammit!* She repeated to herself, standing up to leave. Heather didn't need time to herself to think about what he said. She needed her friends.

Fifteen minutes later, Heather, Lily, Cat, and Rory were sitting at a round table in the Lexington break room. Fortunately, there weren't too many customers in the store and Cat and Rory were able to slip away from the main floor. Lily had just ended her work day at Bellismo and informed her that Hera had plans with Byron and his friends.

While Heather relayed the conversation with Nick, she tried to remember everything. She didn't want to leave out any details. They had to know everything.

"So, tell me what I should do," Heather prompted her three friends who just stared at her, letting the conversation sink in. "Tell me what I should do."

Lily, Cat, and Rory looked at each other before looking at Heather again.

"We can't tell you what to do," Rory finally said, shaking her head. "This is your decision."

"What would you do?" Heather asked, emphasizing the word "you."

Rory smiled and shook her head. "That's not going to work, Vodka Four."

"Fine, tell me what you think."

"I think he loves you," Lily offered.

"But," Heather said, knowing Lily wasn't finished.

"But I would be hesitant about continuing the relationship," she confessed slowly. "OK, I know couples argue, but Nick really didn't handle things well. I see his perspective, but I would have a hard time trusting him."

Vodka Four

"Tell us what you want to do," Cat said. "What are you thinking?"

"I miss him," she admitted. "I must sound like a complete ninny, but I miss him so much. Part of me really wants to give him another chance. I want to believe this won't happen again. I believe he loves me, and I know I'll fall in love with him. We had a great relationship.

"But the other part of me says to end it, because he's so insecure about my independence. I can't spend every waking moment with him, and I can't be constantly thinking about how he will react and what he's feeling. If I give him another chance, I know we'd be walking on pins and needles for awhile. But for how long? So, you guys really need to tell me what I should do."

"We can't tell you what to do," Rory reminded gently.

"Give me any kind of advice, please," Heather begged. "I really don't know what I should do."

Rory stood up and started pacing around the break room. "Ladies and gentlemen of the jury," she began. Heather, Lily, and Cat snickered with amusement. "I believe Nicholas Reed should not be given a second chance. Under certain circumstances, I believe in second chances, but in this situation, I believe it will cause more hurt and pain. Two people in a nurturing and stable relationship shouldn't have to walk on eggshells around each other. They should feel comfortable to be who they are without judgment or fear.

"If a second chance is given, conversations that were once well connected and long lasting will become superficial, awkward, and short. If two people who deeply care about each other are unable to communicate freely and openly without hurting one another, then how can a relationship work?

"Nicholas Reed has professed his love for Heather, which has caused his insecurities about her independence to increase. He knows she doesn't love him and says that doesn't matter. But it does matter to him, as this is evident through his childish and immature outbursts. He called her life boring. He pushes her to go out more. He lashes out at her and her friends. He says he wanted to hurt her because she didn't love him. Is this how an adult behaves in an adult relationship? No.

"I'm sorry, but I feel Nicholas Reed has done too much damage to this relationship. He has caused a tremendous amount of hurt, pain, and confusion — not just to Heather, but to her friends and his friends. I feel a second chance would cause more harm than good. Thank you."

Rory sat back down at the table, smiling.

"You watch way too much *Law & Order*," Lily said, shaking her head.

Cat stood up and took a minute before launching into her "closing."

"Everything that Rory said about Nicholas Reed is true. Yes, he hurt Heather. Yes, he lashed out at her. Yes, he lashed out at her friends. Yes, he caused a tremendous amount of pain and suffering. Yes, he let his insecurities get the best of him. But he is sincerely sorry for his words and behavior. He has made himself vulnerable by confessing that he loves Heather when he knows she doesn't feel the same way. But yet he wants a second chance, knowing she doesn't love him. Why? Because he loves her and is willing to do anything for her.

"At this point in time, trust is a tentative issue. But I ask you to look at Nicholas Reed's history. Even his best friend testified he had never seen my client act this way before. Yes, Nicholas Reed is guilty of numerous charges, but he is also guilty of being in love."

Rory burst out laughing. Lily rolled her eyes. Heather groaned, closing her eyes. Cat giggled. The cliché was too good to not use in her closing.

"Before the night in question occurred, Heather Jennifer Kincannon and Nicholas I-don't-know-his-middle-name Reed were in a nurturing, stable, and adult relationship. Most relationships experience a few hiccups and heated arguments, but should that end a relationship? No. You have to ask yourself one question."

Heather stared at Cat, waiting to hear what she had to say next.

"Ask yourself one question, Heather," Cat repeated, looking at her. "Is Nick worth fighting for? Is he worth your time and effort? Is he worth a second chance? Is he worth fighting for?"

Heather, Rory, and Lily applauded, and Cat curtsied at the praise.

"Thanks, guys," Heather said, with a hint of sarcasm. "You guys gave really good perspectives, but really, you didn't give me an answer."

As Rory and Cat headed back to the main floor, complimenting each other's closing arguments, Heather and Lily headed toward the parking lot, making plans to meet at a bar in a few hours.

Heather sighed heavily as she thought about the excellent points that Rory and Cat made. They didn't make her decision any easier, and Heather still had no idea what to do.

CHAPTER 28

Saturday, March 12

Heather decided to give Nick an answer sometime Saturday. She still had no idea what she wanted to do, but she also didn't want to prolong her decision, believing the wait was probably killing Nick.

Throughout the night, Heather tossed and turned in bed, dreaming about what she would say to him. She dreamed about giving him another chance or walking away from him. Even her dreams didn't reveal a definite answer.

When Heather hauled herself out of bed, she decided to meet Nick at noon at the coffee house. She still didn't know what to do, but she had to tell him something. With crossed fingers, Heather hoped an answer would magically appear.

Part of her wanted to give the relationship a second try, because she genuinely cared for Nick and had a good time with him. The other part was telling her to walk away from Nick, because he wasn't worth her time. They would need time to repair their relationship. She knew it wouldn't be the same, but could it be better? Heather didn't know.

"Still don't know?" Cat asked, over the phone as Heather paced around her apartment, with her cell phone in hand.

"No idea. I'm meeting him in half an hour, and I still haven't made a decision."

"Tell him you need more time."

"I don't want to torture him, Cat," Heather explained. "If I was in his situation, I would want to know something as soon as possible. Waiting would kill me."

"It would kill me, too. So, what are you going to say?"

"I don't know. I really don't. I'm praying to God that he sends me a sign or something."

"Maybe if you tell Nick your thoughts and feelings, maybe something will come to you."

"I hope so."

"I don't know what else I can tell you, kid," Cat said, sighing. "I'm glad I'm not you."

"Thanks for your brilliant words of wisdom," Heather replied sarcastically.

Heather prayed for an answer or a sign as she walked slowly to the coffee house to meet Nick. It didn't. She saw Nick's car in the parking lot and took a deep breath before pulling the door open. He was sitting at the same corner table that they had occupied last night. On the table were two mugs of coffee.

"Hey," he said, with a faint smile. *He looked nervous,* Heather thought. *He almost looks sick.*

"Hey," she replied, taking off her jacket before sitting down at the table.

Heather carefully and slowly sipped her coffee. "I have a question for you. I've been meaning to ask you this, but I kept forgetting. Every now and then, you call me Willow. No one has ever called me that."

Nick smiled. "When I was younger, my grandmother had a porcelain plate decorated with pictures, and the pictures seemed to tell a story. I asked her about it, and she told me an ancient Chinese fable about a young man who falls in love with a beautiful girl. However, the girl's father thinks the young man isn't good enough for his daughter. The guy and the daughter fall in love and run away to be together, but her father sends his troops after them to kill him. I think the couple escaped and lived together for awhile, but then something happened — I can't remember."

Heather chuckled at his lack of memory, shaking her head.

Jennifer Elliott

"Hey," he said defensively, smiling at her. "It was a long time ago. It's a miracle that I remember the story at all."

"Continue by all means."

"Anyway, the couple lived together for awhile, but the girl's father managed to track them down. His troops kill the young man. Seeing this, the girl kills herself by setting the house on fire as she's still in it. Apparently, the gods took pity on the young lovers and transformed them into doves."

"You made that up," Heather accused jokingly.

"No, I didn't," he protested, shaking his head. "I swear to you I didn't make it up. Look it up on the Internet."

"I'm going to," she challenged. "So, that story inspired you to call me Willow?"

"I've always thought you were beautiful, Heather. For some reason, the first night we hooked up, I thought about that story. It's a tragic story, really, but I thought about the beautiful girl and then thought about you."

She didn't say anything. An answer still hadn't come to her. *Shit, what am I going to do?* Heather thought. She couldn't sit here and talk with Nick forever, could she?

"My grandfather overhead my grandmother telling me the story, and he told me an old tale about the origin of pussy willow trees."

"Ooooh, tell me the story," Heather said, excitedly. She really did want to hear another story, but she also needed a little more time to stall.

Nick grinned at her. "There was a farmer who had a cat that gave birth to a litter of kittens in the spring, but there were too many kittens for the cat to nurse. So, the farmer threw the kittens into the river — "

"What?" She interrupted, horrified at the thought of someone dumping a litter of kittens in a river. "This is an awful story."

"Let me finish."

"Fine."

Vodka Four

"The farmer threw the kittens into the river, but this devastated the mother cat. She went to the river to save her kittens, but she wasn't strong enough to save all of them. So, the mother cat started crying to mourn — "

"I think I'm going to cry. This is a horrible story," Heather interrupted again, looking seriously sad. The thought of drowning kittens saddened her deeply.

"It's just a tale," Nick reminded gently, covering her hand with his. His hand felt warm. "The mother cat started crying, and her cries were carried by the wind and could be heard throughout the valley. The kittens also cried as they struggled in the river."

"I don't like this story at all. This story sucks ass."

Nick chuckled. "Stop interrupting me. The willow trees along the river heard the cries, and each willow dropped its branches into the river. As the kittens floated by, the willow trees scooped them up into their branches and saved them. My grandfather says that's how pussy willows were created."

Heather breathed a sigh of relief, knowing the kittens were OK. However, she wanted to kick the farmer's ass. Who dumps kittens in a river?

"You're missing the point," Nick said.

"What?"

"You're totally thinking about kicking the farmer's ass, aren't you?"

Dammit! How did he know? She thought. "No, I'm not," she protested weakly.

"I call you Willow because of the beautiful girl in the Chinese proverb and for your love of cats. That and I think it's a cool nickname."

"Thanks for sharing," Heather said. "I like the nickname. It's different."

"Just like you," he replied, winking at her.

And that's when Heather realized what she wanted. She had a definite answer.

"I'm not going to lie to you, Nick," she began, taking her hand away from his and setting it in her lap. "You said a lot of things that hurt. I know you apologized for everything, but that doesn't erase the memory."

"I am really sorry," he said quietly.

"I know," Heather said, looking in her lap for a second before returning her attention to him. "First, I want to trust you that you didn't mean to say those awful things about me, Rory, and Cat. I know people say stuff they don't mean when they're upset, but I'm giving you the benefit of the doubt that your anger got the best of you.

"You can trust me," he said.

"I want to trust you, Nick," she replied simply. "But you have to realize that I'm not perfect. My life can be boring, and I like that. And you need to understand that I want time with my friends. Just me. Not you and me. Just me. I love my friends, and that includes Eli.

"You don't have to like my friendship with him, but you have to understand that he will always be one of my closest friends. I've known him for more than 10 years, and I'm not going to give him up for anyone.

"I'm tired of defending our friendship to you. If you can't handle it, then we have no future, Nick. I want to stay with you."

When the words came out of her mouth, Heather realized she meant it. She wanted to be with Nick, because he made her happy. He made her smile and laugh.

"I want to stay with you, but if you're going to have an issue with my friendship with him, then I can't be with you."

"I don't have a problem, I swear," Nick said quickly, beaming at her. He had a second chance with her. He was going to do everything in his power to not screw anything up. "Honestly, I'm a little jealous of him because you two share a history together and have this tight friendship. I want that with you."

"In time, we will have that," Heather reassured him, covering his hands with hers. "I want that with you, but you need to give me some time. You need to remember that while we've known each other for years, we've only started to learn about each other in a very short period of time."

"I know, Willow," he agreed.

"Can we think of another nickname? Because I'm not sure I like Willow anymore."

"What?"

"Dead kittens are attached to the nickname," she exclaimed, with enjoyment and a little bit of sadness. Really, who wants to drown adorable kittens?

"The kittens were saved!"

"But the farmer tried to drown them, and that's sad."

"But the willow trees saved them."

"It's kind of a morbid tale," Heather said thoughtfully.

"It's a story of hope and inspiration," Nick countered, reaching for her hand.

"We'll think of some good nicknames for each other," she insisted, holding onto his hand and smiling brightly.

Cat was right about a lot of things, Heather decided. Couples fight and argue every now and then, but should their argument end their relationship?

Maybe Rory was right, Heather thought. Maybe Nick did too much damage to repair the relationship. Maybe their relationship will never be the same again, but it could be better.

Heather didn't know the answers to her own questions, but somehow, she was OK with that. For right now, she didn't need to know the answers.

Acknowledgements

The very first person I have to thank is my dad who always had faith in me and knew I had talent. He never directly pushed or forced me to work on my book, but always silently supported me. He was the first person who realized I wanted to write a book and believed I would someday become a writer.

Thanks to my mom for taking me to the library before I had my driver's license (especially when it wasn't within walking distance) and stood by me when I was old enough to receive my first library card. She always supported and encouraged my love for reading and writing.

A huge thank you to my two wonderful and always younger sisters, Krissy and Becky, for being mean and bratty to me during my childhood. Thank you for the countless memories and deep and meaningful (and the not so meaningful) conversations that I now have the privilege of using in my books. My sisters are always more than willing to share their criticisms and point out all of my flaws and inaccuracies. Because of their naturally spoiled nature, our parents realized I truly was special and gifted (except in math ... and science ... and probably social studies).

I also have to thank Jason and Pat, even though I never told them about my dream to write a book but more than likely knew because my sisters can't keep secrets (from anyone). And if I didn't acknowledge Jason and Pat, they wouldn't hesitate to make me feel guilty for leaving them out.

Heartfelt thanks to Charlie Goetzman, who has given me everything — support, faith, encouragement, time, laughter ("Jenn, this quesadilla is really good), and patience. Being able to hold your hand through everything makes me smile and somewhat grateful for your sarcastic wit and dry sense of humor.

Special thanks to Jeanne LaRose, Becky Remiger, and Terry Gray for reading the first super rough draft of the book and giving me honest opinions. Tremendous thanks to Jill Smolinski, Amanda Ashby, C.L. Friere, R.M. Hamilton, and Justin Olson for patiently answering my questions and giving me much needed advice. Thanks to Heather Tourville, Shonté Kinstler, Betsy Bloom, Tennille Spears, Kerri Johnson, Megs Milling, Curt Trnka, Emily Wilson, Jeremy Schneider, David Bohlander, and Kariann Farrey for letting me lean on them and giving me support and encouragement.

About The Author

Jennifer Elliott lives in Onalaska, Wis., with her two cats, Calvin and Riley, who absolutely love and adore her. She refuses to play "Duck Duck Goose" with anyone who insists the game is called "Duck Duck Gray Duck." Jennifer loves taking victory laps around the croquet course after winning and counts running around the yard for 30 seconds as solid exercise. Backgammon, Scrabble and any game involving pop culture knowledge are her favorite board games. She seriously considers Scattergories her nemesis. Currently, Jennifer is working on mastering the game of Quiddler because she doesn't like losing to her two sisters, Kristen and Becky.